PENGUIN CRIME FICTION
DALLAS DROP

Richard Abshire was with the Dallas Police Department for twelve years and was a private investigator for two. He coauthored *Gants* and *The Shaman Tree* with Bill Clair. Abshire lives in Dallas, Texas, with his wife, and is currently working on his next Jack Kyle mystery.

D1509610

Dallas Drop

Richard Abshire

PENGUIN BOOKS

PENGUIN BOOKS
Published by the Penguin Group
Viking Penguin, a division of Penguin Books USA Inc.,
40 West 23rd Street, New York, New York 10010, U.S.A.
Penguin Books Ltd, 27 Wrights Lane, London W8 5TZ, England
Penguin Books Australia Ltd, Ringwood, Victoria, Australia
Penguin Books Canada Ltd, 2801 John Street, Markham, Ontario, Canada L3R 1B4
Penguin Books (N.Z.) Ltd, 182–190 Wairau Road, Auckland 10, New Zealand

Penguin Books Ltd, Registered Offices: Harmondsworth, Middlesex, England

First published in the United States of America by William Morrow and
Company, Inc., 1989
Reprinted by arrangement with William Morrow and Company, Inc.
Published in Penguin Books 1990

10 9 8 7 6 5 4 3 2 1

Copyright © Richard K. Abshire, 1989
All rights reserved

ISBN 0 14 01.3347 X
(CIP data available)

Printed in the United States of America

To Carol

Dallas Drop

Prologue

THIS TIME THE BOAT was a Carver 32, brand new. I liked that. It was stocked for a long stay out on the water, and I felt good. The twin gas inboards purred at an easy two thousand on the tach. That meant about eight knots, with a range of better than one hundred seventy nautical miles. I told myself my trophy tarpon was half an hour away, playing in an easy swell under a dazzling Gulf of Mexico sky. I was sure of it, the way a fool is sure.

Ahead of us was blue water forever. I tied down the helm and eased into the cockpit. From there I could see forward through the saloon into the stateroom beyond. The boy was asleep already, curled into a ball on my bunk.

On the Carver the gunwales are wide and flat. That makes for a bit of a reach when you are landing a big one over the side, but it is an easy stroll forward from the cockpit to the forward sun deck. I stopped even with the windshield to look at the woman, a lean and leggy blonde.

She was on the deck on her back, slathered with oil and shiny in the sun. The strings of her bikini were pink against the glistening copper of her thighs, her breasts sloshed against her ribs with the rhythm of the boat. Her nipples were like rosebuds.

Mozart was playing on the stereo piped out across the water, bright and well made, like the new boat and the half-naked woman on the blindingly white deck at my feet. I stood looking down at her until she sensed that I was there.

She raised herself, poised on an elbow. She looked at me for a moment, then made a pretty line of her throat as she turned her head to look forward. She knew how she looked.

I peeled off my shirt and knelt beside her. She gave herself up to my kiss, for a moment. Then she pulled away.

"Where is the boy?" she asked.

"Below," I answered. "Asleep."

"Good," she said, smiling a hungry smile. "Come here."

I moved toward her on my knees and she kissed me. I felt her hand at my waist, then inside my trunks. I looked beyond her at the endless blue water ahead. Clear sailing, I thought. The boat could look after herself for a little while.

My arms closed around her and pressed her to me, her breasts against my chest, the fragrant oil of her spreading over me.

Her fingers closed around my sex and I felt my trunks slipping down.

There was a click, a metallic mechanical menacing click that did not belong anywhere in the scene of me and the copper shining woman on the prow of the silver-and-chrome new boat charging out across the azure water toward my trophy tarpon beneath the near and searing tropical sun. It did not belong, but there it was, the click of a switchblade knife opening. I looked down to see that she held my rigid cock in one hand, the knife in the other. She laughed softly.

An alarm sounded. The depth-finder! Beneath us the bottom was rising. Our sleek new hull was slashing through beguiling blue water toward . . . what? Something was reaching up to tear our bottom out. A reef maybe, or a wrecked ship.

She would not let me go to run to the helm, to save us. Laughing, she held me there, and the knife swept down as the alarm bell rang and rang and . . .

I awoke and slapped the cheap clock off the desk into a trash can. It rang on, muffled, and I sat up, alone in cool gray morning light.

Chapter One

IT WAS A QUARTER to seven.

The place where I found myself was not a boat at all, but my office. The boat, the sweet new Carver, belonged to another time. My office, on the other hand, belonged to Metroplex Properties. It was one of a hundred or so offices in a four-story building that overlooked the Lyndon B. Johnson Freeway in north Dallas. It was on the second floor.

Mine was one of the cheapest floor plans that Metroplex offered, what they called a "starter," for new little businesses like mine. Ten by twelve feet, unfurnished. About the size of the tent I bought a few years ago to take my son camping.

All the offices on the second floor shared a receptionist who sat out front in the lobby, facing our two elevators. Some of the offices had two or three rooms and private secretaries as well; KYLE AND ASSOCIATES was just me, with the one room. I had a Private Investigator's License, Class B, issued by the State of Texas, a desk, three chairs, a file cabinet, and a trash can with an alarm clock in it. There was a potted plant, too. Della the receptionist kept it alive.

My file cabinet had four drawers. In the bottom one I kept a pillow and a blanket; in the next one, socks, shorts, and a shaving kit; a few books and a chess set in the next. The top drawer was for my case files. It was empty except for a dozen manila folders stuffed with blank typing paper, for show. When

I was not sleeping on it, my army surplus cot was kept tucked out of sight behind the file cabinet.

I have it on good authority that there are people who can bounce right up out of bed in the morning when their alarms go off, but getting up was a chore for me. Had been for a couple of years, since I got run over by a car in the line of duty as a member in good standing of the Dallas Police Department. My attorney was working on my disability claim, the same guy who had handled my divorce. I was no more than cautiously optimistic about my chances of getting a pension.

Me getting out of bed in the morning sounds like one of those preschool rhythm bands I remembered from my childhood, which mothers and teachers probably do not have time to be bothered with anymore. A lot of castinets and rhythm sticks, all popping and crackling as my vertebrae worked themselves more or less into single file. When I was finally out of the cot, I stored it away and hobbled out to the coffee maker behind Della's desk and put on a pot. While the coffee was brewing I fished my shaving kit and some clean shorts and socks out of the filing cabinet and made my way down the hall to the men's room. I was fresh and clean-shaven by the time the coffee was ready.

The morning papers lay in their respective stacks between the elevator doors. I poured myself a cup of coffee and picked up one of the papers, a *Dallas Times Herald*. Dallasites tend to think of the *Herald* as liberal and the *Dallas Morning News* as conservative, which is a laugh. The *Herald* was supposed to be owned by the *LA Times* people, as if that meant anything one way or the other. There might have been a difference if you were prone to study the editorials, but I picked the *Herald* because of the crosswords. With the *Herald*, the object was to finish; with the *Morning News*, the idea was to see how fast you could finish. And I do like "Doonesbury," which the *Herald* carried and the *News* did not. Maybe that made the *Herald* a liberal paper in Dallas, where it did not take much.

None of the other occupants of the second floor had come

in yet. Della had told me once that my neighbors thought I must be a real early riser, being the first one in every day. If they had known I lived in my office, they would have had me thrown out for violating my lease or a zoning law, or something.

I put the coffee and the paper on my desk and dressed myself in my cleanest shirt and the tan slacks. I owned exactly one suit, a navy-blue one. The jacket went with my gray slacks and my tan ones, for a total of three outfits. Four white shirts and a couple of ties rounded out my wardrobe. I kept it all in a plastic suit bag, hanging on a coatrack in the lobby.

Dressed and fresh, I settled down to the *Herald*. Page one above the fold was all about the Middle East and some local entrepreneurs who had gotten busted for dealing cocaine. It could have been any day of the last five or ten years. But when I unfolded the paper, Brendan O'Bannion's face caught my eye. It was a file photo, in a black border.

DALLAS POLICE NARCOTICS LIEUTENANT
SUSPENDED IN SHOOTING

My heart leaped with glee. I would have been happier only if the headline had read "O'Bannion Killed." I did not want to rush this, so I laid the paper down on my desk and went out into the lobby to warm my coffee. This was going to be good.

O'Bannion was in trouble, all right. According to the story in the box, he had killed a man, an unidentified Latin American, the night before. Beyond that, the story was vague. It just said that an investigation was underway, and that O'Bannion had been suspended pending the outcome. That was all. I thought about calling my friend Lieutenant Cochran in Homicide, but I remembered that he was working evenings, and would not be in his office until around three in the afternoon.

After pouring myself one more cup of coffee, I took the newspaper to the community copying machine and photocopied the story about O'Bannion. Then I copied the crossword puzzle, refolded the paper neatly, and put it back on top of the stack by the elevators. It belonged to one of my neighbors.

With the crossword puzzle and the O'Bannion story side by side in front of me, I lit my first cigarette of the day, a generic ultra-lite. That was breakfast—coffee and a cigarette. With not quite enough money left in my checking account to cover that month's child support, I was cutting back.

The O'Bannion story was fishy. There was not much to it, which was odd in itself. News stories of cop shootings were usually full of information, most of it wrong. And O'Bannion was the furthest thing from a street cop you could imagine. I had no idea what might have lured him out at night to a place where he could get into anything like this. A woman maybe, but I did not like thinking about that. Obviously, the deal was shaky; that was why he had been suspended, which meant without pay, not just put on administrative leave. The Department was treating him like a bad guy.

The phone rang eight times. Had to be somebody I owed money. Nobody I liked would be up that early. Naturally, I did not answer it.

I had finished the crossword except for a four-letter word for a Philippine musk ox when I heard an elevator door open and looked up to see Della walk in. She was a perky blonde with short hair and long legs, just a kid. She came in smiling. Everyone else on our floor was in some dull line of work, accounting or brokering of some kind. Della liked me because I was a private eye, and she was a fan. Mike Hammer was her favorite.

"Good morning, Jack. You look spiffy this morning."

Her voice was musical; she really brightened up the place.

"So do you, kid," I said. "You always look spiffy."

We chatted for a while, and she asked me about the big case I was working on. I did not like to admit that I had no cases of my own, just a little something here and there to help out other guys who had gotten behind their workload now and then. Since I did not want to have to keep up with any lies, I always just told her it was too big to talk about. She loved it. She probably knew it was bullshit, because she was the one who was supposed to type up any contracts I signed with clients, but she loved it anyway. I sat on the edge of her desk while she puttered around getting ready for her workday to start, and we kidded back and forth.

When our neighbors from the other offices started coming in, I went back into my office and closed the door. Before I could decide what to do next, my phone rang again. Della took it at the switchboard and buzzed me on my intercom.

"It's a Mister O'Bannion, Jack. Sounds urgent." she said.

"Brendan O'Bannion?"

"He just said Mister. He said he was a friend of yours."

I was surprised, to say the least.

"Jack, he said it was urgent."

"Take a message."

"Whatever you say."

I had one solid gold reason for not talking to O'Bannion. In a perverse way, I did want to talk to him, though. A call from him on the same morning he was page-one news was no coincidence. I did not believe in those, not anymore.

Della buzzed me again to give me O'Bannion's number. I smoked another cigarette. On my austerity program, I was trying to hold it down to a pack a day. Usually I smoked more at night. When I was through, I mashed the butt out and dialed the number Della had given me. No answer.

"Della, are you sure you got the number right?"

"That's what the man said, Jack."

The number she had given me was not O'Bannion's home number, but it was the same exchange.

I was wearing my last clean shirt. The other three were down in my car, waiting to be taken to the cleaners. I was about to leave to take care of that when Della buzzed me again.

"Mister O'Bannion."

"Okay, I'll take it." I sat down. "This is Jack Kyle."

"I know. Have you read the papers?"

"You know me, I did the crossword."

"I guess that's why you were too busy to take my call the first time."

"I was in conference," I said. "With a client."

"Sure you were."

"What do you want, O'Bannion?"

"I want you to come over. To the house."

"You've got to be kidding."

"I only kid people I like."

"What is this number you gave my secretary?"

"It's a pay phone. So what?"

"So I got no answer there a minute ago."

"I changed phones."

"A tap? You're worried about a tap?"

"Just being careful, that's all," he grumbled.

"You should know," I said, thinking about the time I was sure he had a tap put on my phone. "So, how's the wife?"

"Leave her out of this. This is business."

"And the kid?"

"There's some money in it for you."

"I don't think so," I said.

"Cut the crap. Leave now. I'll meet you."

And he hung up. He was sure I would come, out of curiosity if nothing else. The disconnected line hummed in my ear while I wondered who he thought had tapped his phone.

Della tapped on my door and came in, not waiting for me to answer.

"It was urgent, wasn't it, Jack? Is that the same O'Bannion who's in the paper?"

"No." I cradled the dead phone. "He's not the same one. Besides that, I didn't get a call from anybody by that name. You got it?"

She nodded and winked, her smile bigger than ever.

Chapter Two

I AM A SUMMER person. The hotter and more humid it gets, the better I like it. Someday I am going to live in the tropics and captain a charter boat. But of the winter months, I think I like January best, when the whole world is hung over from the holidays and bummed out from realizing that another year is shot to hell. It was a January day when the story about O'Bannion came out, and cold enough that by the time I made it from my building to my car I could feel it getting into my bones. That is the thing about the cold when you have a bad back, everything tightens up on you and you feel so damned old.

I drove east on LBJ Freeway and watched a light mist fall on a gray and somber landscape that looked the way I felt. I left the freeway at Preston and drove south toward downtown. It would have been quicker to stay on until Abrams, but I had a stop to make.

Taylors bookstore at Preston and Northwest Highway is a place I like to waste time in on occasion. Taylors Books is a locally owned chain and it's a big place with a hell of an inventory. I went straight to the psycho-babble section and found half a dozen books on dreams.

The first one I thumbed through said that dreaming about castration had something to do with getting your anima and animus mixed up, not paying enough attention to the feminine

15

side of yourself, or else maybe you really secretly wanted your cock whacked off for some reason. I liked the second book better. It said that a dream about castration, whether you were the one doing it or the one having it done to you, meant that some long-standing issue that had been troubling you was about to be dramatically resolved. I quit while I was ahead and left.

From the bookstore I drove east again, on Northwest Highway, across Central Expressway, then south on Abrams to Mockingbird. I went that way so I would pass within sight of White Rock Lake. I liked the lake because I could pretend it was the Gulf of Mexico if I tried hard enough, and because neither of us had panned out. The lake was dug around 1910, and the city fathers figured they had their water problems licked until the year 2000. But they did not figure on the Sun Belt boom, and the little lake got swallowed up in the maw of prosperity. Now it was an inner city curiousity, peopled on one side by mansions built by oil wildcatters in the first boom, by plucky cottages on the other.

Mockingbird Lane skims a low ridge across the north end of the lake, and as I passed, I could see the sailboats moored here and there, and the piers. Nobody was sailing. I remembered taking my little boy to feed the ducks at the lake.

O'Bannion lived in Casa Linda, east of the lake on the other side of Garland Road. Most of the houses there were fifteen or twenty years old, and there were lots of trees. It was a solid, family neighborhood in most places, where the people who lived in the houses were buying them.

Mrs. O'Bannion answered the door, and I wished that she had not. Her face looked tired, her eyes pleading. In the suspicious crack of the door, I could see that the chain was still on.

"Jack. What do you want?"

"I came to see O'Bannion," I answered.

"Leave us alone."

"Who is it, honey?" It was O'Bannion's voice, from behind her somewhere.

She closed the door and I heard them talking about me. When the door opened again, O'Bannion and I stood face to face. Mrs. O'Bannion was nowhere to be seen.

"I guess you know how hard it was for me to call you," he said.

I said nothing. I did not care how hard it had been, and I did not know what to expect. I was not even sure why I had come. He moved to one side and I stepped inside.

The room was quiet; O'Bannion looked away from me, fiddling with an unlit cigar. I started to smoke a cigarette, but did not. He picked up a transistor radio from the table beside his easy chair and walked out of the den, toward a sliding-glass door at the rear of the house. He motioned for me to follow and I did.

The patio was roofed and stocked with lawn furniture, several chairs, and a table. He sat in one of the chairs and pointed at another one for me. His backyard ran uphill to a stockade fence, and there were two oak trees you could hardly reach around for shade. The way it was laid out, it would have been hard for anyone outside to see into the yard without being seen themselves. As cold as it was, somewhere in the low forties and damp, O'Bannion had not bothered to put on a coat. I figured he did not plan for my visit to be a long one.

He put the radio on the table between us and turned it on, loud. It was playing rock and roll, of which I knew he was not a fan.

"Think you're bugged, too?" I asked.

He shrugged, as if to say he did not know, but that he was taking no chances.

"If you think so, I mean if that's the reason for the radio, you really ought to turn it to KRLD."

"Why?"

"Because music is not much good at beating a bug. It's too easy to filter out. It's better if you play an all-talk station, makes it tougher for the listeners."

He did not change the station. That was how pig-headed he was. He would wait and do it after I left.

"Reporters have been all over me," he said. "Like maggots on a corpse. Did you see how they trampled all over the yard, the flower bed?"

I had not noticed and I did not care.

"The wife's had about all she can stand. I don't know if she can hold up to all this crap."

O'Bannion caught himself and stopped talking about her. He was quiet for a while. Maybe he was hurt that I was not more sympathetic. Surely he was a better judge of character than that. We sat on the cold damp patio and listened to rock and roll.

He was a big man, but soft-looking, puffy. His face was pasty white and he wore a toupee that did not match what was left of his hair. His hair had been red, but now it was mostly a wild, wiry gray. The dark-red toup set atop his head like a cow turd. His eyes were watery blue, almost washed out to gray. Aside from his vaudeville hair, the only color about him was his gin-drinker's nose. At six foot six, he used his height to intimidate people, but I had never thought of him as strong. Devious, but not strong. Looking at him while I waited for him to start talking, I realized that he had aged hard in the year or so since I had seen him last. Booze and using people will do that, I thought. He had a lot on his mind.

"Aren't you curious about why I called you, Jack?"

"I guess that's why I'm here."

"Jack, it's a hell of a deal. There's a lot more to it than you read in the paper."

"There'd have to be. There was next to nothing in the paper."

"There's just a hell of a lot more to it. Stuff I can't even go to the Department with yet. That's why I'm suspended. I know it looks bad right now. But when the whole story comes out, everything will be all right. Better than all right."

Then you don't need me, I thought.

"Did you kill the guy?" I asked.

"That's not the point. The point is who he was and what he was. . . . There's just a hell of a lot more to it, that's all." He looked me in the eye for the first time. "I was working on something kind of on my own, a deal I came across. It runs parallel with something. . . . Anyway, I was working on this deal, and some things happened. It couldn't be helped. Now I'm out of action. I can't do anything now, with this shooting thing hanging over me. That's why I called you."

"I don't follow."

"There are still a couple of things to be done. I want you to take care of it for me."

"You're kidding."

"I've never been more serious."

"Well, it doesn't make a damned bit of sense. For one thing, you and I have never been friends, anything but. For another, I've been a PI for just less than a year now, and you are tight with a dozen ex-cops who have established agencies. For that matter, you know everybody in this town. You could get more done in a day on the phone than I could running my ass off for a month." I realized I was leaning toward him. I lit a cigarette and eased back in my chair.

"I don't blame you for being a little hesitant. You're right, you're hard-headed and I don't like you. You're not a team player and you don't know how to get along with people. You're a smartass, with your crossword vocabulary and all that crap. You were a cop for what, twelve, fifteen years or whatever it was?—and still you never connected with the people who count anywhere in this town. The people who run things never heard of you."

"So what are my good points?"

"In a wierd way, the same things. You're hard-headed. Once you start on something, you won't quit, even if you should. And you're not connected. This deal I'm working on . . . was working on, involves some big people. Real big. And there may be a rat in it somewhere. I don't know who to trust,

19

and that's why I can't go to the Department. I have some friends, like you say, but if any of them got involved, it would make waves. It might queer the whole deal."

I thought that over. If he was on the level, it sounded like something way over my head. What I had in mind when I got the license was divorce work, maybe an insurance scam now and then.

"Besides," O'Bannion went on, "the people on the other side of this thing play rough. If they found out a guy was working for me, he might turn up dead or something."

"And you wouldn't want that to happen to a friend of yours."

"That's right, Jack. You I could live without."

I laughed. I could not help it. As far as I knew, it was the first time he had ever told me the truth.

"What I'm talking about doesn't involve a lot of brain work. If I didn't think you could handle it, I wouldn't have called you. I remembered your background in the service."

That bothered me. My "background in the service" had been shooting people. I had been a sniper in the Marines. But I had not shot anybody in four or five years, and I was not looking for a chance to do it again.

"Two hundred dollars a day plus expenses, right?" he asked, then added, "that's standard."

I had worked for less, but O'Bannion did not have to know that.

"I'll give you a thousand," he went on. "Go as far as you can on that and call me if you need more. But that should cover it. I don't want daily reports. I'll give you a number to call. Use a pay phone. She will set up a meet. Go along with her, whatever she says."

"A woman?"

"That's right." He cut me a mean look with his watery eyes and fished a bill out of his pants pocket.

I took it. It was a thousand-dollar bill, the first one I had ever seen. Folded inside it was a handwritten note: the name Pilar and a phone number.

"You don't want to hear from me unless I turn up something," I said. "So I'll use your thousand to cover my rent and child support, spend a few days rereading Dashiell Hammett in my office, and then tell your friend here that I drew a blank."

"Nah, you're too dumb to cheat. You'll give it your best shot, Jack. I just hope it's good enough. Besides, it's not that kind of deal. Just call her, that's all. She'll take it from there."

"You have this kind of money to throw around?" I asked.

"What the hell's that supposed to mean?"

"Just thought I'd ask. *If* I decide to take the job, I'll need more information."

"Not here. You've been here too long already. Talk to Pilar. She has everything I have—more. She'll fill you in."

"Sounds like you trust her."

He did not answer. He stood up, and I followed him back through the house to the front door.

"I'll think it over, Brendan," I said. "If I decide to pass on it, I'll return your money."

He ignored me and opened the door.

"Don't go see her today," he said. "Don't take the money to your bank today. Better yet, don't put it in your account at all. Break it somewhere. Make it a straight-cash deal, no paper trail. And don't send me any contracts to sign. If you have to keep any records, which you shouldn't, do it in longhand, or tape it. Don't have your secretary type any of it. Don't leave anything lying around your office. And don't contact me again. Use Pilar for everything."

I stopped on the porch and turned to face him.

"Brendan," I said, "you haven't changed a bit. Still like to boss people around."

I smiled at him. I could tell he did not like my calling him Brendan. I did not blame him.

"Why," I asked, "do I get the feeling you're trying to set me up for something awful?"

"You're paranoid, always were. There's one more thing. It could be that somebody's watching my house, watching us right now."

21

I looked both ways, up and down the quiet street. He's the one who is paranoid, I thought. Then I noticed the plumber's van at a house four doors down. A couple of doors up the street in the other direction, I saw a house with a FOR SALE sign in the front yard. Maybe not.

"Jack," he said. "It would be better all the way around if people didn't get the idea that you and I were buddying up."

I was about to say that I did not think there was much danger of that when I saw the punch coming. He was not very quick, but I was not looking for it, either. I rocked back, flat-footed, and brought my left arm up, almost in time to block him. Not quite, though. His hammy fist with the pinky ring brushed inside my forearm and caught me on my left cheek as I leaned away. It was not much of a punch, but I was off balance, and I fell back a step or two, almost going off the porch into poor Mrs. O'Bannion's flower bed.

He yelled at me to get my ass out and stay out. I did not bother to feint or to pretend that I was going. I did not even hit him with my right hand. A straight left with a little snap to it, aimed somewhere just beyond his eyes, and he went down. He landed flat on his back, like a sack of fertilizer thrown off a truck. Mrs. O'Bannion appeared from a hallway, running to her fallen champion. She screamed and I left.

I always knew O'Bannion could not take a punch. As I drove away in the swirling mist, I felt terrific! I was almost back to my office when I noticed the blood. My cheek did not hurt, but that did not mean anything; it was too cold to hurt much. I looked in my rearview mirror and saw that O'Bannion's pinky ring had opened my cheek a little. I was bleeding on my last clean shirt.

Chapter Three

"YOU'RE BLEEDING!"

Della's eyes bulged and her smile disappeared when I walked off the elevator. She ran to meet me as if I were dying.

"Jack, what happened to you? You're bleeding!"

Heads popped out of offices here and there around the floor as people looked to see what all the fuss was about.

"It's nothing, Della, really. Calm down."

"God, Jack, you are tough."

I saw a little light twinkling in her eyes.

"Yeah," I said. "Just like Mike Hammer."

"Sit down at my desk, Jack. Sit down and I'll fix you right up."

She took me by the hand and led me to her chair.

"Don't worry about it, Della. I'll get a Band-Aid. It's nothing."

"Nothing? You probably need stitches. At least let me put something on it so it won't get infected."

I sat down. I did not want to spoil her fun. She went to a cabinet beside the coffee machine and rumbled things around until she came up with an old first-aid kit.

"I knew this would come in handy. It came with my first-aid course I took at the Y." She brought the kit to her desk and set it down. "Just relax. I won't hurt you."

She produced a bottle of disinfectant and an applicator.

23

She stood in front of me and leaned toward me, daubing the stuff on my face. I cocked my head to one side and looked down her blouse. She had wonderful breasts. The French are supposed to have a saying that the perfect breast just exactly fills a champagne glass. I read that somewhere, also that the champagne glass was first modeled after the breast of some French queen. Della was wearing a chemise, no bra. She finished with me all too soon.

"There, that's better." She stepped back to admire her work. "You're my first real-live victim."

She had taped a chunk of gauze over the nick, when a Band-Aid would have been plenty.

"It feels better, too. I think you saved my life, Della."

"Any time." She repacked her gear in the kit and returned it to the cabinet. "I don't suppose you'll tell me what happened."

"Too big to talk about, kid."

"You sound a little like Bogart when you say that. I mean when you call me 'kid.'"

"Whatever turns you on."

I smiled at her, but I was the one who was turned on, from looking down her blouse and getting the scent of her. I tried not to be obvious as I studied the lines of her legs under her skirt. Della was no tease. She dressed sensibly for the office, and she did not try to show off her figure. But she had one of those tight, leggy bodies that could not help itself. I really did not think she had any idea of the effect she had on men. I could have been wrong.

"Is there anything else I can do, Jack? Do you need any help?"

"Not right now, kid. You've done plenty. I feel much better, no kidding." I got up from her chair. "I'd better let you get back to work."

"I think you'd better change your shirt. That one's ruined."

That was when I remembered about the run to the cleaners that I had not made. My other shirts were still out in the car.

Della thought I should lie down with my feet elevated or something, but I convinced her that I was up to running an errand. I dropped the shirts off at a little one-hour shop near the office. It was nearly lunchtime when I got back, but I had decided to skip lunch. The way my day was going, I might feel like a drink by evening, and I did not want to go over my budget.

When I got back, Della told me someone was waiting in my office. She said she thought he looked like a live one, and gave me a big wink.

I did not explain the blood on my shirt to the man and he did not ask. He was fortyish, about my age, but he had taken better care of himself. He was about my height, too, maybe a fraction under six feet, but well fed and prosperous-looking. His face was so ruddy and shiny-clean it was pink. The suit was expensive but understated banker's gray with subtle pinstripes. I noticed a school ring and no wedding band: a company man. The tortoise-shell frames of his glasses made his eyes look enormous, like a frog's. He smiled. A lot.

"Mister Kyle, my name is Arthur Crandall. I'm with Amalgamated Enterprises."

"Never heard of it."

We shook hands. His grip was firm, stronger than I had expected. He sat back down in one of the chairs in front of the desk; I sat in mine.

"We're rather a large operation, Mister Kyle. Very large, as a matter of fact. But I can understand how you might not have heard of us yet, especially if you don't follow the financial news."

I thought he lingered over that a bit. Screw him, I thought. If he's looking for a *Wall Street Journal* type, he can look somewhere else. I did not have anything against the WSJ. I mean, if one of the accountants on my floor subscribed, I would read it.

"We like to maintain a low profile, Mister Kyle," the well-fed man was saying. "Operate discreetly, as most holding companies do. We are headquartered in New York City for the time being. But we plan to relocate our corporate headquarters here in the near future, to Dallas."

"There's a lot of that going on."

"Yes, quite a lot. And that is why I am here today."

"What is?"

"The move. We may be in need of your services."

"Oh."

"Is that all you have to say?"

"For now. I'm kind of a low-profile type myself."

"I see." He laughed a little, without losing the smile. "I've heard about you Texans. You are all supposed to be . . . laid back, I understand."

"Or backward, depending on where you're from." I did not bother to tell him what Lyndon Johnson was supposed to have said about talking slow and thinking fast. "Which of my services do you think you might be in need of?"

"There is practically no end to them. We will be hiring people locally, and we insist on thorough background checks. That would be a job in itself. In addition, we will be interested in property, which means that a man who knows his way around the courthouse, who has longstanding local sources, would be valuable. It could work into something really nice for you in the long run."

"Sounds great." I studied him, but I could not make anything out behind the smile and the glasses. "How did you happen to pick me? Did somebody recommend me?"

"Not exactly. We contacted the State Board. You are what we are looking for, a new, one-man operation hungry for business, someone who doesn't already have a big client list. We want someone who can give one hundred percent of his time and attention to our needs. We intend to make it worth your while. Believe me, money is not a problem with us when it comes to paying for a job done right. We are accustomed to paying New York prices. We don't mind paying the most to get the best."

"When would I start?"

"Ah, there's the rub. And it is something I need to go over with you. In our kind of operation, it is impossible to keep regular business hours. We're international, so our workday never really ends. The next step would be to arrange an interview for you with our board chairman. He likes to eyeball a man before he's hired for any sensitive position, one with the kind of future we are talking about here. We expect the chairman to make a stopover here in Dallas some time within the next few days. Unfortunately, I can't say with any degree of certainty what day or even what time of day. He may very well show up in the middle of the night, our time. Here is the question: Could you be available on short notice if I call you at any time, day or night, within the next, say . . . three or four days?"

"I'll be honest with you, Mister Crandall, because that's the best policy and because if you've checked up on me you'd know if I were lying. I don't have what Howard Cosell would call a plethora of clients standing in line to get in here. So, as far as I know, I should be available. But you never know. As you walk out somebody else may walk in and dump a big case in my lap. It's not likely, but stranger things have happened. I mean, I am in the yellow pages."

He laughed, very pleasantly.

"Naturally, I understand completely. I can appreciate that. We wouldn't ask you to pass up business without compensating you. Look, I've come in here and talked a lot of big business with you. You and I both know that talk is cheap. You're a businessman and what you're interested in is money. Naturally, I propose to pay you a retainer, your going rate for, say . . . four days. You won't lose any money and I won't have to feel guilty about asking you to sit by your phone waiting for our call. Is that agreeable?"

I said that seemed fair and buzzed Della to bring in a contract. She did a good job of not letting on that this was my first.

When the papers were signed and notarized and I had Mr. Crandall's check for eight hundred dollars, made out on a corporate account at a local bank, he stood and we shook hands again.

"One thing, Mister Crandall."

"What? And call me Art, please."

"Okay, Art. It's my image. You look Ivy League to me. Am I going to have to spring for a three-piece suit and a manicure?"

"Not at all." Hearty laugh. "Not at all. Don't worry about that for a minute. Amalgamated takes us where she finds us. No, don't go by me, as they say. We have all types and kinds. *De gustibus*, I say. That's Latin . . ."

"Short for *de gustibus non est disputandum*. I know. It means 'there is no accounting for taste.'"

"I am impressed, Mister Kyle."

"Don't be. And call me Jack."

I walked him to the elevator and we shook hands a third time as he left. Della followed me back into my office. Everyone else on our floor was gone to lunch or eating in. I could tell Della was excited for me, about my first real client.

"Well, Jack, things are looking up, huh?"

"Sure seems that way."

"Eight hundred dollars, just like that. Is there more where that came from, do you think?"

"According to Mister Crandall there is. According to him, there is plenty more. He said it could work into something really big for me in the long run."

"Art."

"What?"

"He said to call him Art."

"How could I have forgotten. Good old Art."

"You don't seem very excited about it, Jack."

"You can't go by that, kid. I'm actually very excited. I'll be even more excited if his check is any good."

"I guess that's an occupational hazard in your line of work. You have to be suspicious of everybody."

I nodded and called the bank. The check was good; I knew it would be.

"What did they say, Jack?"

"Good as gold, maybe better. In fact, this check is so good, I am going to buy you lunch."

"My god, you are excited."

"You bet. Anything you want, sky's the limit. I'll watch your switchboard while you run out and pick it up."

"Anyone ever accused you of being cheap?"

"A time or two. Here's some money."

I gave her the ten I had been nursing for the last couple of days. Before Art came along, it was all the discretionary funds I had. "And get me one of whatever you're having."

Della threw her big purse over her shoulder and left by way of the stairs, which she often did because she said it was good for her legs. When she was gone, I noticed that one of her phone lines was flashing. It only took a minute to put all the lines on hold so I would not be bothered. Then I settled down to think.

For openers, O'Bannion was right about being watched, and maybe about his phone being tapped. That I was sure of. Another thing I was sure of was that it was not being done by the police. Whoever was keeping tabs on O'Bannion had sent their boy Crandall around to look me over, and to fix it so they could keep an eye on me. If I was waiting around for a call from the chairman of the board, a call that would never come because there was no chairman and no board (although there was almost certainly a multinational conglomerate operating out of New York City named Amalgamated Enterprises, just in case I wanted to check it out), then I could not be out stirring up things for O'Bannion. Art was not from the Dallas Police Department. And neither was the good-as-gold check for eight hundred dollars. The city cops did not have the budget to operate that way, handing out money to get nothing tangible in return. Could be some kind of federal deal, I supposed, something big-time and high-tech, the kind of operation I wanted no part of.

O'Bannion had not told me much, except that he was into something big and there might be a leak somewhere, a rat. That left me in the dark and feeling a chill, like there was a window open behind me somewhere.

My first instinct was to mail O'Bannion's thousand back to him, or maybe stash it somewhere until the heat was off. The way people were passing out money it would not be long. O'Bannion had paid me in advance for five days, Crandall for four. Whatever was coming down, it was due before the week was out.

I took the thousand-dollar bill out of my pocket to put it somewhere safe, and I remembered the note. Pilar. Why should I wade into deep, dark water for Brendan O'Bannion? The only nice thing he had ever done for me was give me an excuse to punch him out.

On the other hand, if this was really a big-league bad deal, I might already be in it too far to get out, just by having been seen at O'Bannion's house. Maybe that was the way he had planned it.

Thinking was getting me nowhere but worried. I had a notion to call Pilar, but thought better of it. I wanted to call Fast Eddie Cochran in Homicide first, get as much background as I could. I started to make the call, but suddenly I did not like phones that much anymore. The thing to do was catch Eddie later that night after work. He usually stopped in at his favorite bar for a beer or two on his way home. As luck would have it, it was my favorite bar, too. The name of it was The Only Good Armadillo is a Dead Armadillo Café.

Chapter Four

"AN ARMADILLO IS A goddamned rat with shoulder pads. I and every other sane person in the world kill the filthy disease-carrying things every chance we get. So would you if you'd ever lost a good horse because he broke his leg in one of their holes, or had to worry about rabies."

Red was in full swing, explaining things to a newcomer at the bar.

"Here lately, a mob of public relations flacks, fakes, and freaks have tried to make something other than a pain in the ass out of the noble rat. Along with all their bullshit about chili, these geeks have tried to make these rats some part of the Texas cowboy hype. They'd promote malaria to make a nickel apiece. And I guess they've done a pretty good job of it, too. I understand you can't walk down a street in LA or Manhattan nowadays without bumping into some ignorant asshole decked out in high-dollar ostrich-hide boots and designer jeans, playing cowboy. Same way in bookstores around here. You can't find a decent read without climbing over enough chili cookbooks and Texana bullshit to pave a freeway. Texana my ass."

Actually, the name of Red's bar was just Red's Bar. He had originally called it The Only Good Armadillo is a Dead Armadillo Café just to make sure that he did not draw the phony Greenville Avenue cowboy crowd. But it turned out that fake cowboys will congregate under any sign that mentioned the great rat. After he got tired of throwing people out of his place for demanding that he throw away the Bob Wills records and put some *real* country music on his jukebox, Red finally took his sign down. I liked the original name, though, and the thought behind it.

Fast Eddie Cochran had two favorite watering holes. Besides Red's place, there was the ever-popular Club 66, a private club for police officers and their guests that was owned and operated by the Dallas Police Association. It was downtown, between the Police and Courts Building at Commerce and Harwood and the police garage on Young Street. It was upstairs over a place that had been a hiring hall for day laborers. Club 66 was named that because of the radio jargon that Dallas officers used to indicate the end of a tour of duty, which was Signal 66. It was like calling a bar for golfers the Nineteenth Hole.

I had not been in the Club 66 since I was kicked out of the Department. There would probably be somebody there who would vouch for me, but I liked Red's better.

Red looked past the guy he was preaching to and spotted me as I moved toward the bar.

"Hey, kid. What've you been up to?"

"Trying to stay out of trouble. How you doing, Red?"

"Can't complain. What'll you have?"

"A draw, I guess."

Red was a retired cop. He had worked fifteen years in Vice. Then there was a scandal, not involving him, and one of the chiefs decided all the old Vice guys should be rotated out to Patrol. Red did not care for the idea, so he quit and married a rich widow he had been seeing for as long as I had known him. He ran the bar because he wanted to. I had no idea what Red's legal given name was and did not know anyone who did, but everybody knew Red Sanders.

In addition to Red himself, a good reason to drink in his place was his jukebox. Red had a theory that nothing worth a hoot had been made since about 1959, and he stocked his jukebox accordingly. Besides Bob Wills there was plenty of the thirties and forties big-band stuff, a little Gershwin and Porter, some Count Basie, and Duke Ellington, really nice stuff to listen to. It was one of my favorite ways to kill time, but I had not been in for a couple of weeks, due to my budgetary problems. Red would run a tab on you if you asked, but I do not like to owe anybody anything.

I took my beer and looked the place over. It was not all that big—what I liked to call intimate. The location was good. Greenville Avenue, but on the lower end, not the part out by SMU. where the fern bars and meat markets seemed to breed one another. Red's was down near the south end of Greenville, where it begins by the old Sears store and takes you north from a moderately sleazy "neighborhood in transition" out through Lakewood, which used to be a classy neighborhood. Lakewood has come back in the last couple of years, since yuppies and urban pioneers started buying the old houses and fixing them up. In a five-minute drive from Red's you could find yourself in East Dallas, where life can be really interesting, in sedate and rebuilding Lakewood, at good old White Rock Lake itself, or out in the Greenville–Lover's Lane singles' city.

When I worked this beat fresh out of the police academy, Red's place was something else, I don't remember what. Charlie Frederick was my training officer, the guy who taught me the ropes. I had not thought of Charlie for a while. That is another thing I like about Red's, you see people and are reminded of people there.

"Hey, Jack. What's happening?"

It was a guy everybody called Speed. I did not know his real name, either. Or why they called him Speed. I had heard it was because he worked fast to make deadlines. He was some kind of free-lance writer or photographer or both, but I had never seen any of his stuff published. He could have gotten his name from using speed, amphetamines of one kind or another. He was that kind of herky-jerky guy.

Eddie Cochran was not there yet. It was a little early for

him. I took a stool beside Speed, swiveling to put my back to the bar.

"Can't kick, Speedy. How about yourself?"

"I'm fighting off a fit of depression, to tell you the truth."

"Sorry to hear it." The guy never heard of a rhetorical question?

"Nuclear war, Jack. Nuclear war."

He leaned toward me like he was telling me a secret, then he suddenly threw his head around, the way punchdrunk fighters are supposed to do. He was quirky, all right. From habit, I kept my eye on the front door and the cash register while we talked. Charlie Frederick had taught me that. You might not care enough to try to stop a robbery or a till-tap if it happened, but at least you want to know about it.

"Which nuclear war is that, Speed?"

"The only one, man." He giggled.

"Guess I missed it."

"Not yet. But when it comes, ain't nobody gonna miss it."

"When, not if, huh?"

"Absolutely. It's inevitable. I've been reading up on it, for a piece I'm doing."

I had heard of people you would call encyclopedic, who knew and could recall everything about everything. Speed was not like that, he was a single tracker, went off on tangents. This week it was the bomb. He could surprise you with the stuff he knew, but only about his topic of the week. I would say this for him, though: He had good sources. I had used him from time to time to run down information on interstate, even foreign deals, and he had come through with righteous information. Maybe he really was a newsman, in his own way.

Speed was telling me something about megatons when I noticed Leslie Armitage at a table near the jukebox. I had not recognized her the first time I looked the place over, because she was looking a lot healthier now than the last time I saw her. She saw me, too, and smiled. When she waved at me to join her, I noticed the ring. It sparkled, even in the dim light

34

of Red's. That told me it was a big stone. There was another woman at her table, whom I did not know.

I left Speed talking and went over to the table to join the two women. Looking back over my shoulder, I saw that Speed had not missed me. He was hunkered over the bar, scribbling something on a cocktail napkin and talking away.

"Jack, how are you, darlin'? I haven't seen you in ages."

Leslie had just about used up her forties, but she looked good. She was decked out in clothes you knew were expensive, the really good stuff that seemed plain until you looked close.

"Evelyn, this is Jack Kyle, a dear old friend of mine."

Evelyn offered her hand, and I took it. She was sporting a little jewelry herself. We chatted nicely for a while, two dear old friends.

"Isn't he sweet, Evelyn?" Leslie smiled at me. "Just going right along with me. He doesn't know you, dear, and he wouldn't do or say anything to give me away. He's such a dear."

"That is sweet. Thoughtful," Evelyn said.

I did not say anything.

"When I was whoring, Jack was my favorite Vice cop. Do you remember the first time, Jack? Our first time? God, you looked like you were twelve. Such a baby. I thought I was going to get to turn you on and turn you out."

"Looking back on it, I wish you had, Leslie."

"Wouldn't that have been fun?"

"You could've called me," Evelyn chimed in. "We could have cornered the pussy market."

We laughed and drank as if we really were old friends.

"What are you ladies doing in here, overdressed as you are? If you're working, I think you should know that mostly only cops come in here. And you know how they are, no tips and they always expect a discount."

The ladies laughed some more.

"We're not working, Jack, just killing time. We're retired."

"Speak for yourself honey," said Evelyn.

"Good for you," I said. "How do you make ends meet?"

"You mean without making ends meet?" Leslie said.

They both laughed at that, impressed with Leslie's wit and with each other generally.

"Okay, don't tell me." I looked up as the door opened and two off-duty cops filed in, neither of them Eddie Cochran.

"We've each made arrangements, dear," Leslie said.

"You've made an arrangement, Leslie," Evelyn countered. "That's what I mean about not being retired. Wifing and whoring, all seems the same to me. Semiretired, maybe."

"Evelyn married a rich man," Leslie explained. Evelyn waggled her hand from side to side to signal "so-so." "And I've found a traveling man who keeps a little home away from home here in town."

They laughed some more and yoo-hooed for more wine. I did not mind seeing Leslie again, since she seemed to be doing so well. But I was glad to see Eddie Cochran walk in, alone.

He acted happy enough to see me, and I bought him a beer at a table off to one side where we could talk. It did not take long for O'Bannion's name to come up.

"I guess you saw the paper this morning," Eddie said.

"Yeah. I hated that about O'Bannion getting suspended."

"My ass." Eddie laughed, and I did, too.

Eddie was a little guy with a sense of humor that showed in his face and the way he carried himself. He was good with people, got along with everybody. He was average-looking in a way that made some people underestimate him. I saw him kill a man once, with the same easy smile he was smiling as we talked. The man gave him no choice, brought it right down to that, in spite of anything Eddie could say. The man thought he had an edge on Eddie.

"What the hell's the deal, anyway?" I asked. "If it's anything you can talk about."

"I don't have any secrets on this one. For once, what you read in the paper was the whole story. You know just about as much as I do."

"You're kidding."

Eddie shook his head. "Lieutenant O'Bannion shot the guy. No debate. Claimed the man had a gun, but we didn't find one."

"Why? What was O'Bannion doing there in the first place?"

"That's the weird part. He wouldn't tell us. Said it would all come out in the wash."

"A killing?"

"Hell of a deal." Eddie studied his beer for a minute before he said anything more. He had not asked why I was asking. Maybe he figured, things being the way they were with me and O'Bannion, my interest was natural. Maybe he trusted me to tell him if he needed to know. "He hinted around about some big deal he had stumbled into. Too big to talk about. How many times have you heard that crap? Whatever it is, when he does lay it all out, it will put him in the clear. Or so he says. That's all."

"It ain't much. Do you believe him?" I asked.

"Nothing to believe. Just O'Bannion smiling in the face of a trial board and a murder rap, singing 'Trust me.' What do you think?"

"Need you ask? He's always been a hustler, playing angles. Aside from that, he's a lying, back-stabbing son of a bitch."

"Don't hold back, pal. Tell me what you really think of him," Eddie said.

"But he's not dumb. Not like he'd have to be to put his ass on the line with something like this. Unless he was drunk. If he were drunk enough, he might pull something without thinking, or panic and overreact. He's not a street cop by any stretch. Then, when he saw what he had done, he might come up with a song and dance to buy himself time to think up a story."

"He wasn't drunk. Blew about a point or two on the breathalyzer. Not even close."

"Then I'm stumped, Eddie."

The waitress, a pretty kid I had not seen before, brought us two fresh beers.

"Is there anything you can tell me, Jack? Do you know anything I don't know?"

I decided to answer those questions one at a time. I said no to the first one, and let the second one slide. Maybe Eddie thought I meant no to both of them. He did not press it. My rule of thumb is don't lie to your friends, but don't volunteer any information either. If he had asked me if O'Bannion had hired me, I would have told him the truth. But I guess it never occurred to him; it wouldn't have occurred to me.

Eddie and I were interrupted then by a young cop in civvies. He had a severe haircut and a scrawny mustache and he wanted to talk shop with Eddie. I did not know the kid, so I turned aside in my chair and lit a cigarette. Before the first young trooper was through, there were others, some as new as the first and some as old as me. It was shift-change time, and the place was filling up with police men and women getting off work. Every one of them did not automatically come over to say hello and visit with Eddie, but more of them did than did not.

I excused myself with a wave, and Eddie nodded. I started for the door, but Speed slid off his stool and had me by an elbow with a thin, nervous hand. He was still going on about the nukes. I interrupted him.

"Speed, you see those two ladies over there by the jukebox?" I pointed at Leslie and Evelyn. They waved at us. "I told them about your bomb research, and they were enthralled. Why don't you go over and tell them about it?"

"Really?"

"Sure. Tell them we're doomed."

"We are, you know."

"They can take it. Maybe they'll suggest something to do with the little time we have left."

He was at their table by the time I made the door.

Chapter Five

BACK AT THE OFFICE, I checked my answering machine. Nothing from Mister Crandall of Amalgamated Enterprises. I tugged the slip of paper O'Bannion had given me out of my jacket pocket and looked at it again. Just the name Pilar and a phone number.

One of the things I had not bought with what was left of my credit union savings when I left the Department was a crisscross telephone directory. One of my second-floor neighbors already had one. No point in both of us laying out eighty-five dollars.

I used the last of my credit cards, the only one I had not surrendered on demand, to let myself into the guy's office. Good thing he had not sprung for the extra couple of bucks to have a dead-bolt lock put on his door. The standard job was a snap.

Pilar's number was listed, which surprised me. It was with the name of Jaime Maldonado, with no mention of a Pilar or anybody else. According to the directory, Señor Maldonado was retired. It did not say from what. I decided to go for a drive and look the Maldonado place over.

Driving north on Preston Road from LBJ, I wondered again at the traffic. In the late sixties, when I first came to Dallas, they had not built LBJ yet. Northwest Highway was still more or less the northern boundary of development. It was a

part of Loop 12, the old outer circle that let you skirt downtown if you were just passing through. Driving toward the Maldonado address, I counted apartment complexes where there
had been only cow pastures and an occasional house fifteen
years before. Work was under way on LBJ in 1968, when I was
transferred from the Northeast Division to Southeast. Northeast was the White Rock station, a cinder-block outpost next
door to a National Guard armory behind Flagpole Hill, across
Northwest Highway from White Rock Lake. At the time, the
Northeast Division had more hero bars per capita than any
other outfit in the Department. That was because White Rock
Creek flooded every year and the troops had to wade in and
save people trapped in their cars. Southeast Division was down
on Bexar Street, backed up against the Trinity River just down-
stream from the railroad bridge and South Central Expressway.
The station fronted a City Service Center across the street from
a housing project. In the wake of the murder of Dr. Martin
Luther King, Jr., the brass pulled all the rookies on training out
of Southeast, and sent one-year men with clean personnel jackets down there in their place. I say *men* because we did not
have any women in Patrol then. About that time, the Corps of
Engineers or somebody fixed White Rock Creek so it did not
flood so much anymore. I remember part of the fix involved
moving people out of houses not far from the Southeast station
because the flooding there was going to be even worse. After
that, the troops in the Southeast Division started getting all the
hero bars. But ours were not usually for saving lives, ours were
usually for some kind of combat. Somebody did a survey in one
of those late-sixties or early-seventies years and figured out that,
on a percentage basis, our casualty rate was higher than the
Army's in Vietnam.

Now LBJ and Preston Road, all the main north Dallas ar-
teries, were never clear of traffic. I wondered who these people
were and where they were going, twenty-four hours a day.

The city had boomed in the seventies and early eighties,
sprawling beyond LBJ, across the line into Collin County. In

the downtown skyline the skyscrapers stood shoulder-to-shoulder like a gang of high-rollers shooting craps and laughing at a private joke. The boom had been the product of a combination of Sun Belt razzle-dazzle, an almost recession-proof mix of business and light industry, available fuel, and cheap labor. It was a right-to-work, Southern Baptist, can-do place, and the growth northward had come so fast that city service had not kept pace. You had traffic jams that looked liked Tokyo at rush hour; and the taxpayers in the far-north parts of town had to wait half an hour or more when they called the cops, who were spread too thin to cover all the beats. Progress.

The address I wanted was way out north, near the Preston Trails Country Club, where women were still not allowed, and where, until the last couple of years, the PGA tour came every spring to play the Byron Nelson in the rain. Now the Nelson was played at Las Colinas, a deluxe development on the northwest edge of town in Irving, the same suburb where the Cowboys played at Texas Stadium. At Las Colinas you could stable your polo ponies at the Equestrian Center while you made a movie at the Dallas Communication Complex soundstages, a sprawling complex that was supposed to be as big and good as anything in Hollywood. There were residential and business parks, too, with a monorail being built to whisk people downtown and avoid the traffic.

It was a big house, the Maldonado place. It rambled up and over a low ridge behind a fieldstone wall eight feet high. I might have been mistaken, but in the blue arc of a streetlight, I thought I saw something glittering along the top of the wall. It made me wonder. North Dallas is security city, but I could not remember ever seeing broken glass on top of a wall before. Not in North America.

Beyond the wall, like some kind of psychic aura, stretched an unbroken band of light. High-intensity security lighting, a firebreak against whatever Jaime Maldonado was afraid of.

I did not linger long enough to be spotted by some watchful neighbor with the police emergency number taped to his phone. I made one pass, then turned around when I was over a rise out of sight of the house. On my way back, I did not slow down when I passed, but I had time to jot down the license number of the dark-gray van that sat across the street from the Maldonado house. I figured that was only fair. Unless I missed my guess, the men in the van had my tag number already, and my picture, too. It was dark as pitch in the street beyond the lights, but the man who lived in that house could certainly afford infrared lenses for his watchdogs' cameras.

There did not seem to be much point in hanging around. I toyed with the idea of checking out the back of the house, to see if the alley went all the way through the block, maybe spot the trash drop—you would be surprised how much you can find out about someone by rifling through his or her trash. And some of the most security-conscious people in town do not give their trash a thought. They just toss it all, letters and receipts, everything. I know private eyes who would rather swipe your trash than tap your phone. But with the precautions he had in the front, Maldonado struck me as the type who ran his trash through a shredder.

I did not like the look of it. The house seemed to bear out O'Bannion's story, at least the part about major leaguers being involved. A man has to know his limitations, and I had had mine pointed out to me by professionals. I felt more and more certain as I drove back toward my office that the best place for me was well out of this deal. I would have been wary with a client I thought I could trust. With O'Bannion, I was down-right scared.

You can never be absolutely sure you are not being followed, but you can be careful enough to feel pretty safe about it. I did a few of the things you do when you just want to be careful, made a few trips around a block, turned out of the wrong lane a time or two, and back-tracked until I figured I was not being followed. Probably. Then I went home.

There were no new messages on the answering machine, so I took my chess set out of the filing cabinet, found the photocopied game descriptions I had gotten out of my neighbor's paper of the Karpov-Kasparov championship tournament being played in Moscow, and set up the pieces to run through a couple of the games. There were half a dozen smokes left in my last pack. I had a few hours until daylight, and I did not feel like sleeping. For one thing, I had a lot on my mind. For another, I was in no mood to spend another night on my dream boat.

Chapter Six

"GOOD MORNING, MALDONADO RESIDENCE."

Naturally, a servant of some kind answered the phone. From the sound of the voice, I pictured a pleasant matron in a maid's uniform. Her diction was precise, with just a hint of an accent. I asked for Pilar and the lady told me nicely to wait. I did.

While I waited, I ran through things once more in my mind. It had been a long morning already, but I had made some progress. Things seemed a little clearer now. Setting aside my feelings about O'Bannion, I was in on this deal so far because I had taken his money and because I was curious to know more. And there was the guy who called himself Arthur Crandall. I was being worked on by the two of them, prodded by one and screened by the other. That is the way it is sometimes, you are on the spot without knowing why, without doing much of anything. I did not like being used and I did not like being kept in the dark. But there was more to it than that. Crandall was smooth, and he used a soft-sell approach. And his check cleared. That was all in his favor. But still, I could only read him one of two ways. Either he thought I was simple or he thought I could be intimidated. Nicely, but intimidated. What it came down to either way was running me off. That I did not like.

O'Bannion was conning me, too. That was a given. But

we had private unfinished business, and working with him on this deal might pay off for me there, whether I ended up bailing him out or burying him. If I could put aside my hatred for the man, look at it coolly, he was an interesting proposition. It had not been easy for him to call me, whatever his reasons. He was an arrogant man, and calling me meant he was desperate.

If I played it safe, Crandall's way, I would never know what it was all about. The only way I was going to get a look backstage was to see what Pilar had to say. I might still decide to back out, but I would not be working blind. That was important. I did not like other people calling my shots for me. This attitude had gotten me into trouble before, but there it was.

I had strong feelings about O'Bannion's taste in women. I wondered about Pilar.

"Yes?"

Her voice was a little throaty, sexy.

"Pilar?"

"Yes."

"I'm Jack. O'Bannion asked me to call you."

"I see. You are a friend of his?"

"No."

"I'm afraid I don't understand."

"I'm certain that I don't." I figured if anybody was listening in, they might as well know where I stood.

"You said your name is . . ."

"Just Jack for right now. Didn't he tell you to expect my call?"

She did not answer. I could almost hear her thinking.

"It is necessary to be careful. Surely you understand, Jack."

"I don't understand a goddam thing, lady. If you don't want to talk, that's fine with me. It just makes life a little simpler."

"When can we meet?"

"Let me check my schedule." I was calling from a pay phone, the way O'Bannion had wanted it. I thumbed a page in the phone book back and forth, close enough to the mouthpiece for her to hear it. "I think I can free up some time this afternoon around three. Is that good for you?"

"Give me the number where you are now, Jack. I'll call you back."

I gave her the number and she hung up. Sitting on the hood of my nine-year-old blue Chevy with the unrepaired fender in front of a 7-Eleven store, I felt very much the patsy, waiting for her to call. A quarter of an hour passed, and I had decided to step inside for a cup of coffee when the phone rang.

"Yeah."

"Jack?"

"It's me. Sorry, but you didn't give me a password or anything."

"I'll meet you right away. Name a place."

"Are you kidding? I have appointments, clients to see. Like I said, I can fit you in around three this afternoon."

"Be serious, Jack. This is important."

"Not to me. Not yet."

"Very well, then. At three. Where?"

I could tell she did not like it, and I was glad.

"Do you know the Wine Press on Oak Lawn?" I asked.

"I can find it."

"Fine. See you there."

"How will I know you?"

"I'll be at the bar, reading *Crime and Punishment*. In paperback."

"Naturally."

She hung up again. Not one for chitchat.

Actually, I would have preferred to see her as soon as possible. But I did not want her to get into the habit of ordering me around. And I did not want her to think she was the only thing on my mind. Whatever her story was, she needed me more than I needed her.

It was not easy filling the time until three. I ran a check on the license number of the van that had been parked outside the Maldonado place, but I did not learn much. It came back to a leasing company.

Della was too busy to kid around with me. I told her I would be in conference and asked her to wake me around two. Then I locked myself in my office and tried to take a nap. I wanted to be sharp when I met the mystery woman. I got some sleep, in fits and starts, which was just as well. No dreams that way.

The Wine Press was a comfortable bar and restaurant in Oak Lawn, which has been described as Dallas's attempt at Greenwich Village. It was in an old building that used to be something else. The ground floor was narrow, just room enough for a long bar and a staggered row of tables, but it was deep. Above the back third of the ground floor there was a balcony or loft, with more tables.

I walked into the place a little after three, acting casual. It was early for the after-work crowd, and there was plenty of room at the bar. I settled down with my ragged old copy of *Crime and Punishment* and ordered a glass of burgundy. I had hoped she would be waiting for me, but she was not there. I did not have long to wait, though.

"It looks as if you've read it before," she said pleasantly.

I looked up to find myself face-to-face with her, and I was impressed. Pilar was tall and trim, her face angular. Like an animal bred to race, I thought. Her long black hair had the carelessly tossed look I understand women pay a lot of money for. As she slipped her sunglasses up onto her head, she fixed me with crystal-blue eyes. I saw the Caribbean in them, the sea and the sky. Her lips were full, with a pout that did not go away when she spoke. She was wearing a white silk blouse that did not hide her breasts and a simple-looking but very expensive tailored suit. I thought of Leslie Armitage for a moment, and saw that Pilar wore no jewelry except a necklace of pearls.

She tapped the open pages of my paperback on the bar in front of me, and I was surprised at her finger nails. They were manicured but not long, almost stubby. Her fingers themselves were long and delicate.

I looked at the book, finally, and saw what she meant. One of the pages was dog-eared and there were notes in the margin.

"Yes," I said. "But I enjoy rereading it."

"That's interesting."

"Hope you're impressed."

She smiled, and it was a nice thing to see. I asked the hostess if we could have one of the tables upstairs, even though the downstairs was not full. I chose one near the railing overlooking the ground floor so that I could put my back against the wall and keep my eye on things. Since we were the only customers upstairs, we could talk freely. I did not ask her the first question that came to mind, about her limp. She had tried to hide it as I followed her up the stairs, but I had been paying particular attention to the way her hips moved. She had been hurt badly, and not too very long ago.

As I looked over the wine list, I found myself ready to believe her because of the way she looked. It is a hard lesson to learn, that looks have nothing to do with what is inside. The lesson after that is even harder: that looks do mean something, but in reverse. It is the beautiful ones you have to watch out for.

Pilar waited while I ordered a bottle of decent but inexpensive burgundy. When our waiter had left, she started talking. I was ready. I reminded myself not to believe her.

"You confuse me a little, Jack."

"How's that?"

"I was expecting a call, but I had been told it would be a friend of Brendan's. Then you said . . ."

"Well, I'm your man, all right. But I'm no friend of his."

"You were policemen together, weren't you?"

"Yes. He was my lieutenant."

"And you are a private policeman now?"

"Private investigator."

"I see. Please do not be offended, but may I see your credentials?"

I showed her the card the State Board had sent me in

49

exchange for a considerable fee and a shoe box full of paper-work. It had my picture on it and my number. She studied it.

"Would you like something to write on? You can copy down all the information and call Austin to confirm everything."

I offered her my ballpoint and one of my business cards.

"It is not necessary. I will remember."

"Nothing in writing, is that it?"

She nodded. "Your card says 'Kyle and Associates.' Who are your associates?"

"There are none yet. Not full time. That's just the name of my agency." She frowned, and I hurried to add, "On my bigger cases, I subcontract with other PIs. It's better that way for tax reasons."

I did not like the feeling that I was auditioning for her. She was here to sell me, not the other way around. Her eyes and that pout were having an effect on me.

"In this matter please, there will be only you, Jack? The fewer people involved the better."

"If you say so." I decided to ask a few questions. "When I called you this morning, you went to a pay phone to call me back, to arrange our meeting, right?"

She nodded and returned my card.

"Which means your phone is tapped, or you think it may be. Are you being followed, too?"

"I don't think so," she said.

"But you can't afford to leave any written clues lying around. Maybe you don't trust your maid."

The waiter brought our burgundy and offered me a taste. I nodded that it was okay and he poured her some, then left us alone again. She tried it.

"Okay," I said. "Fair's fair. Let's see your ID."

She produced a passport from her purse without having to fumble for it, as if she had expected me to ask. According to the little book, she was from Santa Rosa, Central America. She had traveled some, to the States and here and there in Latin

America. I did not see any stamps that looked like Cuba or Nicaragua. Her name was Pilar Maldonado.

"You chose a nice wine, Jack."

"I imagine you're used to better."

"Explain yourself please, Jack. It is important that I trust you."

"Okay, I'll go first. I have no secrets." I lit a cigarette and offered her one, which she accepted. She surprised me a little when I lit it for her, because she did not give me that sexy look up through the lashes the way they sometimes do. "My education is self-inflicted, what there is of it. Right out of high school I joined the Marines. One tour in Vietnam before it really got hot there and made it back without a scratch. When I got out of the service I joined the Dallas Police Department. I worked beats in East Dallas and South Dallas for about six years. I got shot once and run over by a car, in separate deals. Then I went to Vice and worked whores for a little over four years. After that, Narcotics, working for Lieutenant O'Bannion. A little over a year ago, I got fired."

"Why?"

"I called O'Bannion some names and threatened to kill him."

"There were witnesses?"

"A few. I did it at an awards banquet. The chief of police was there, and the mayor. Also a couple of hundred kids from the Police Athletic League. And one of the police chaplains. The chaplain was saying grace at the time. I interrupted him to call O'Bannion an ass-faced sack of motherfuckers."

"Ah, you are a man who speaks his mind, no matter the consequences."

"I was drunk at the time."

"I see. Why were you so upset with Brendan?"

"Earlier that evening I had been served with divorce papers and a court order that said I couldn't go home or see my little boy or pick up my stuff or anything. The constable served me at work, at the police station. I was locked out of my own house."

"But what did Brendan . . ."

"It turned out that O'Bannion had been sleeping with my wife. The men I worked with all knew about it. He'd send me off on some wild-goose chase and then he and Betty . . . They got married as soon as my divorce was final."

"Oh."

Chapter Seven

I HAD NOT MEANT to tell her so much, but she was easy to talk to. I drank my wine and decided to tell her a little more.

"The last time I talked to O'Bannion before yesterday was a couple of months ago. He wanted me to sign over the kid so he could change his name to O'Bannion. John O'Bannion. We used to call him 'Little Jack.'"

"The child is yours?"

I gave her a look that must have scared her, just a little. Her face colored and she looked away.

"Do you hate him?" she asked.

"When I think about it."

"And your wife, do you still love her? Or do you hate her, too?"

"I . . . I don't hate her."

Pilar refilled both our glasses.

"Have you met Betty?" I asked.

She gave me a look then, one eyebrow cocked.

"No," I said. "I don't guess O'Bannion would introduce you."

"Why are you helping him, Jack? Do you hope somehow to get your wife back? How?"

Good question. It had been in the back of my mind, I had to admit, a notion along those lines.

"He gave me money," I said.

53

"Ah, a mercenary." She seemed relieved.

"I'm in this to make a living, if that's what you mean."

"Don't be offended, Jack. I have learned to prefer dealing with mercenaries over idealists. It makes everything simpler. But to help a man who did such a thing to you. Surely there is another reason. You hope to protect her from him, perhaps?"

I had told her too much, and she was too good. I did not like her questions. Answering them put too sharp an edge on things. I liked them better the other way.

"Sorry," I said. "You're time is up."

"You must be good at your work if Brendan turned to you in spite of everything."

"Not particularly, Pilar, and you can hold the bullshit."

"I beg your pardon?"

"I never believe flattery, I don't need your sympathy, and I don't like being patronized. You asked about me and I told you, because I think you have a right to know about the people you're doing business with. So now it's your turn. I want to know about you, and I want to know about the deal. Keep it basic: who, what, when, and where. Why if you think I can handle it."

"Fair enough, Mister Kyle."

Calling me mister was supposed to make me feel bad, I guess, as if I had had a shot at something personal with her, but I had blown it by being rude. I did not let it bother me.

"As you know from my passport," she went on, "I am Pilar Maldonado. Perhaps you know of my father, Jaime Maldonado."

"Not until I looked in the phone book last night. But then I don't read the papers, except for the crosswords and the sports page during football season. Is he famous?"

"If you have to tell them you are famous, you aren't. Who said that, Winston Churchill? or . . ."

"Actually, I think it was Gregory Peck, one night when he had trouble getting a table at the Pyramid Room. But go ahead with your story."

"Before the revolution in my country, my father was Minister of the Interior. You *have* heard of Santa Rosa?"

"Banana republic. In the twenties and thirties, the Marines used to scrimmage down there, when they weren't busy in Nicaragua. I hear the fishing is excellent on the Caribbean side."

"There is not much sport fishing since the revolution."

"Damned shame."

"When the government fell, my father went into exile. He went first to Miami, then he came here to Dallas."

"What about you? Your English is better than mine. Were you already living here?"

"No. You may as well know, Mister Kyle, I was a revolutionary. I fought with the liberation forces, against my father and his friends in the government."

I did not react to that, and she seemed disappointed.

"I am not ashamed of it, Mister Kyle. If you could have seen how the people lived in my country, the *campesinos* in the hills, the children in the city slums . . ."

"I've been south of the border. I know there's poverty in Latin America. Just like in places here. I could show you things in Dallas that would break your heart. Get back to the facts."

I did not care if I made her mad, better if I did. As she talked, I was feeling out of my depth again. To tell the truth, I would not have minded if she had walked out on me right there. I would not have minded an alibi out of the deal.

"The facts, Mister Kyle. When I was at university here in your country . . . look, let's just say that I had good reasons for doing what I did." She stopped talking and her lips quivered. For a moment the seductive pout was gone. She sipped her wine, and I saw that her eyes were moist and full of pain. It was real, or else she was the one who was good at her job. When she looked at me again, I could tell there was something she had decided not to tell me, something she did not think I deserved to know. I did not like that, but I let it go.

"Anyway, the point is that we won the war, Mister Kyle.

55

We won, but the junta that came to power then sold us out. We had fought, all the people had fought, for a nonaligned socialist government, one that would not choose between the East and the West. What business do we have worrying about the East and West? We fought for a government that would concern itself only with making life better for our people."

"But it didn't work out that way."

"No. The junta sold us out to the Cubans and the Soviets. They have betrayed . . ."

"I've heard this part before, or seen the movie. Keep it simple, all right?"

Her face colored again, and she lit a cigarette of her own.

"Yes. Now you know who I am. The *what* is a trade meeting that is scheduled for later this week at the Santa Rosan consulate here in Dallas. The junta will send its Foreign Minister to meet with representatives of U.S. companies who did business in Santa Rosa before the war. The minister will try to persuade them to reinvest in Santa Rosa. He will deny that he has entered into secret agreements with Castro. I don't care about that. But one of the men in the minister's party is an agent working for my father and his friends in the counterrevolution. This man will be carrying a microfilm list of agents and a breakdown of vital Santa Rosan defense information. With this, my father's friends, with the help of your government, could launch a series of strikes that would topple the junta. If the microfilm should fall into the wrong hands, hundreds of loyal Santa Rosans would die. They would be executed by the junta. The counterrevolutionary movement would be destroyed."

"What does any of that have to do with O'Bannion or me? Surely your father can handle making the drop, or has people who can do it for him."

"You don't read the papers, do you? My father is dead. He was murdered three days ago."

"I'm impressed. I've seen a little of his security setup. How did it happen?"

"In such a way that it seemed a common robbery, but done by a professional sent by the junta."

"Don't you think that means they are onto your plans for the drop?"

"It does not necessarily follow. My father was one of many men the junta wanted dead, to prevent a return of the old government. He was not the first to be killed in this country."

"Where were your father's security people?"

"That is the problem, Mister Kyle. My father put his life in the hands of an American, a former agent in your Central Intelligence Agency. I do not trust him. And he claims not to trust me because I was a revolutionary. When the time comes to make the drop, I want to have someone I can trust beside me. Brendan O'Bannion was to have been that man, but . . ."

"But he took himself out of the picture with his shooting the other night. Now he is being watched. And, since he is suspended and a murder suspect, he doesn't have much weight to throw around if you need it."

"Exactly."

"Then why don't you import somebody? Surely the movement has people who could come here to handle this."

"I'm afraid you don't appreciate the security problems with which we are faced. Double agents are everywhere. It is impossible to know whom to trust. And many of my father's friends do not trust me, especially since his death."

"Then I don't see what good the microfilm would do you. How can you organize a takeover, no matter how good your information is, if you don't know who's on your side?"

"Your point is well-taken. But without the information there is no hope at all. I intend to take the microfilm to your government, as proof of our capabilities and the assets already in place. With so many factions in the resistance, your government has been reluctant to involve itself directly. I hope I can prove that we are worthy of their support."

"Sounds like another Bay of Pigs to me. How does O'Bannion's shooting figure into all of this?"

"The man he killed was my father's assassin."

"And the missing gun—the one O'Bannion claimed the man had but the cops couldn't find?"

"I have it. The two deaths must not be connected until after the drop is made. It could ruin everything. The whole trade meeting might be canceled."

"You were with O'Bannion when he shot the guy?"

"Yes. We did not intend to kill him, you must believe that. We hoped to turn him, to pay him to keep quiet until the drop. We could not afford to have him active because he might uncover our plans."

"And O'Bannion trusted you enough to let you skate with the gun and the eye-witness testimony that would clear him? That's not like him."

"He understands the situation. He knows that hundreds of lives are at stake."

"I see." In a pig's eyes, I thought. For O'Bannion, a motive always had a dollar sign in front of it. That or something even more personal. Pilar had the face and the body to tempt a better man than Brendan O'Bannion, and the brains to use him. I tried to imagine the two of them, the slender sultry Santa Rosan and fat pink O'Bannion in bed. Then, without meaning to, I thought of Mrs. O'Bannion. The three of them rolled around together in my mind until I forced myself to listen to Pilar again.

"After the drop is made, all of this will be made public and he will be cleared. Brendan knows that. As much as we can afford will be made public, that is. We have to protect our sources."

"I see."

I poured the last of the wine into my glass, not bothering to offer her any.

"So you just want me to ride shotgun for you when you make the pickup off the drop, keep an eye out for this ex-spook you don't trust. Is that it?"

"Allowing for the idiom, I believe that is correct, Mister Kyle."

58

"Do you think your dad's man just looked the other way when the hit went down, or did he actually engineer it?"

"With the murderer dead, there is no proof. We had hoped to learn from the man who did the shooting if my father's American spy had a direct hand in it. But I think my father's friend was behind it. He is a fanatic, the most dangerous kind of a man in this business."

"Not that it will mean anything to me, but what is his name?"

"He calls himself Arthur Crandall."

Chapter Eight

I HAD BEEN WATCHING the front door of the bar the whole time we talked. Of course, when you are sitting across the small table from a woman like Pilar and looking into her eyes and lighting her cigarettes, it is hard to remember about the front door. It was possible that someone had come in without my noticing. Of the people I had seen, none looked suspicious. That does not mean much, since the first thing you learn is not to look suspicious, but sometimes you can tell. We were still alone in the loft, and none of the people downstairs seemed interested in us.

"I must get back," she announced.

"Afraid you'll be missed?"

"I try to be careful, Mister Kyle. Perhaps I am followed, perhaps not. Perhaps someone notices when I come and go."

"Mister Crandall?"

"That is what I think. What do you think?"

"I think you're crazy if you're telling me that you and Crandall are sharing that big house. You have to sleep sometime."

"It is a risk, but easier to keep track of him this way, too. Do you think the risk is too great?"

"You already laid out my job. Thinking wasn't part of it."

"Then you will do it? You will help me?"

"No."

"You confuse me again."

"I'm going to do the job, for a couple of reasons. One is this feeling I have that I'm already in it up to my butt anyway. The rest is none of your business, like I said. But I'm not helping you, and I'm not working for you. O'Bannion paid me and I'm working for him. That's the way it is with us mercenaries."

"It's the same thing, helping him and helping me."

"Maybe. In fact, if you're leveling with us, it is the same. But remember I'm working for him. And part of my job is to see to it that you stick around to clear him after all this cloak-and-dagger business is over."

"Of course." She rose to leave. "I will call you. Have you a pager?"

"No, just an answering machine. But I'll make it a point to check for messages regularly."

Her eyes disappeared behind black glass as she dropped her sunglasses back into place.

"Before you run off, why don't you tell me when the drop is supposed to be?" I said.

"The minister's party arrives tomorrow. The meetings will last three days, maybe four. The drop will be made during that time. We should have sufficient notice."

"I'll be waiting by my phone," I said, as she rose and turned to leave. "One more thing."

"Yes?"

"The gun. The one O'Bannion needs to beat the murder rap."

"What about it?"

"I want it."

"Don't be silly. It's in a safe place."

"Of course it is, but I'm not sure you are. I want it. Before the drop, you give me the gun. That way, if you get lost in the excitement, O'Bannion still has something to back up his story. And another thing. There was no ID on the guy when the cops got there. You have that, right?"

She nodded.

"I want that, too. Whatever he had on him that showed who he was. I want that stuff and the gun before we do anything else."

"You're being silly, Mister Kyle, but I understand. I don't mind."

"I don't give a rat's ass if you mind or not. Just get the stuff to me before the drop, or all bets are off."

"Whatever you say, of course. Good-bye."

"Bye."

I leaned over the railing and made another careful study of the way she moved as she walked the length of the bar and out the door. Even with the limp, I knew she had not learned to move like that in the jungle, whoever's side she was on. She knew I was watching, but she did not look back.

I thought I had handled her pretty well, until I started thinking of questions I should have asked her but had not. And I did not like that I had told her so much about myself. Never volunteer information. The main thing was to be sure I got that gun before things got hot. Once we got into it, I had a feeling I might have my hands full staying in one piece, much less keeping an eye on her. After a little review, I had to admit that her looks had gotten to me more than I liked. And her fragrance. It lingered at the table, and was like nothing I had ever smelled before on a woman. A blend of tropical vegetation and the earth after a rain, it put me in mind of fertility rites. It was not overpowering, but it stayed a long time after she had gone, and made it hard to think about anything else.

I paid the check and went downstairs to the pay phones. Aside from my license and car keys, about the only thing I always carried on me was my book of phone numbers. I did not have that many women to keep track of, but almost everybody I knew had unlisted numbers. There were four different numbers for Speed. One of them was supposed to be his apartment. No answer there. The others were either friends of his or places where he worked from time to time. Somebody at one of the work numbers suggested still another number and Speed answered there after three rings.

"Hey, Jack. How's it going?"

"Fine, Speed. I need a little help."

"Anything, Jack. You know that."

"Well, I don't want you to strip any gears, but how about changing subjects for me?"

"This ain't about nukes?"

"No, I'm sorry."

"Oh. Okay, I'll try. What's it about?"

"Latin America. Santa Rosa in particular."

"Hey, I did a piece on that. They had a revolution down there, right?"

"That's what I hear."

"You want more?"

"A little. Whatever you can get on Jaime Maldonado, former Minister of the Interior. And a daughter if he had one. Pictures if you can."

"Sounds familiar. How soon do you need it?"

"As soon as you can get it. A hundred dollars worth."

"Can I get back to you at your office?"

"Yeah, I should be back there within the hour. If I'm not in, just leave a number."

"You got it."

"One more thing, Speed."

"Yeah?"

"I need to borrow your camera."

"I don't know about that, man. I seem to recall you're kind of hard on equipment. I mean, my cameras are my eyes."

"You got me mixed up with somebody else. Another fifty and you can hold my deer rifle as insurance, as soon as I get it out of hock."

"Okay, but I don't want no guns around here. You keep the gun. What lens do you want?"

"You know I don't know from lenses. When we talk later, I'll tell you what I want to do, and you tell me which lens, okay?"

"Okay, Jack."

Next I called the office. Della answered.

"Hi, kid. You busy?"

"Not very. Been beaten up lately?"

"Not since the last time you saved my life. Any calls?"

"Your client called."

"Which one?"

"Excuse me, Jack. How many do you have?"

"You mean Arthur Crandall?"

"That's the one."

"Did he leave a number?"

"No, he just called to see if you were in. That's all."

Another coincidence, in which I did not believe. I go to see O'Bannion and Crandall shows up in my office. I drink a little wine with Pilar and Crandall calls my office. It stood to reason I was due for another visit from my smiling friend with the big glasses. I told Della I was on my way back to the office, and she told me to be careful. It would not be easy, I thought.

As far as I knew, I had never met a CIA agent, current or former, unless you counted Crandall, about which I had my doubts. All I had on him was Pilar's opinion. The thing was, CIA types and spooks generally were an unknown quantity for me. I had no idea what mood Crandall would be in when he dropped in next time. I had an idea that there might be trouble. I did not flatter myself that hustling whores and dope dealers was the kind of background a person needed to jump feet first into the international spy business.

I tried to be careful again when I drove away from the bar, looking for a tail. I drove circles and figure eights up and down the boulevards for a while. If anybody was following me, either I lost them or else they were so good I did not spot them. When I felt silly enough, I cut across to North Central and headed home. As I drove north, it occurred to me to try to get hold of a handgun of some kind. A lot of people do not know this, but private investigators in Texas are not authorized to carry guns. If I were a straight citizen, I would probably keep a piece in the glove box like everybody else, but I did not want to risk losing my license. Besides, I had sold my only pistol long before. All I had was the deer rifle, which was in a pawn shop run by a friend of mine, another ex-cop. I thought about running by there, trying to swap it for a snub-nose.

There were no vans in the parking lot at my office building, and I did not see anyone loitering around. By then, I was pretty fatalistic about it.

Della looked up from a magazine as I stepped off the elevator. When she saw it was only me, she put the book back on top of her desk and smiled hello.

"Hi, Jack."

"Hard at it, I see. What're you reading?"

"Nothing."

I looked over her shoulder as I passed behind her, and stopped in my tracks. The magazine was mostly pictures, and I could not believe my eyes.

"What *is* that, Della?"

She showed me the cover.

"'Suck My Whip'? Where in the world did you get that?"

"There's a place on Harry Hines Boulevard. I ran over there on my lunch hour and picked it up. What to you think?"

In the photo on the cover a tall woman decked out in black leather stood posed like a big game hunter, one foot on a stool. Garter belt, whip, and everything.

"Della, I had no idea."

"Now you know." She giggled naughtily at me.

"So how long have you been into whips and leather, kid?"

"It's for a party, silly."

"Can I come? I'd like to watch."

"A costume party, Jack. I'm trying to get some ideas for a costume."

"Whatever you say."

She laughed, and I could not tell what was behind the laugh.

"Jack, you can help. I'm having a problem."

"Anything."

"We drew for costumes. You know, a bunch of us drew slips of paper out of a hat. Mine said 'sex kitten.' I thought of the old movie *Kitten With A Whip*, but I'm not sure what to wear. I thought about leather, but do you have any idea what that stuff costs?"

"No, I haven't shopped for leather in ages."

"Too darned much. So I thought I might make do with just some black lingerie. I picked up a few things. What do you think?"

"It's hard to say. I'd have to see it on you."

"Good idea. I know I can trust you. You'll tell me if I look just too silly, won't you?"

"I promise. But where? You know *I* won't complain, but I'm not sure about some of the other tenants."

She thought for a minute.

"What about in your office, Jack?"

"Yeah, that might work."

"It's been quiet on the switchboard. I'll slip into your office and change. You can come in and take a look. Promise you'll be brutally honest."

"Trust me."

She hopped up from her chair and grabbed a big paper sack from under her desk. I smiled and she disappeared into my office. I had a lot of fun imagining what was going on in there for a while. After five minutes, I rapped lightly on the door. I noticed she had not locked it.

"Do you need any help?" I offered.

"It's the garter belt, Jack. But I think I've got it figured out now. I'll just be a minute."

The attorney in the corner office, the one whose crisscross directory I borrowed sometimes, had a secretary with a face like J. Edgar Hoover. She was all right once you got to know her, but I had the impression she did not care for me. It stemmed from the time I caught her passing around a petition demanding that I be evicted for the general good. Her name was Mrs. Farragut, just like the old admiral. It happened that, just about the time Della was solving the mystery of the garter belt, Mrs. Farragut appeared at the outer door of her office on her way to the copying machine. She stopped in the doorway so she could devote her full attention to giving me a cold stare.

"Jack, I'm ready," Della called, a touch of excitement unmistakable in her voice.

"Be right with you, kid."

I could not help smiling. Farragut turned on her heel and marched back into her office, slamming the door behind her.

My hand was on the door knob and little Della was on my mind when I realized that an elevator door had opened behind me. That is the way these things usually happen. Even if I had a pocketful of snub-noses, Crandall had the drop on me if that was what he wanted. As I turned to face him, I guessed by the look of the big man he had brought with him this time that he might very well be thinking along those lines.

Chapter Nine

THEY WALKED TOWARD ME, passing on either side of Della's desk. The big one looked more than businesslike enough for me. He was tall for a Latino, well over six feet, and I guessed his weight at around two fifty. But he did not look fat, and he moved well.

"Mister Kyle, how nice to find you in." Crandall put an edge on his voice, and only smiled a little this time.

"Mister Crandall, how nice of you to drop in, but you needn't have. I know how busy you must be. If you had left a number with my secretary, I'd have gotten back to you."

I offered my hand and he took it. He squeezed it harder than he had the last time, but I let that go. I did not care to match grips with him. I felt better when the handshake was over and I was free of him.

"But that wasn't our agreement, Mister Kyle. Our agreement was that you would be available, here at your office, if I needed you."

"Did you need me?"

"Let's go into your office and discuss it further, shall we?"

I remembered Della. I turned toward my door and saw that it was open a crack.

"Jack, I'm ready," Della cooed.

I eased the door open and reached inside. I intended to push the button and pull the door shut, locking Della inside in case things got dicey out in the lobby. But the big man, who moved even better than I thought, muscled in behind me and shoved the door open. I was bumped pretty good in the process, and I stumbled across to the filing cabinet. Della's mischievous smile died on her face as the big man bulled his way into my office, shoving the door back hard, barely missing her with it. She fell back against my desk and tried to cover herself with her hands.

I could not help looking, anymore than the big man could. This party she was going to must be for very close friends only. She would not be safe with strangers, dressed like that. Her outfit only showed about as much of her as your average string bikini, but all that black nylon and lace had an effect, as did the hose and spike-heel black pumps. I could see she was embarrassed—she was blushing all over.

I got over it before the big man did, and I took advantage of that. He had better than sixty pounds on me, and I figured there was a gun somewhere under his white linen jacket. Not the kind of odds I would buck as a rule, but this was the exception. The office was not much, but it was all I had. And I did not like the look on Della's face. I did not like that he had scared her.

He figured to be a bodyguard by trade, which probably meant he was wearing some kind of body armor. No point in trying to gut him with a punch. And he had a head that looked like a bowling ball. But a knee is a knee. He had turned a little toward the girl, and I was looking at his left knee broadside. I was no karate expert, but what I wanted to do was not all that complicated. Pivoting on my left foot, I brought my right knee up as far as I could and then put everything I had behind the kick. Mrs. Farragut, three doors down, must have heard the pop when the big man's knee joint went. He screamed and went down, banging his face on my door frame on the way. He squealed like a burned pig, all in Spanish that was too fast for me. He wrapped both his catcher's-mitt hands around the knee like he was trying to hold it together. He had forgotten all about the girl and me. Before he could remember me, I reached inside his coat. No gun. All the way around his waist. Both ankles. Nothing.

Crandall stood just outside the office door. He was watching me closely, but he was cool. There was nothing in his face for the big man. He did not care how badly the big man hurt. Behind those silly glasses, his eyes were fixed on me with interest, but there was nothing beyond that. His right hand was in his jacket pocket, his left at his side.

The big man's pain must have been very bad because he started to puke. I used my foot to push his face outside my door, so Della would not have to see it. There was blood on my shoe from his face. I stepped over him and squared off with Crandall.

"Well?" I looked him in the eye, but it was his right hand in the jacket pocket that I was concerned about.

"Well what, Mister Kyle?"

"I don't like being pushed around. Not here. If you've got anything in mind, let's settle it right now, while I'm in the mood."

I was feeling cocky. The big man had handled easier than I'd expected. And if Crandall had something in his pocket that he intended to use, he had waited too long, let me get too close. Now was as good a time as any.

"So you crippled my chauffeur. Impressive. If you'd allowed me, I would have apologized for his pushing his way into your office. I imagine he thought you were going to lock us out for some reason."

"Or maybe he thought my receptionist was somebody else and he got excited." I probably should not have said that, I thought.

"Possibly. Who knows what they're thinking, the kind of help you get these days."

Mrs. Farragut and her lawyer had come out of their offices, and another secretary from somewhere else. I did not know how long they had been watching us, but the big man was still making enough noise to draw a crowd.

"Nothing to it, folks," I told them with a wave. "Man here has a trick knee. No problem."

It was not easy, but I got leverage on one of the big man's arms and dragged him out into the lobby. When I reached back inside to close the door, I saw that Della had moved behind my desk. She was sitting in my chair, bent over so that I could only see her face and her shoulders. I gave her a smile I hoped was reasuring and pulled the door to.

"Now what, Mister Kyle?" Crandall said.

"First thing, I'd recommend you take your driver or whatever he is and drop him off somewhere for repairs. Then we can talk if you still feel the need."

"I should do something with him. I can hardly hear myself think with all the racket he's making. Would you give me a hand?"

Between us we got the big man off the floor and into Della's swivel chair.

"Roll him out on this. Send the chair back up in the elevator," I said.

"Right. I'll drop him off and meet you back here."

By the time he did that the office building would be empty. Everybody left early on Friday. And who knew who he would bring with him next time?

"Not here," I said. "Make it at Vincent's, on Midway Road."

"Right." His smile this time was more of one than when he first got off the elevator. "Vincent's. Let's say in about an hour."

He wheeled the cripple to the elevator and pushed the down button. The door was opening when I thought to peel off the big man's jacket. It was fully lined, good stuff.

"What is that for?"

"To clean up the mess he made."

Crandall shrugged and dragged the overloaded chair onto the elevator. As the doors were closing, I looked into the big man's face. He was crying with the pain, and he said something to me in Spanish, again too fast for me to catch.

"What did he say?"

"You don't want to know, Mister Kyle." Crandall laughed. And then they were gone.

I tossed the big jacket over the mess on the carpet and worked it around with my foot. When I looked up, everyone had gone back to work except Mrs. Farragut.

"Mrs. Farragut, I'm sorry. Did you want to look before I clean this up?"

She humphed and disappeared.

Della did not answer when I tapped on the office door. I eased it open and saw that she was still in my chair. When she saw that I was alone this time, she straightened. I closed the door behind me and locked it, so no one would barge in on us. Della leaned back in my chair, all the way back against the wall. I could see her body again. It was still blushing, the redness almost like a rash across her chest and throat. She was breathing hard. I went behind the desk and put my hand on her shoulder to calm her. She gripped my wrist tightly with both hands.

"Oh, Jack," she said, in a tight little whisper. "I love it. I really love this stuff."

Chapter Ten

I LEFT DELLA IN my office to change her clothes and went out to her desk. Out came the little book of numbers again, and I started calling around for Speed. No luck.

People were beginning to leave the building by this time, some of them eyeing me as they passed. One of the accountants found Della's chair on the elevator and rolled it in for me. I sat down and called Speed's home number again. One of my two phone lines lit up on the switchboard and I answered it.

"Jack, how's it going?"

"Speed. It's about time you called."

"Yeah, yeah. I got all I could on short notice. You want me to come by your place or what?"

"First I want the number you're calling from."

He told me and I called him back on one of my neighbor's lines.

"Okay, Speed, so what did you find out about our man from Santa Rosa?"

"Maldonado, Jaime. One of your basic oligarchs, last in a long line. He was a minister of one thing or another for thirty odd years, until his side lost the war. He was Minister of Interior during most of the fighting, which made him like the chief of police for the whole country. He stayed until the bitter end, long after most of his friends and neighbors had taken everything that wasn't nailed down and lit out for healthier climates.

He was very anticommunist, pro-American. In the end, though, even he snapped that the jig was up. He supposedly caught one of the very last planes out."

"I've seen his place, Speed. It doesn't look like he left with just the shirt on his back."

"Hard to tell who got what. He was quite a hero to his side, so the Santa Rosan old-boy network probably took care of him once he made it to the States. They could afford to be generous. From what I hear, when the big boys cut out while he was still trying to win the war, it was like Somoza's guys in Nicaragua in seventy-nine. They took everything. Besides, they all were taking money out of the country all along, for generations. A lot of it they banked here, and there are supposed to be millions stashed in Bahamian bank accounts, too. There have been all kinds of rumors about numbered accounts here and there which maybe nobody has the numbers to anymore because the guy who pulled the scam didn't make it out of the country. Who knows?"

"Okay. So when he got out of Santa Rosa, then what?"

"He went to Miami first. Then, about six months ago, he moved here. Nobody knows why. And just the other day he gets bumped off in a parking garage downtown. But you already got that, I guess."

"I heard about it, but not from a very reliable source. What do you have on it?"

"Not much. He parked in a garage downtown and never came out. It was supposed to be a robbery I think."

"Yeah. Did you check on that with anybody in Homicide?"

"No. I figure you and Eddie Cochran are tight, you would ask him if you want. Paper said it was a straight robbery, though, I have it right here in my notes. You want me to talk to Eddie?"

"Yeah. I've already talked to him about another deal, and I wouldn't want him to put the two together just yet. I won't lie to him, but I'll try to avoid the hard questions if I can."

"Makes sense."

"How about family? Did Maldonado have any kids?"

"A daughter. His wife died a long time ago, and the old man never remarried."

"Did you get a description of her?"

"A looker, by all accounts. A friend of mine on a paper in Miami pulled a file photo, from when she was a deb down there or something. Says she's a real Latin lovely, only with blue eyes, light blue. Tall, like a model."

"That fits."

"I'm glad."

"Listen, Speed, the hundred is for your time. Let me know the tab on these long distance calls you had to make."

"No problem. This place where I'm working on the nuke thing has a WATTS line."

"Good. There's something else . . . hang on a minute, Speed."

Della was standing beside me, holding the paper sack tightly under her arm. She had her dress on again.

"Are you all right, kid?"

She nodded. There was something else.

"You want me to walk you to your car?"

"No, I'm fine. Thanks."

"I'm sorry it happened. I'm sorry you got mixed up in it."

She shook her head and walked away toward the elevators.

"Have a good time at the party," I called out after her. She stopped, then walked back toward me. When she reached the desk, she fidgeted with the sack before speaking.

"Jack," she said. "Could you put him on hold for a second?"

"Sure. Speed? I'm going to put you on hold, okay? Just hang on."

"No problem, man."

I punched the hold button and Speed's light blinked at me.

"What is it, kid?"

"I want to tell you something." She hesitated again. "I

didn't change, I just slipped my dress back on. I'm still wearing my costume, the lingerie, under this."

"Thanks, that's good to know."

She raised her skirt to show me her outfit again. This happened to be the same time the elevator door opened and the little guy riding down dropped his briefcase when he saw Della. She laughed and blushed and got on with him and then the door closed and they were gone. I thought to myself that if we had many more afternoons like this one we were both going to have to find a new place to work. Me, anyway. Della might get a raise.

I was left in a hell of a state, and it was a couple of loud heartbeats before I noticed Speed's light blinking on the switchboard.

"Speed, you still there?"

"Natch. What's up?"

"I am, Speed. I am."

Chapter Eleven

"SO, SPEED. YOU WERE telling me about the daughter?"

"What's going on over there, man? You sound strange. Are you all right?"

"Yeah, fine. You got more on the daughter?"

"Right. Name's Pilar. Seems like they had a bit of a generation gap during the war. She was on the other side, which is to say the bad guys. Of course, that depends on your foreign-policy perspective, human rights vis-à-vis containment of the communist menace, and all that."

"Speed, please. Without the trimmings."

"Right. There wasn't much said about her being with the rebel's during the fighting. Of course, the S.R. press was run by the government, and they weren't about to print that story. The rebels put out some stuff about her, but that was generally dismissed as propaganda. Then, after the rebels won, she showed up, at least her photos did, in some highly visible locales. It was pretty clear she had played a hand in things on the rebels' side. But I don't think the rebel high command, the ones who made up the junta, thought very much of her."

"Anything else?"

"Rumors. There were supposed to be a couple of American kids with the rebels. Probably more, but a couple of them bought it. Martyrs of the revolution and all that crap. Anyway, there was some noise that maybe she had been involved with one of these guys. But the junta played down the romantic angle. Could be that was why they were down on her. Doing it for love is bad motivation for a revolutionary. There has not been anything in the press down there about it, but that doesn't mean anything either way. The press is being run by the government again now. After a couple of months of freedom of the press, the junta decided real reporters were a pain in the butt. They shut down all the papers but one and the radio is theirs, too. Nothing changes but the uniforms and the slogans."

"Is the junta in bed with Castro and the Russians?"

"Bound to be. Stands to reason they ain't in our camp, not with what we've got going in El Salvador and Nicaragua."

"I heard they promised to be neutral if they got in."

"No way. After five or six years of civil war, they need help feeding their folks. Not to mention putting the place back together again."

"Terrific. Anything else?"

"Sure, but that's all you asked for. The rest is trimming."

"You're a good man, Speed. Got your camera?"

"Always. You still want to borrow it?"

"No, the plan's changed. I want you to take some pictures for me."

"When?"

"Half an hour."

"I made plans already, I got a date tonight."

"Bring her. It's another hundred."

"What do you need?"

"I need you to get some shots of the guy I'm going to be having drinks with at the Vincent's on Midway Road at LBJ, without him knowing it."

"I can do that. I have this lens, see . . ."

"I don't mean to be rude, Speed, but I am really pressed for time. Just get the shots for me, okay?"

"I'll do my best."

"That's usually good enough. Later."

"Yeah."

When I got off the phone I checked my watch. It was ten after five, and the place was empty. I had a touch of nerves on the way out. In fact, I took the stairs. Outside, everything looked kosher.

Vincent's was a nice seafood restaurant in a good location, a block or so from an LBJ on-off ramp in the middle of a part of north Dallas, full of industrial parks and office buildings like mine on the north side of the freeway. On the south side of the freeway there was a solid upper-middle-class residential area big enough to have its own zip code. Vincent's was the kind of place I wanted for my meeting with Crandall: respectable and full of witnesses.

I found a spot at the bar and ordered a beer, out of habit. Then I remembered that I was loaded for a change. I had Crandall's eight hundred, less two hundred for Speed, and all of O'Bannion's thousand. There was probably an ethical question about keeping both retainers, but I was not in the mood for considering it. I did not figure either of these guys was going to bother filing a complaint with the board. It also occurred to me that there was better than a long-shot chance that I would not live to spend it all. I caught the bartender before he drew the beer and changed my order to my favorite, Pinch on the rocks with water by. It had been a while since I had had the good stuff.

The first slug was good to me. It lit a fire in my belly and sent a chill up my spine at the same time. My friend the bartender had poured me a happy-hour double for the price of a single, and I had to drink straight scotch for a while to make room for some water in the glass. By the time there was room for water, I decided I did not need it anyway. I should have been nursing my drinks to keep a clear head, but the scotch tasted too damned good by itself.

Crandall was late. My second glass of Pinch was half empty when he walked in. I waved and he saw me. There was no sign of Speed yet.

"Sorry to have kept you waiting, Mister Kyle."

81

"That's all right. I've managed to amuse myself."

He looked at my glass and his lips smiled.

"So I see. I have some catching up to do."

"Let's move to a table."

We found an empty table, a small one with two chairs, against a wall. There was a pretty good crowd in the place, making enough noise that no one would overhear us. I grabbed the chair I wanted, the one that faced the door. From the look on his face, I could tell that Crandall wanted that one, too, and I offered it to him. Easier to get his picture that way.

The waitress reported in and Crandall ordered a dry martini. When she had gone, he shook his head and smiled again.

"You really did a job on poor Mario, Mister Kyle. You really did."

"Call me Jack."

"Quite a job. They're not sure how long he'll have that leg in a cast. Probably limp the rest of his life."

"Yeah, but who gives a shit, Arthur? Not me and certainly not you. If we're going to talk, let's get down to it."

"You don't bother with the amenities do you Jack?" His drink came and he smiled at the waitress, too.

"Not much. It's come up before."

"I can imagine."

"So let's move on to the next topic. Any word on when your chairman of the board will be in town?"

"No." He studied his martini as he stirred it, as if he could read our futures in the gin. "I will be candid with you, Jack. It is risky, but I think you deserve to know the truth."

It is always a bad sign when somebody starts out promising you the truth. Out of the corner of my eye, I saw Speed sweep into the bar. He had a chestful of cameras and gear around his neck and Leslie Armitage, the franchised whore, on his arm. I pretended not to notice.

"So much of life is illusion, Jack. We survive by maintaining our illusions. In a manner of speaking, illusions are my business. If you had done as I asked, as, I might add, I paid you to do, you might have maintained the illusion I offered you, and stayed clear of trouble."

When Crandall stopped talking, I saw that he was watching Speed. So was everyone else in the place. Speed was prancing around Leslie at the bar, posing her this way and that on a stool. He stuck what I guessed was a light meter under her chin and then described a theatrical semi-circle around the alternately smiling and pouting whore, saying things like "That's it, baby. Give it to me. Make me want you." I thought it all a bit overdone, but everybody gave him room. The bartender stood back from the bar, two fresh drinks in hand, waiting for him to finish. Two waitresses stood watching enviously. Leslie was dressed to the hilt in an off-the-shoulder gown that showed most of her rebuilt tits. The fur and jewelry looked real. When he had shot a dozen pictures with each of two cameras, Speed waved to the customers and the hired help, and he and Leslie trooped out. I was puzzled because he had never aimed a camera even in our general direction. But it was a hell of a show. The people in the bar buzzed about them for a long time after they had gone. Crandall looked at me questioningly, one eyebrow up.

"Hey," I said. "That's Dallas. You never know what to expect. It's the Third Coast."

"Yes." He finished his drink and motioned the waitress to bring us another round. I did not protest. "My point exactly. Illusion. That was a perfect example. A glamorous woman, whose photographs will be used to sell toothpaste or disposable douche or something, by selling the illusion that using the product will make other women look like her, or help men get women like her, or whatever the case may be."

It occurred to me that Arthur was not much of a drinker. One martini had thickened his tongue considerably. Of course, it had been a happy-hour double. I had not bothered to explain about that. I figured he was a man of the world.

"I could use a little truth, Art. I've been doing without it

83

ever since you showed up in my office the other day. For openers, what is your real name?"

"Need to know, Jack. Now you will know the truth *that you need to know*. That is key. If anyone knows more than he . . . or she . . . needs to know, then he or she is a threat to the operation and to every person in it. Need to know only, Jack. That is very important."

"And you decide how much I need to know."

"Absolutely. That's how it works."

"Who decides how much you need to know, Art?"

Our refills came and Crandall downed half of his in a gulp.

"I'll say one thing for you Texans, you make a decent martini."

"Gin is gin, Art. Go on with your story."

"Yes. Let's see, where to begin?"

"Why don't we start with you, whatever your name is. If you can't tell me who you are, how about what you are? Are you CIA? Maybe you're Mafia. International drug smuggler?"

"I am none of the above, Jack. I was with the Company, but I've retired."

"You don't look old enough."

"Disability. My back."

"You don't say."

"Yes. I still have to watch myself, take my medicine. Once you hurt your back, they say you're never the same again."

"Tell me about it."

"That's right, how stupid of me. I'd forgotten about your back injury. Got run over by a car. Terrible. Damned shame about their not giving you the pension."

"You've done your homework. I'm impressed."

"You oughtn't be. It's routine when you have the contacts. Actually, that's about all I remember about you, that and your service record. I believe you're the first sniper I've ever met."

"That you know of."

"I was impressed with your score, especially since you were there early in the war, before the action really got heavy. What was it, sixty-seven or sixty-eight kills?"

"Sixty-nine. One of them was pregnant."

He laughed until he choked, slapping the table and making such a fuss that everybody in the place turned to look at us, until he finally got control of himself again.

"Great, Jack, terrific sense of humor."

"It's a standard sniper joke. I don't care for it myself."

He gave me a queer look, as if he had begun to like me, but now he was having second thoughts.

"But let's get back to the subject, Art. Who are you working for if you're retired?"

"Free-lancing."

"For whom?"

He finished his drink and waved to the waitress for another before answering. The booze was hitting him pretty solid and his eyes were beginning to show it. I figured he had been a good boy and taken his pain pills.

"Can't tell you that, Jack. But I can tell you, and this is key . . . this is absolutely *critical*, Jack . . ." He leaned across the table and whispered, "I am a *good guy!*"

I could not help laughing.

Chapter Twelve

"GO AHEAD AND LAUGH. You laugh, Jack, but I am serious. We are living in troubled times, when the issues facing us are complex, bewildering. It helps to simplify things."

"You don't think there's a risk of overdoing it?"

"Risks in everything. Risks in my talking to you. But if you stop to consider, understand everything, all the nuances and facets, all the points of view, you never act. You become paralyzed by the enormity of it, and you do nothing."

"Don't think, do."

"What?"

"That's your motto, then. Don't think, do."

"By God, I like that."

"I thought you would."

"But seriously, Jack, I am a good guy. That is key."

"Got it. Need to know and you're a good guy."

"What?"

"Those are the two key things you've said so far."

"That's right, Jack. You are listening. Good." He tried to get a little more gin out of his empty glass. "She's beautiful isn't she?"

"Who?" I was feeling a little buzz myself, and I was not sure if I was holding my third or fourth scotch.

"You know very well who, Jack." He leaned toward me again and he may have winked. "Pilar. Damned beautiful woman. Pity about her leg. But don't deny it, Jack. It's imperative that we level with each other."

"What ever you say, Art."

"Damned right." He looked up as our waitress put his drink in front of him. "Wait a minute, miss. Where's my friend's drink?"

"That's all right. I'm fine."

"Won't hear of it. We're in this together, Jack. Drink for drink, tit for tat. Miss, another one for my friend."

I nodded and the waitress left.

"She's not to be trusted, Jack. Believe me. She's played your friend O'Bannion for a fool, and she'll do the same for you. I mean it."

"If you're talking about Brendan O'Bannion, he's no friend of mine. And what do you know about him?"

"Goddamnit, you haven't been listening!"

"Or maybe you left something out."

"Could be." He took another pretty good slug of gin. "Could be, but I've told you plenty. Figure it out for yourself the rest of the way. Here's the cruncher, though: It's all going to happen in the next few days, and you have to decide once and for all whose side you're on."

"What are my choices?"

"Good guys or bad guys, pal. That's always the choice."

"Your side or hers, you mean?"

"Us or them."

We both drank without talking for a few minutes. The waitress brought my refill and went away. I was careful not to slur my words when I finally asked, "What's at stake here, Arthur?"

"The usual. Future of the free world, democracy or communism in Latin America. The domino theory, basically. Maybe you've heard of it."

"It came up a time or two in Vietnam." I watched him finish his drink. "You want to know what I think?"

He did not seem to be listening. He was staring into his empty glass.

"Listen to me, Arthur. This is important. I'm going to tell you what I think." I thought that if he was wired for sound I might as well get on the record. I waited until he looked at me. "Arthur, I don't care about politics. I don't care who wins in Central America or anywhere else. It doesn't make a rat's ass to me if the Republicans or the Hottentots are in office, as long as they don't outlaw deep-sea fishing. I wish the Third Worlders had a third choice, I wish they didn't have to play on either team. Just don't screw up the fishing, okay? That's all I care about, because some day I want to buy a boat and live in the tropics where it's hot all the time because cold weather makes my back hurt. And maybe my kid will come down and work the boat with me when he's out of school in the summer. That's it, that's all I want out of life. And you can count me out of the rest of it. Understand?"

"Naïve, Jack. You're naïve. Everybody's in it, whether they know it or not. There'll be no lamb's blood on the doorposts this time. No Passover. You especially. The sidelines are out-of-bounds to you, my boy."

"They're out-of-bounds for everybody, Art. But that's where you go when you take yourself out of the game."

He stood. He was unsteady on his feet, and there was a disheveled air about him.

"That's all for me," he said. "I've things to do. Remember all that I've said."

"And you remember what I've said, Art."

"Not a chance. Good night."

I stood and we shook hands.

"I'll be in touch, Jack. Remember."

I nodded and watched him make his way out of the bar. When he was gone, I sat down and lit a cigarette. When I thought Crandall had had plenty of time to get out of the building, I left some money on the table and went out to the foyer to a pay phone.

There was only one message on my machine: "Speed, the crib." It meant he was at his apartment if I wanted to see him, and I did.

Nothing looked out of place in Vincent's parking lot as I walked to my car. Pretending to check my left rear tire, I looked the back of my car over thoroughly. There was no reflecting tape on the bumper, no luminous spray paint on the treads of the tires, none of the gimmicks I like to use when I am working a tail to make a car easier to stay with at night. I did not take the time to check for a transmitter.

It was dusk and traffic was still heavy, but the worst of it was over. I went through my routine again, checking for a tail. Again I did not see anything. Using a transmitter, though, they would not have to follow me closely enough to be seen. I decided to be sure before I went to Speed's place. One of the worst things you can do is lead people to a friend. It is a responsibility not to do that.

At Preston and Royal, I timed it so that I went under an amber light in the intersection. It was red for the cars behind me. A block south of Royal, I turned right out of the left lane, across two traffic lanes, up a side street that led past a savings and loan into an apartment complex. Inside the complex, I made the first right, then a Y-turn to face the way I had come.

When I ran my hand along the inside of my rear bumper, there was nothing. But when I reached a little farther, I found it. It was a plastic box about the size of a cigarette pack, held to the underside of the fuel tank by a magnet. There was an antenna wire, too, with tape to hold it in place. Once I had yanked the works loose, I could see in the gathering darkness the glow of a tiny red bulb at one end of the box. That meant it was working, sending its signals. Not far away, someone was listening to those beeps on a receiver set, someone who could use them to home in on my car wherever it went. By now that someone probably had figured out that my car was stationary. He or they would wait a few minutes before they came into the complex to pin down the position. They would not come in too soon and chance being spotted.

I did not know whose car I put the little gizmo on, but it was a sporty, high-powered job, the kind people buy to drive fast. Someone had left it in a fire lane in front of a laundry room. I hoped that meant the driver had popped in to put a load in the wash and would soon be on his way. I hoped he would take my tail on a nice run before they got wise.

There was another way out of the apartment complex, on the opposite side of the way I had come in. I went out that way, onto Royal Lane. Then it was half a block to the Dallas North Tollway, south on the tollway, and I was gone.

You cannot be too careful, and it was still half an hour before I made it to Speed's. I parked a couple of streets over from his apartment on Live Oak in east Dallas. Being careful to check behind me as I went, I cut across a couple of parking lots and made my way to his door.

I was developing a knuckle ache and a worried feeling by the time I finally heard the locks and chains working behind the door. It opened, and there stood my man Speed, with his big grin, zipping his pants.

"Hey, Jack. How's it going?"

"You tell me, Speed. May I come in?"

"Sure. You bet."

Speed is ordinarily slovenly, but his place looked especially trashed. Dozens of magazines and old newspapers were scattered all over the place, and Speed's whole wardrobe must have been thrown up in the air at some point. Socks and shirts were everywhere.

"Speed, did somebody break in here? Did somebody search your place and leave it like this?"

"Nah, man. It's cool. It's okay." He giggled, and did his little tic motion with his head, jerking it around. Only this time, it was in slow motion. I could not remember ever seeing Speed so slow, so mellow.

"What have you been smoking?" I asked him, as he tried to refasten the chains and deadbolt locks on his door.

"Hey," he smiled goofily over his shoulder at me. "Damned if I know."

Chapter Thirteen

"LET ME HELP YOU with that." I locked his door for him, all three deadbolts and both chains.

"Come on in, Jack. Have a seat. I'll get 'em."

"Get what?"

"Hi, babe." Leslie Armitage appeared in a bathroom door, wearing a pair of boxer shorts.

"Hi, Leslie. Nice tits."

"You're sweet."

She was wearing high-heeled shoes, too. She had an empty champagne bottle in one hand and a joint in a roach clip in the other. I could smell the marijuana now. On the floor of the bathroom behind her, I saw the gown and furs she had worn for the photo session at Vincent's.

"Thanks for your help, Les," I told her.

"Don't mention it, dear. I'm having fun tonight."

"It shows."

She giggled and followed Speed into the walk-in closet he used as a darkroom.

It was an efficiency apartment, one room and a bath, with a sofa that made up into a bed. That was why the place was usually a little messy, because Speed's closet was full of camera stuff. Everything else he owned he stacked around in the living room.

I cleared off the sofa and sat down. On a coffee table in

front of me a typewriter lay buried under a stack of books and magazines. I checked some of the titles, and was not surprised that they were all about nuclear war.

Speed joined me shortly, excited. He spread four glossy prints across the top of the mess on the coffee table. They were surprisingly good shots of Arthur Crandall, black-and-white eight-by-tens. Two were head-on, Crandall apparently looking directly at the camera. The other two were at angles. He was smiling in a couple of them, and looking heavy-lidded, a little drunk.

"These were the best of the bunch. It's about as big as I could make 'em fast, without worrying about resolution. I hope they're all right, Jack."

"Are you kidding? They're great. But when did you take these?"

"While Leslie and I were putting on our show at the bar, naturally." He was proud of himself, and I was proud of him, too. "You didn't see it, did you?"

"Speed, I swear I never saw you point a camera in our direction."

"And you're absolutely right. That's the beauty of the lens I was telling you about. It's called a right-angle lens. I aim the camera over here . . ." He made an imaginary camera of his hand and squinted through it at the wall in front of us, ". . . and I take a picture over there." Still squinting at the wall, he pointed his finger at me. "Neat, huh?"

"Absolutely." I peeled two hundreds off the roll in my pocket, Crandall's money, and gave them to him. "You do good work."

"I aim to please."

"Speedy," Leslie called from the darkroom closet. "Come back in here and let's see what develops." She giggled some more.

"Well, I can see that you two kids would like to be alone," I said as I stood up. "So I'll be on my way. Thanks a million."

Speed slipped the photographs into a manila envelope and handed me the envelope.

"Thank you, Jack. Thank you for bringing me and Leslie together. I can't tell you how happy you've made me."

"Yeah, about that. Uh, listen, Speed, I don't know how much she's told you, but . . ."

"Neither do I, and I don't care. Who listens? Did you see those tits?"

"Hey, they're great. I mean, the guy does good work. But . . ."

"And you know what else? She's a hooker!"

"No!"

"Cross my heart. I love that part."

"Whatever." I went to work unlocking the door. "Listen, I've got to run along. I'll see you later."

"It was the nuclear war thing that did it."

"Did what, Speed?"

"Turned her on to me."

"You're kidding."

"Swear to god. It's a complex psychological dynamic. Has to do with the sense of impending doom, a release of . . ."

"Not now, Speed. I'd really like to hear all about it another time. I really would, because I may want to use it myself. But right now, I have to go. I have people to see, you know."

"If one of them's Eddie Cochran, you might try Red's about eleven-thirty. When I called his office this afternoon about the Maldonado guy, the desk man said he was planning to stop by there after work."

"Thanks."

"Anytime."

Speed and Leslie made a nice couple, in a way, and I was happy for them. I thought about them as I worked my way back by a different route to my car, the photos tucked under my arm. It was just eight-thirty when I climbed into my car. I had a couple of calls to make.

There was a 7-Eleven at the Y where Collett and Fitzhugh divide, a couple of blocks east of Central Expressway. Charlie Fredericks used to take me in there all the time when he was my trainer. It was open all night, and Charlie and the night manager were friends. As I drove that way, I watched the build-ings pass by, and seemed to remember something about almost every one of them, something that happened there to somebody I knew, or a call that Charlie and I answered. I remembered the week before I graduated from the police academy. I was so gung-ho that I went around on my own time, handing out my business card to everybody I could find on this beat I had been told I would be working. Used car lots, cleaners, liquor stores, you name it. It scared the hell out of some of those guys, hav-ing a cop walk into their places without being called like that. God, I was green in those days.

Our 7-Eleven had changed, like everything else. The kid behind the counter was Vietnamese, and having almost as much trouble with our language as I had had with his. I poured myself a large coffee from the freshest-looking pot and won-dered how Charlie would have gotten along with this guy. He would have found something to talk to him about. That's the way Charlie was, a bullshitter in a way, but really good with people. The job was fun to him.

The pay phone was outside the store, next to an all-night laundromat. I dialed O'Bannion's number and he answered. I had hoped Mrs. O'Bannion would, for no particular reason.

"O'Bannion, it's me."

"Are you crazy?"

I gave him the number of the pay phone and hung up.

A friend of mine once told me that being a private in-vestigator was equal parts lying and loitering, and he was right. You're either hanging around waiting for somebody to do some-thing, or you're passing yourself off as something you're not to get information out of people. O'Bannion did not make me loiter long. I still had half a cup of coffee when the pay phone rang.

"Yeah?"

"Goddamnit, Jack, I told you not to call me! I told you . . ."

"Shut up and listen."

"Don't you tell me to shut up! Have you talked to Pilar?"

"Yes."

"And she told you everything, right?"

"Hell no, just what she wanted me to know. Nobody has told me everything yet."

"Who else have you been talking to?"

"A man who says his name is Arthur Crandall, for one."

"Crandall? Jesus Christ. Why? How?"

"It was easy. He was waiting in my office practically by the time I got back from your house yesterday. He hired me."

"To do what?"

"To stay where he could keep an eye on me. Do you see what that means?" O'Bannion did not answer. "That means you were right, you are being watched. I recommend you check your car for a 'rabbit.'"

"A what?"

"A 'rabbit,' a 'bumper beeper.' You know, a transmitter. An electronic homing device." I described it to him, and told him where to look. Hard to believe he did not know about the things. Maybe he had forgotten, or always had people to know that stuff for him. I told him about the gadget I had found on my car. Then I filled him in on my meetings with Crandall, leaving Speed and Leslie out of it.

"What else?" he asked when I had finished.

"That's about it, except that I think you and I are in over our heads. What do you know about Pilar?"

"What you do, basically."

"'Basically' is a weasel word, O'Bannion. If you don't know any more than I do about her, you sure as hell don't know enough to stick your neck out the way you have. Don't be cute with me. If you're holding a trump of some kind, let me in on it."

"Hold your horses. I'm on my way to a meet right now. Afterward, I'll get back to you."

"Damn you, O'Bannion, if you're setting me up . . ."

"Hold on, hold on. It's not like that, I swear."

"You swear. Big deal. Listen, you put me in this and that's all right. Maybe I'd have done the same thing in your spot. You're on my blind side anyway because of Betty and the kid, and you know it. But I'm giving it to you straight. This deal's too big for us, and I'm telling you your best bet is to go to the Department with whatever you have and take your chances. Because if you're counting on me to get you through this somehow, I can't promise you a thing."

"Maybe you're right," he said. "I'll know more after the meet."

"Who's it with?" I asked.

"I'm late now."

"I'll go with you."

"That's not necessary. It's not like that."

"How do you know? How can you be sure of anything in this deal?"

"I'm sure. Don't worry about it."

"I'll be at Red's later. Call me there."

"Right."

"O'Bannion?"

"Yeah?"

"Watch yourself."

"Always."

He had not sounded worried enough to suit me, not by half.

Chapter Fourteen

MY NEXT CALL WAS to Homicide. Lieutenant Cochran was not in, the clerk told me, and he was not expected to return to the office before the end of the tour of duty at eleven. If it was an emergency, she assured me she would try to get a message to him. Was it an emergency? I told her it was not. I would try another time.

I was worried about O'Bannion. Either he was holding out on me or he really had put his life in Pilar's hands. Unless he knew more than I did, that was not a smart move. I did not believe her, and I had a lot less at stake than he did. O'Bannion could take care of himself, as far as plots and schemes were concerned. That was what I told myself, and I was the one to know. But I did not like it, just the same. I could not shake a feeling that things were about to go bad. Real bad.

I had shaken my tail, but it was a cinch that he or they would be waiting for me to show at my office. Maybe at Red's, too. I decided I would call Cochran at Red's and ask him to meet me somewhere else. No sense getting him into this if I could help it. Not until something happened that made it his business.

That left me with time to kill and no place in particular to go. So I cruised for a while, and thought about the hands O'Bannion had dealt me, the thing now with Pilar and the other one, with Mrs. O'Bannion. I was still turning it over in my mind when I found myself at White Rock Lake.

I pulled off West Lawther into a parking lot on a point of land that jutted out into the lake across the road from a big dark house. From where I sat, only a hedge and a gate were visible behind me across the road. The house itself was on a hill beyond.

The lake was calm in the moonlight, like a slab of ice. Looking at the water made me feel better after a while, but I could not forget O'Bannion. I hated him for what he had done, hated him every time I thought about my son. I especially hated him when I thought about him and Betty together, the fat pink man and the leggy blonde. I thought of them now. I thought of Betty.

O'Bannion's house was not far from the lake. I was there before I had time to ask myself why I was going there. When I parked in front, I saw that the house was dark except for a light in the master bedroom.

I knew when I got out of my car that I was being watched. I knew they had his house covered, that I was putting myself back into their net. But I did not care. They would have found me again anyway, sooner or later. Screw them.

She answered the door and I did not say anything.

"What do you want?" she asked.

"I'd like to see the boy if you don't mind."

"He's not here. He's with my mother."

I did not know what to say, but I did not make a move to leave.

"Come in."

She opened the door wide for me and I went in. I stood in the entry hall while she bolted the door.

She looked awful. Her hair was short now, and it looked as if she had been asleep. The brown terry bathrobe sagged off her shoulders and the sleeves dropped beyond her fingertips. O'Bannions, I guessed. She was not wearing any makeup, and almost looked her age.

"Go in the den, Jack, and make yourself a drink. I'll just be a minute."

I found the booze without any trouble. O'Bannion did not stock Pinch, but there was a bottle of Chivas. I poured the scotch into a heavy tumbler that looked like real crystal and made myself comfortable in O'Bannion's overstuffed chair.

She was more than a minute, and I amused myself by making a fire in the fireplace. It was going nicely when I felt her watching me.

Now she looked the way I remembered her, like the woman on the boat in my dreams. She had fixed her hair and her face, and slipped into something that fit. It was a gown with a lot of lace in front that made you think you could see her, and a robe that matched. She had not bothered to pull the robe closed in front.

"I'm sorry you missed the boy, Jack. He's been away since the shooting. If I'd had any idea you were coming . . ."

"It's all right. I just thought I'd take a chance."

I envied the boy. When I thought of her folks' place outside of Paris, the three-hundred-acre ranch with work to do and aunts and uncles living within a couple of miles, I could not think of any place I would rather be. Except maybe here, with her.

"Are you all right?" she asked.

"I never know how to answer that. How do you mean?"

"Generally, I suppose."

"I'm fine, generally. And you?"

"I'm scared, Jack."

"You don't look scared."

"Oh? How do I look?"

"Not scared."

She cocked her head to one side as she smiled at me. Her arms crossed around her, pulling the robe closed over her gown with the lace, but she did not tie the sash. Its ends hung loose on either side of her. I did not have anything else to say to her then, and I turned away to keep from looking at her anymore, leaving her in her pose on the step that led down from the entry hall into the den. She looked good there, but she knew that. She always knew exactly how she looked. She had cut her hair short because she looked a little younger that way, when she took the time to fix it. To give myself something else to look at, I took in the furnishings in the den.

The room was well-appointed, as they say, but I stopped looking when I spotted the fish on the wall opposite the fireplace. I had not seen it there before. I had not seen it at all in a long time. It was a respectable marlin, mounted on an oak board with a brass plate. I read the inscription on the plate, then stepped back to get the effect.

"Can you tell me what you're doing?"

"Admiring my fish."

"I don't mean that. I mean what are you doing with Brendan? What has he got himself into?"

"He had the plate replaced on my fish. Why would he do a thing like that?"

"What difference does it make?"

"My name was on the original plate. On this one, there's just the date and the name of the village where we chartered the boat."

"Little Jack likes the fish. He wanted it up there, and Brendan said it could stay if we took your name off."

"'Little Jack'? I thought you didn't call him that any more. I thought you called him John."

I studied the fish, remembering.

"Does he tell people he caught the fish?" I asked. "I mean, when you have people over, does he tell everybody how he caught the big marlin?"

"We seldom entertain. And you said yourself, Jack, that it's not a very big marlin."

"Whatever. Has he ever told anybody that this was his fish?"

"Good Lord, Jack, you're being childish. What is so important about the stupid fish?"

"I don't know. He's taken everything else and made it his . . . I thought you said you'd lost it."

"I found it again. And it's not Brendan's, it's the boy's."

"I caught the goddamned thing before the kid was born. It's his after I'm dead!" I had not meant to make such a thing of it. "I'm not dead yet."

She left the step and glided like a runway model across the floor to the couch. She forgot about the robe. When she moved, it fell open again. Maybe she wanted to get my mind off the fish.

"Do you remember when I caught it?" I asked. "It was your first trip with me. Your first fishing trip." She settled on the couch, and I thought she was careful about the way she arranged herself. Her gown was slit on one side and showed her thigh. "When I think about you, it's on the boat . . ." I stopped myself from telling her anything else about how I remembered her, because I did not want to tell her about the dream.

"Do you think of me often?" The question was soft, like her voice, but there was machinery behind it. Never let an opening pass. "Do you think of me fondly, Jack?"

"You know me and boats. I remember all my times on boats."

"The time I remember is the first trip we took with Little Jack. He was just a baby, remember?"

"He spent all his time asleep in the cabin. And you spent yours sunbathing." I drank some of O'Bannion's scotch. "I think about that sometimes."

"I was a bitch to you then, Jack. Women can be like that after a baby."

"How long after? And how long before?"

"Jack, don't let's fight. You're a man of appetites, and . . ."

"Okay, we won't fight. You said you were scared. Of what?"

"Would you make me a drink?"

I did. The stuff was not hard to find. I handed it to her and she smiled up at me through her lashes.

"How sweet, you remembered what I like."

"Lucky guess," I said, moving away from her a little. I did not sit beside her.

She downed all but a little of her gin and tonic in one toss. That was not how I remembered her handling her booze. Then she finished it off and asked for another. When I knew her well, two drinks were her limit for an evening. I wondered if this was a special occasion.

"Why did you come here tonight, Jack? Tell me the truth."

"I told you, I just took a chance the kid was on the premises."

"You didn't know we had sent him away? Brendan hadn't told you?"

"We don't talk about the kid very much."

"I suppose not."

She did not waste any time finishing her second drink either, and she laid her head against the back of the sofa. Only it was too low, so she slid forward, then leaned back again. The thing was, when she slid forward, her gown rode up a little and the slit with it. She had nothing on under the gown and I found myself looking at a very nice hip and remembering things. Her robe was hardly in the picture at all. It was lying on either side of her, not covering anything but her shoulders.

"You knew Brendan wasn't home."

"Yeah."

"Good."

She studied her empty glass carefully, but she did not ask for a third and I did not rush her. She ran her finger around inside the glass, down to the bottom. Then she put her finger between her lips and sucked it, slowly. She did it again, taking her finger deep inside her mouth. If I had not known her better, I might have thought she had forgotten about me, she seemed so engrossed.

"I am afraid . . ."

"Of what?" I asked. I felt better when she was talking.

"It's Brendan. He hasn't been himself lately, even before the shooting. I know you don't want to talk about him, but I can't help it. He's keeping something from me."

"Or someone?"

"Don't be petty, Jack. It's beneath you."

She raised her glass for another drink and I obliged her.

"I'm not worried about another woman, Jack. It's natural for you to think so because of . . . well, our background. But it's worse than that."

No, I thought, you are not the kind of woman who would lose her man that way, not if that were all there was to it. She paused to take down the top half of her third gin and tonic.

"It's a feeling I have, Jack, a premonition. I can't shake this feeling that . . . something terrible is going to happen and there's nothing I can do about it. Jack, I feel . . . death."

She cried then, because she thought that O'Bannion was going to die. I did not care about that, I did not need ESP to know that he was asking for trouble. The bad thing was that the same feeling she was talking about had been working on me too, nibbling at my nerve like a rat on a dead man. I knew exactly how she felt, but it was not O'Bannion I was worried about.

"Tonight I felt it more than ever," she said, and I could see it in her eyes. She meant it. "When I saw you at the door, I thought you had come . . . that it had happened and you had come to tell me . . . he was dead. Then I thought maybe it was just that you felt it, too. I thought maybe you had come to say good-bye."

"To the boy."

"To me, I hoped. Whatever brought you, I'm glad you're here. I mean that, whether you believe me or not."

I guessed that she meant it, from the way she lay back against the arm of the sofa, not caring where her legs were or how much I saw of them. They were even better than I remembered.

"I'm glad, too," I said.

I poured myself another drink. I felt her eyes on me. Why had I come? A kiss-off, I told myself. Short and sweet and then you're out of it. That is what I told myself. I felt her hand on my arm. I turned.

Her eyes explored mine from inches away. Her face was turned toward mine, and the hint of a smile told me she had seen what she was looking for.

"Hold me, Jack."

Her scent was warm and sweet. Her arms moved slowly to embrace me and the robe fell away from her shoulders. I put my hands on her waist to push her away, but the feel of her stopped me. She held me tight and pressed herself against me.

"Just hold me. I need you, Jack."

Her voice was low and soft, a little throaty with what might have been lust. I was losing myself in her touch, her aroma.

"Can you ever forgive me?" she whispered. "Can you?"

"I knew you were a whore when I married you."

My voice did not sound the way I wanted it to.

"I deserve that." She raised her head again, and I watched her lips as she spoke. "Forgive me."

She kissed me and I did not try to stop her. The heat from the fireplace behind me was nothing to the warmth of her against me. It was beautiful and I felt alive for the first time in a long, long time. My heart was breaking, remembering my times with her. Even knowing what she was, I could not help myself. I did not care if she meant any of it or what it meant, or what it made me. I would have killed to have her one more time.

But not like this.

"I have to go," I said, and pushed away from her. She did not fight to keep me.

Chapter Fifteen

WHAT HAD SHE WANTED so badly tonight?

Her premonition was real, and it fed mine. But what beyond that, beyond her need of kindling my urgency against the chill, had she hoped to gain? Maybe she hoped I knew more than she and would tell to have her. What did she suspect? I knew what I thought.

I thought that Brendan O'Bannion had met his match in Pilar. She had given him something to want more than he wanted to keep Betty for himself. Betty could not imagine losing O'Bannion to another woman, and I knew she was right, if it were only a woman. But what was she up against in Pilar? Another seductress, of course, but what was the extra angle, the tie-breaker? I knew O'Bannion pretty well, too, and I figured dollar signs, the icons of his religion, were there somewhere.

What had Speed said about the Santa Rosans? They had been salting the national treasury away out of the country for generations, some of it in numbered accounts. The kinds of accounts that pay off like slot machines for whomever shows up with the winning numbers. Maybe that was it. Maybe Pilar had shown O'Bannion a little green and a promise of more to come. Do this for me, baby, and then it's you and me and the palm trees, and more money than we can spend or lose if we live to be a hundred. That would do it. That would lure O'Bannion away from anything.

I hope to hell I am right, I said, talking to myself as I drove in no particular pattern, generally making my way toward Greenville Avenue and Red's. It would be justice for her to find herself alone, her man gone with another woman and a pot of gold. I thought about that, and I liked it at first. I liked it a lot. She was not a woman who would go it alone, and I knew she would come to me when O'Bannion was gone. Deep down, I knew she would come to me until and unless something better came along. It was hell to know that about the woman I loved, but better to know than to be blind. I loved her anyway. It would be that way, I told myself. A doublecrossed doublecrosser, she would come back to me for as long as I could keep her this time. It was not what I wanted, but I would take it.

I knew how I wanted it to be. I knew now, if I had not admitted it to myself before, that I had gone along with this deal, that I would go along to the end of it, to get her back. I worried about her premonition and my suspicions. I did not want anything to happen to O'Bannion, nothing that would take him out of the picture. The way I wanted it was the three of us, all the cards on the table, and her choosing me over him. It could be that way, I told myself. I could make it that way.

The clerk in the off-brand convenience store where I stopped eyed me when I walked in, and he looked tense. I guess I looked like a man with things on my mind. Being careful not to make any quick moves, I showed him my dollar bill and asked for change. He looked relieved when I left.

From the outside pay phone I called Eddy Cochran. Red answered and fetched Cochran for me.

"Cochran."

"Eddie, this is Jack Kyle."

"Hi, sleuth. How's business?"

"Picking up. I have something for you."

"Come on over. I plan to be here a while."

"It might be better if you met me somewhere."

Just in case they had not picked back up on me at O'Bannion's house, I thought maybe I could still keep Eddie out of it.

"Why?"

"I could explain when I see you."

"Well, Jack, let me ask you something. Are you worried about me for some reason, or about you, your deal? Because if it's on your end, I'll meet you. You know that."

"I'm better than even to have a tail right now, Eddie. I shook'em earlier, but I think maybe they're back. Either way, I think they may be set up on Red's. I don't want to get you involved in it, that's all."

"Well screw a bunch of that crap. I've had a hard day, and I'm due some serious unwinding. You come on over here and we'll talk. If somebody wants to shadow me around, fine. But they'd better be watching their own ass, too."

I did not argue, I just said I'd be right over. I could remember being that strong when I still had a team behind me. It makes a difference, but I had a hunch Eddie would be the same either way.

Eddie was in front of Red's when I cruised by looking for a place to park. He was standing in the open door of his unmarked take-home car, his radio microphone in his hand. The take-home car meant he had the call for any police-involved shootings that might happen before seven the next morning."

"Jack, pull it in here and go with me."

He backed his squad car out and I parked my heap in his space. When I climbed in beside him, he wheeled away, making the old Volare squeal the tires in the process.

"Eleven ten," he said into the microphone.

"Go ahead."

"I'm en route on the signal twenty-seven."

"What's the deal, Eddie?"

A twenty-seven was a dead body.

"I got another call after I talked to you. Business."

"I can wait, talk to you later."

"No problem. Go ahead and tell me about it."

I laid the manila envelope with the photos of Arthur Crandall on the seat between us. My mind was working pretty fast, figuring the angles, what to tell him and what to hold back.

"What's in there?" he asked, meaning the envelope.

"Pictures of a guy I'd like to know more about. He goes by the name of Arthur Crandall, uses a front he calls Amalgamated Enterprises. I've been told by unreliable sources that he is supposed to be CIA, maybe retired. I thought you could show him around a little to your friends down at the Federal Building."

"Would this have anything to do with Brendan O'Bannion's deal?"

"Probably. But I'm not sure how it fits in."

"What are you sure of, Jack?"

"That O'Bannion hired me to protect his interests. And that this Crandall guy doesn't want me to. He's been nice so far, even gave me some money. Hired me on a blind to keep me out of circulation for a few days."

"I see. Your business is picking up, ain't it?" After he had thoroughly chewed a toothpick, switching it from one side of his mouth to the other and back the way he did when he was thinking hard, he added, "What else can you tell me about it?"

He was leaving me some operating room, putting it like that. I could not be sure whether he was making it easy for me or laying a trap. It depended on how much he knew. You could never tell with Eddie.

"Not much that you don't already know. O'Bannion gave me the same story you said he told you, about the deal that was too big to talk about. He just wanted me to be handy whenever whatever is supposed to happen happened."

"Why?"

"He figured he was out of it because he was being watched and because of the shooting thing. He was too hot."

"He was being watched by who?"

"I can't be sure, but it figures that is how Crandall got onto me. I haven't made anybody tailing me, but I found a rabbit on my car earlier this evening."

"You still got it?"

"No."

"Too bad. Sounds like somebody's working with a big budget. How much did Crandall give you?"

"Four days worth. It's soon, whatever it is."

"Tonight maybe?"

"I don't think so."

"What else, Jack?"

"That's about it." I was not sure why, but I had decided to keep Pilar out of it if I could. Call it a hunch. "Maybe you know more than I do."

"Maybe. Where were you the hour or so right before you called me?"

"Why do you ask?"

"For the same reason that I won't ask again."

"Then I don't mind telling you," I said. There was a tone in his voice I had heard before, but never aimed at me. It was a stone deadly edge that I knew meant business. I did not want to lie, because I knew if it counted I could not afford to change my story later. "Most of it, I was at O'Bannion's house."

"Got a witness?"

"Betty."

"And your boy?"

"He wasn't there."

"And what the hell were you and Mrs. O'Bannion doing?"

"Putting together a Brendan O'Bannion scrapbook. None of your goddam business."

"Jesus."

"What is it, Eddie? What's going on?"

"It's O'Bannion. He's dead."

"I was afraid of that."

"You don't sound surprised."

"You knew him, are you surprised?"

"No. But I wish to hell you were."

Out of the corner of my eye, I saw Eddie Cochran studying me on the sly. The kind of a cop that Eddie was and that

111

I used to be, the good kind that gets the job done. They can, in a way be closer, have more in common with the crooks than the squares. I knew that and so did Eddie. When you are in the Department, there are things that help you stay on the right side of the line. Your partner, your friends you work with, maybe even your family sometimes, a lot of things. But when you leave that, when you are on the outside working solo, it can be different. It is a very fine line. I thought Eddie was thinking about that as we drove, neither of us talking. I know I was.

Chapter Sixteen

WHEN EDDIE AND I drove up to the cabin, I could see through a window without curtains, the lab guys coming and going inside. Their strobes jumped like lightning flashes out the window and door, across the drive. We passed a sign with its neon tubes burned out that said this was the WAGON WHEEL INN. It was a row of sheds that passed for what used to be called a motor court, set off by a gravel drive shared by a liquor store from Harry Hines Boulevard. The place had been there over twenty years, since the days when Hines was the highway north to Denton, before I-35 went in.

I spotted O'Bannion's car, parked head-in at the front of the cabin, the farthest one from the street, with an overgrown vacant lot beyond and beside it. You never pull up right in front of a place like that and get out of your car where whoever might be inside can see you. You park to one side or the other, preferably the near side. You get out quietly and ease up to the place, give yourself a chance to look things over on the way in. You learn that early working a squad. Like I said, O'Bannion was no street cop. He had been inside a long time, but being careful is something you do not forget, not if you had a good trainer. It becomes a part of you. Myself, I never knocked on a door and then stood in front of it waiting for an answer. Not if I was just taking a box of candy to my maiden aunt. No matter whose door it was, I would stand to one side, out of the line of fire. It is second nature. But O'Bannion had been away from it too long. He had been too much of a big shot, with nobody to be afraid of. It was being afraid that kept you alive.

There were half a dozen cars there besides O'Bannion's, a couple of marked patrol cars, a Homicide car and one for the lab team, plus an ambulance. The ambulance crew was in no hurry. Both the attendants were leaning on a fender, smoking and joking. Eddie got as close as he could, then parked and got out. I followed. Eddie stopped on the cabin porch to have a word with one of his investigators. I trailed behind and took the time to check underneath O'Bannion's car.

It was too dark to see, but I ran my hand all along the underside from the rear bumper as far forward as I could reach. Nothing. I borrowed a flashlight from a very young-looking uniformed cop who did not seem to have anything to do. He was probably supposed to be watching the victim's car, to keep anybody like me from screwing around with it. But maybe nobody told him, or he figured since I came with the lieutenant I was okay. Either way, he seemed happy to help. I did not tell him what I was looking for.

By the time I gave the kid back his flashlight, I had covered every inch of the belly of the car. Not only was there no transmitter, there was no sign there had ever been one. There are a lot of ways to put one on a car, but most of them leave traces. The car was as dirty as you would expect, and there should have been some scratches or marks, something. I wondered. A feeling that had begun to work on me cranked up a notch. A second feeling, aside from the premonition I shared with Betty. Eddie was waiting for me when I finished.

"Find what you were looking for?" he asked.

"Yeah, but not what I wanted to find."

"Anything you can tell me, or don't I have a high enough security clearance?"

I did not take long to decide to level with him, within reason. This was no time for semantics.

"O'Bannion thought he was being tailed, like I said. I was just checking for a transmitter."

"And?"

"Nothing I could find. You might want to have somebody go over it again."

"Yeah, I might. Who was doing the tailing?"

"I'm not sure. Maybe the Crandall character, the guy I told you about."

"And who is he, Jack? Who is he working for?"

"I don't know."

Eddie did not think much of that.

"On the level, Eddie. That's why I called you tonight, remember? I wanted you to check the man out. You tell me."

"What made O'Bannion think he was being tailed?"

"I don't know what made him think it at first. Crandall showed up right after I was over at O'Bannion's house. That's what made me buy it."

"When were you at his house?"

"The morning the story broke in the paper about his shooting. He called me and I went over. He took me outside to talk, kept a radio playing the whole time. He even took a swing at me in his front yard. Said if anybody was watching, he didn't want them to think we were chummy."

"Is that how you got the nick?"

"Yeah." I had forgotten about the cut on my cheek. "He clipped me with his pinky ring."

"And then what?"

"I laid him out."

"Bad?"

"Nah. He couldn't take a punch."

Eddie spat a gnawed toothpick between his feet and fished a fresh one out of his shirt pocket.

"You were always good for a theory, Jack. You're bound to have some ideas. Talk to me."

"Crandall is supposed to be ex-CIA. He may still be working for them. Could be O'Bannion stumbled into something they were interested in."

"The CIA."

"I know how it sounds."

115

"I'll check into it. Aside from that, if you're talking taps and transmitters, surveillance, that kind of manpower, budget . . . you know what that sounds like, don't you?"

"To me, it sounds like the feds. I don't know as much as I'd like to about wiretaps, but the big boys tell me that about half of the ones you find have fed court orders behind them."

"The big boys? And who would that be, Jack?"

"Lighten up, Eddie, it's a figure of speech, for Christ's sake."

"Oh."

The kid in the uniform was eating this up. I guessed it sounded pretty big-time to him, but I did not like it that Eddie was cutting up our business in front of him. I could not help thinking that maybe he wanted a witness."

"Anything else?" Eddie asked.

"Like what?"

"Don't dance me around on this, Jack."

"I wouldn't dream . . . hey, I'm leveling with you, god-damnit."

I had not seen Eddie like this before, not with me. It did not feel good.

"So what else, Jack? Anything in particular come to mind here? We're talking a high-dollar operation covering a man's house, his phone, the man himself, around the clock. Not to mention putting a tail on you to boot."

"If it's not the feds, maybe a high-powered private investigator. We have one or two in town. But that doesn't figure."

"Let me help you out, Jack. Let's say for the sake of argument that it is the feds. Think you could narrow it down any from there?"

"I know what you're getting at. All right, it could be DEA. They have the budget, and with O'Bannion being in Narcotics, it could make sense. Is that what you're getting at?"

"Maybe."

Eddie paced a circle, like he was mulling things over. I

looked past him and saw the lab men packing up their gear. I wanted to take a look inside before they put things back, but I decided not to push it.

"Tell me what you were supposed to do for O'Bannion. I won't ask you why he would pick you, or what in God's name would possess you to go along with it. I'm not up for any of the deep stuff tonight. Just give me the easy one: He hired you to do what?"

"I don't want you to think I'm being coy, Eddie, but he wasn't very clear about that. Look after his interests was how he put it. Something was supposed to happen in the next few days, and I was to kind of represent him."

"What was supposed to happen in the next few days?"

"I'm really not sure. Maybe some kind of a drop."

What I was doing was dangerous. I had a choice to make. Either I could give Eddie everything I had and let him take it from here on out or I could hold out on him and try my hand. Ordinarily, I would give it to him and call it a day. Not just because he was probably better at the work than I was, but for the obvious reason that it was his job. He had the authority and responsibility and the machinery behind him to get it done. But this was not ordinarily. The truth of this whole deal lay somewhere between Pilar and Arthur Crandall. They were not people Eddie could get to. If he found them, he would never be able to do anything with them. They were pros from another league, like the Yankees coming to town for an exhibition game. Neither of them would talk, they would both have alibis and backup alibis, and both of them would get out of the country before the locals could get as much as indictments, even if they could put together enough evidence to make a case. Besides, nobody I knew even knew who these people were for sure, including me. I had read enough Le Carré novels to know they had more sets of identity papers than I had old parking tickets. I wanted to give him enough to steer him in the right direction if I could, at least save him from a wild-goose chase that might stir up problems for him with the feds. The trick was to do that without giving myself away. I had to make him think I was telling him all I knew. If he thought I was holding back, he would find a way to put me on ice until it was all over. That was why I was telling him what I had to tell him in installments. That way, maybe he would think he had gotten everything out of me. I knew I was taking a chance.

"It took you long enough to get around to it. What kind of drop?"

"Just some information," I said. "Political stuff."

"You're shitting me."

"I swear."

"O'Bannion told you that?"

I nodded. It was my first lie to him. But I had to lie to keep Pilar out of it. If Eddie had already got wind of her, I was in deep trouble. I did not have that many friends, and right now Eddie was the last man on earth I wanted to cut myself off from. But this felt like the way to play it.

"Christ almighty, Jack, did you buy that? When did you ever know Brendan O'Bannion to get mixed up in anything more political than kissing some chief's ass?"

"Can't say I ever did. You think it's a dope shipment?"

"You tell me. You knew O'Bannion better than I did. Maybe you don't think he was the type to try for a big score, a one-time deal that could set him up for life."

"Damned right he was. But it doesn't have to be dope. There could be money in politics, couldn't there?"

"Not without being elected. What the hell kind of politics do you think we're talking about here?"

"Latin American maybe, like the dude O'Bannion shot. Maybe O'Bannion got a line on something he found a market for. That could fit in with the feds being in it. Or maybe Crandall really is ex-CIA, or still on the payroll, for all I know. Either way, if he came down on the other side from O'Bannion, he could have been the one who threw a net over him. Or he and O'Bannion could have been in something together, freelancing, and the feds got onto them. It could be something like that."

"You got a couple of good stories there, if you don't stop to count the maybes."

"You wanted a theory," I said. "That's it. You know as much as I do."

The look Eddie gave me cut deep. There was a lot on the line, and we both knew it.

"I hope so, Jack. I sure as hell hope so."

Inside my head the seconds passed like soldiers on a funeral march. Eddie was thinking, and I had nothing else to say.

Chapter Seventeen

I WAS THINKING, TOO, trying to figure what Eddie would do next. I had a couple of ideas, and I did not care for them. If he was giving me time to change my mind about anything, my time ran out, and he turned to the kid with the flashlight.

"Get a wrecker out here and impound this car. You stay with it. I don't want anybody else screwing around with it. Stay with it until the Crime Scene Search people get at it. Go in the wrecker to the pound. Get them to put it someplace where we can hook up some lights and get a good look at it. You got that?"

"Yes, sir."

I thought the kid almost saluted.

"Eddie," I said, trying to sound nonchalant. "You mind if I take a look inside?"

"You seen one, you've seen 'em all."

Somebody inside the cabin waved, and the ambulance attendants went in, wheeling their stretcher along.

"Yeah, I know," I persisted. "But I might pick up on something."

"Like what?"

"How do I know from out here? You know, something."

It was lame and we both knew it. I did not even know myself at first why I wanted so badly to go inside. There was something to be said for seeing O'Bannion dead. I had thought about that a time or two in the last year. But that was bullshit. I did not really want him dead at all. Victory by default. Who needs it? I wanted him on his feet, I wanted to beat him on his best day. It came to me then that a part of me did not want to be there at all, not inside the cabin, not anywhere near the sleazy little dump called the Wagon Wheel Inn. Part of me did not care about that at all anymore. That part of me wanted to be with Betty. She would need me. Her intuition had been right, and she would need me to make her know she would not be alone.

But another part of me wanted to go inside, for reasons bigger than seeing the body or picking up a clue. Inside there was for members only. I wanted in more than the shabby cabin, I wanted in the club again. Not as a member, not really in. I knew that was over for good. I wanted in on an honorary ticket, as a guest at least. I had put in my time and I had my wounds. That ought to count for something.

When they started out with the body, Eddie put a hand on my arm and turned me away. He walked me off a little distance. He was almost gentle about it, but there it was. He was the gatekeeper and I was the outsider.

That hurt, but not as much as the look on Eddie's face. It was coming clearer now, and knowing it went to work on me. I felt light-headed, and the gravel drive under my feet started a slow spin. There are almost always a couple of things about a murder, about the scene or the body, that you do not let out. These things nobody knows but the cops and the killer. That way, if a guy slips and lets something out, something that was not in the papers, not on the TV news, maybe not even in the official reports, if the guy drops his guard, he is telling you that he was there. He's hanging himself. That was why Eddie did not want me inside before they finished, why he did not want me to get a look at the body. I was not just out of the club, I was a suspect! It made sense if you looked at it from Eddie's point of view. But from mine, I felt as if I were off a beach somewhere trying to swim but the tide was going out.

"I guess there's no harm if you want to go in and look around."

The ambulance eased past us as Eddie motioned toward the open door of the cabin for me to go in. One of the patrol cars, driven by a sergeant I used to know, was backing out, leaving. I saw the lab men loading their gear into their car.

"Thanks," I said.

We walked up to the door and started inside, then stepped back to let the two Homicide investigators pass on their way out. I knew one of them, the one who did not look at me. The other one was new. He looked almost as young as the kid Eddie had left in charge of O'Bannion's car. I did not know why, but I looked back toward the kid as if I were looking back through time at myself at his age. There he was with his flashlight, obeying orders like a good scout. He was watching me, but he turned away when I looked at him.

It was stuffy inside after standing so long in the cold drizzle of the driveway, and it did not take long to look at it all. There was a ratty little bed with its spread tousled and a dresser opposite, all the drawers opened and stacked upside down on the floor. That was it except for a cheap dinette table and two chairs. One of the chairs was busted. The floor was linoleum.

Either they had straightened up the place or else O'Bannion had not made much of a fight. There was not much, but except for the overturned dresser drawers, nothing looked out of place. A light bulb with a dingy shade hung head-high between the bed and the table, and there was a garish print on the wall behind the table near the back door. It depicted a romanticized cowboy on horseback.

I went to the bed and pulled the cover back. I did not bother to ask Eddie if it was all right. His men had finished. It was all over or I would not be there.

Something happened when I pulled the cover off the pillow, something so subtle that it did not register at the time. I did not know what it was, I mean, only that something there meant something. Something out of place somehow.

"Do you mind telling me how it was done?" I asked.

"You know better than that, Jack."

"The hell I do."

"It's confidential."

"Bullshit. Cause goes on the death certificate, for Christ's sake. It's public record."

"Once it's filed."

You go just so far and then you turn, no matter what is at stake, no matter how you feel about it or anything else. I was getting there, and Eddie knew it.

"Overdose," he said.

"Now you're the one who's kidding."

"That's what the medical examiner told my guys."

"Overdose of what?" I asked.

"We'll have to wait for the autopsy. We didn't find anything here."

"No needle, no works?"

"I didn't say it was an injection. If he used pills, there wouldn't be anything to find."

"No, and your M.E. wouldn't have called it an overdose. Natural causes, he would have said, until he did the post and found the junk in O'Bannion's system. Don't you dance me around, Eddie."

"The syringe was clean. No traces as far as we could tell without a microscope."

"Prints?"

"None on the syringe."

"None at all or none but O'Bannion's?"

"No prints at all."

"So you are calling it a murder."

"Naturally."

"What else, Eddie?"

"What do you mean?"

"What I said. You're not telling me everything."

"And you are. You're telling me all you know about this."

"That's right," I said. In for a penny, in for a pound.

"There was something else."

"Is it confidential?"

"It sure as hell should be, but I'll tell you. Marks on his throat. M.E. says he was choked first, that's his guess for now. Like somebody choked him out and then shot him up."

"What did they use?"

"An arm from behind, probably. That's preliminary, of course. A pretty strong arm, to handle a man O'Bannion's size."

"Right."

"Jack, do you understand what I'm telling you?"

"Yeah, that somebody used a chokehold on him."

"That's right. A standard DPD chokehold."

"I get the picture."

"The kind you've used a hundred times. Right, Jack?"

"Right."

"The kind you used on . . . what was his name? Ringwald. Yeah, that's it. Clovis Ringwald. You remember him, don't you, Jack?"

"The name sounds familiar. Yeah, Eddie, I've choked a guy down a time or two in my life. So have you. So have a couple of thousand other cops. That's here in Dallas. That's not counting Houston, LA, every other town in the country."

"You've got a point, Jack. There's a lot of cops in this country. How many of them do you figure were ever married to Betty O'Bannion?"

Chapter Eighteen

WE WERE GOING DOWNTOWN.

Eddie said nothing about arresting me and he did not start that business about my rights. He just needed a statement from me, he said. That was the way to do it, the soft sell. Just need you to come down to the station with me and get this straightened out. No need to fight them if you can con them. I had done it plenty of times myself.

He was backing off. I thought about that. Maybe he was easing up because we were friends. Or because he knew in his bones that I was not a murderer. He was hard to figure, the whole deal was. It had taken off on me, gotten complicated as hell, and I needed time to think things through. He did not press me to talk on the way down, and I did not volunteer any conversation.

It occurred to me that Eddie might be easing up because he figured I *was* his man, and he did not want to screw up his case by pushing too hard, too fast. Get a statement out of me, get my story on paper, something to go after. Break the story and you break the man. If he leaned on me, I might decide I did not want to give him a statement or anything else. I might start talking about lawyers, might start talking about rights myself. I liked my first view of it better, that he was giving me the benefit of the doubt. That was what I wanted to believe. By the time we crossed Ross Avenue, I had stopped trying.

I closed my eyes and leaned back against the headrest. And that was when it hit me. That was when I knew what the something was, the subtle something that happened when I pulled the cover off the pillow on the bed in the cabin at the Wagon Wheel Inn. A scent, a fragrance. Gardenias and musk, like a cat in a flower garden. Pilar.

Whatever hunch I was playing by not telling Eddie about Pilar, it did not offset my need to stay clear of a murder rap. But tell him what? Would it be worth admitting that I had been holding out on him to tell him I suddenly had a better suspect? Would he believe me, or just think that I was trying to get out of the spotlight by swinging it onto my mystery lady? There was no mistaking her scent. But that did not prove anything to anybody but me.

Nobody was going to be filed on for murder because I was willing to swear on my nose. If Eddie were in the mood to go fishing, he might use it to run a bluff on her, but it was not much. I decided it was not enough, even if I could have made him believe me. If anybody was going to work on Pilar it would have to be me. All I had to do was find her, after I talked my way out of Eddie Cochran's office.

Then I thought about Betty again, and it occurred to me that Eddie did not have much of a case against me, either. He had not volunteered the time of death and I had not asked. I knew it had to be between the time I spoke to O'Bannion on the phone and sometime before I met Eddie at Red's. I had a little time there that would be blank when I was wandering around and wound up at the lake. But I had been with Betty most of the time. An innocent man's alibi is seldom perfect. I figured that with any luck at all mine was good enough. It was hell the way things had worked out. I had gotten into all of this in the first place to save Betty from O'Bannion. Now it was up to her to save me from him, in a way.

Homicide was about what you would expect, green walls and steel desks, a lot of crap on bulletin boards. It had not changed since my days. It looked like it had when I used to walk down the hall from my office in Narcotics and drop in on my friend Fast Eddie.

He did not put me in one of the interrogation rooms where they stuck suspects. He showed me to a desk that was not being used at the back of the squad room and handed me a legal pad and a ballpoint.

"Make yourself comfortable, Jack. You know the drill, just write down what you know about this, where you've been this evening, anybody who saw you. You know what I need."

I nodded and went to work. The sooner I got this done, the sooner I would be out of there. I had not gotten very far when I thought of something.

"Say, Eddie. When we finish here, you want to give me a lift back to my car?"

"I wouldn't count on it. Looks like I may be tied up here for a while."

"Oh. Maybe one of your guys . . ."

"They're all out. It's been that kind of a night."

I knew he usually did not have anybody working after eleven, but there were bound to be a few called in because of O'Bannion. There were always the uniforms. It was standard practice to provide transportation for witnesses who came down to give statements. To hell with him.

"No problem," I said. "Mind if I make a call?"

He looked at me as if he would rather I did not, but he did not say so, so I punched up a line on the desk phone and called Speed. There was no answer at any of his numbers, and none at his apartment on my second try. I checked my little book of numbers and called Della at home. I could not think of anyone else. Besides, I felt like I owed her an explanation. I wanted to tell her what was going on before she heard it from someone else. I wondered as I dialed why it mattered.

She sounded a little husky when she answered and I was afraid I might have awakened her. She said she had not been sleeping.

"What is it? Jack, are you hurt again?"

129

"No, it's nothing like that. I'm okay."

"Then what is it?"

"It's O'Bannion. Somebody killed him."

"Mister O'Bannion, the man who didn't call?"

"Yeah, that's the one."

"What's that got to do with you? Where are you?"

"I'm down here in Eddie Cochran's office at Homicide."

"Homicide? Did you kill O'Bannion?"

"Della!"

"It's okay if you did. I mean, if you did I know you had a good reason. Do you need an alibi? I'll *swear* you were here with me . . ."

"Della, stop it."

It occurred to me that a kid who trusted you that much could be a big responsibility. And she was serious about it, I could tell from the tone of her voice.

"I appreciate your confidence in me," I told her. "But I had nothing to do with it. Lieutenant Cochran just asked me down to give a statement, that's all."

"Is there anything I can do?"

"I could use a ride back to my car when I'm finished here. Are you in any shape to drive?"

"Of course I am. I'll come right down."

"Do you know where it is? The old Police and Courts Building, at Commerce and Harwood, not the new City Hall."

"I'll find it."

"Okay. Come down Central, exit to your left before you get to the elevated part. Come on down to Elm and take a right. Go west on Elm past Harwood to St. Paul, because you're not supposed to turn left at Harwood. This time of night it shouldn't matter, but I don't want you to get pulled over. Left on St. Paul, then left again on Commerce. It's one way coming back toward Central. Pull over to the curb on the lefthand side of the street. If I'm not there, you should be able to wait for me. If there's any traffic, you can make the block. Okay?"

"Got it. I'll be right down."

"There's no hurry. They'll have to type my statement, and Eddie will probably want to go over a couple of things with me. Take your time. I don't want you to get a ticket or anything."

"Don't worry about me, Jack. Just be careful of your friend Cochran."

"I will. Listen, don't come inside looking for me. There are all kinds of creeps in this place this time of night."

"All right. Be careful."

"Thanks, kid."

"Don't worry, Jack."

I looked up from the phone and Eddie was staring at me. He had not said anything when I had told Della that I was not in trouble, that I would be ready to go soon. I hoped that was a good sign.

"Say, Eddie," I said. "What times do you want on this?"

"This evening."

"Yeah, but what times? Give me a hint."

"Make it from about five P.M. until you met me at Red's."

"Five P.M.?" I asked.

"If you don't mind."

"Sure. No problem."

That meant after my run-in with Crandall and Mario in my office, which was fine with me. No use clouding the issue. I wondered why he wanted me to start at five. I knew O'Bannion was alive long after that; I had talked to him on the phone around eight or eight-thirty. Of course, the medical examiner might not have nailed the time of death down very tight in his preliminary. Or maybe Eddie was doing a little fishing.

I started the statement with my meeting with Crandall at Vincent's. I did not like it, but I could not see any way around involving Speed and Leslie. That would tie in with the photos I had given Eddie, and anyway, I could not afford to leave a lot of things out. This was official, and it was in writing. I did not want to have to go back later and try to patch it up. I covered my conversation with Crandall, but I did not put anything in that I had not already told Eddie. Then my little adventure with the transmitter, my stop at Speed's apartment, and my phone call to O'Bannion. I put in my conversation with O'Bannion word for word as best as I could remember it. Then my cruise by the lake and my visit to Mrs. O'Bannion. To see my kid, who was not there. As for what we did during the hour or so I was with her, I covered some of our conversation and left it at that. All that was left was what Eddie already knew firsthand, the part where I called him and then met him at Red's place.

It did not take long to write. When I had double-checked it to make sure I had covered everything, I stood up and handed the legal pad to Eddie. He read it and looked at me.

"This is your story?"

"That's it."

"You wouldn't want to look it over, maybe think about it again? It's not too late to change it."

"Eddie, all I can do is tell the truth."

"Pick a story and stick with it, is that it?"

"Honesty is the best policy."

"Right. Have a seat, I'll get this typed."

Eddie left me to myself at the back of the empty squad room while he went up to the typist's desk by the front door. He did not offer me any coffee, and he did not say it would be all right to smoke. I smoked a couple of cigarettes anyway, while I waited. There were just the three of us in the place, me and Eddie and the typist. He did not have anything to say to me while she was typing. He was handling this strictly business, and going out of his way to be obvious about it. Like the thing about the ride back to get my car. It was not a big deal, but I was getting the message.

I was about to light my last cigarette when Eddie returned. He had two copies of my statement in his hand, my handwritten original and the typed version. It was on a printed form titled "Voluntary Statement, Not Under Arrest," and it had a preamble that said I was giving this statement voluntarily and all the rest of the boilerplate. There were Xs typed in across the bottom to show that nothing could be added after I signed it.

Underneath the place for my signature there was the usual stuff to be filled in by a notary. From her desk the typist was watching me, waiting for me to sign the paper. Then she would notarize it.

I looked the thing over pretty carefully, just in case they had changed anything, slipped in a little something that might trip me up. It looked kosher and I signed it.

"Is that it?" I said.

I smiled at Eddie and got to my feet. I wanted this to be over. I had things to do.

"Not quite."

I reconsidered my decision to keep Pilar out of it, now that it was too late. Eddie looked like a man with a secret, like he was holding a fat hand on a fat pot.

"There's somebody I want you to see," he said.

"Any friend of yours . . ."

Eddie opened a door in the wall opposite the desk where I was standing. He stuck his head inside, and I heard voices. When he turned back toward me, standing to one side of the door, I heard the scuffling of feet beyond the door.

I did not know who I expected to see, but it was not Betty O'Bannion. She was the last person I would have guessed, but there she was, with a uniformed policewoman on one side of her and Eddie on the other.

"Betty, what are you doing here?" I could not make out the look in her eyes, and I could not figure out what was happening. "Have they told you?"

She did not move or speak at first, and her eyes fixed on mine. I started toward her, started to ask Eddie what the hell he was doing dragging her downtown at a time like this. She should be with her folks. I was thinking about Betty's folks when she hit me.

It was a big purse, the kind she always carried, full of junk and heavier than a field pack. I came nowhere close to getting out of the way of it, and it felt like a hammer on the side of my head. I staggered back until the desk hit the backs of my legs and I sprawled backward across the top of it. She was on me like a panther, screaming and crying and swinging the big purse.

"Murderer! Murderer!"

Over and over she screamed the same thing as she flailed at me with the purse. I tried to catch her arms, to hold her still, but she came at me with a vengeance. "You killed him!"

She bore down over me like a cat and I thought she would bite through my throat if I let her get close enough. But then, as her lips brushed my ear and just before Eddie and the policewoman managed to get control of her and pull her away, she whispered something.

"Trust me," she whispered. "Trust me."

And then she was gone, half carried out of the room by the two cops, limp and crying between them, as if all her strength was spent. She was sobbing with the loud jerky noises a kid makes when he is inconsolable. Eddie closed the door behind her and wiped a sleeve across his forehead. He looked at me as if he wanted me to make the next move. I did not.

"Well?" he said finally.

"Well your ass, Eddie. What was all that about? You've got no business dragging her down here for all this crap. Has anybody called her parents in Paris? She ought to be with them."

"Oh, I appreciate your concern, Jack. Don't worry about that right now, though. That's been taken care of." He paced away from me, then back. "You know, you're about the damnedest thing I have ever seen. You really are. You're really worried about her, aren't you? You dumb sonofabitch! Didn't you hear her? Didn't you hear what she was calling you? Are you so goddamned hardheaded you don't even know she tried to beat your brains out?"

"She's upset."

"No shit. And you would be too, if you had the brains of a pissant."

"What are you talking about?"

"This."

He handed me a typed statement, the same kind of form I had just signed. It was not easy to focus my eyes enough to read it. She must have hit me harder than I thought. When the words on the page did come clear, I could not believe it. I saw Betty's signature at the bottom of the page, I recognized her handwriting, but I could not believe it.

"What is this?" I asked. "What the hell is going on here?"

"You tell me." Eddie said.

All I could do was shake my aching head and read the thing again.

"She says you were not with her tonight, not at any time. She says there that she has not seen you since the other day when you came over to her house to give O'Bannion a hard time for getting his name in the paper. She says you got out of line that day, badly out of line, and that O'Bannion kicked your ass for it. She says you threatened to get even, that you threatened to kill him."

"Eddie, you know this is bullshit. You can't take this seriously."

"Can't I? Stop me if you've heard this one before: 'You have the right to remain silent. If you give up the right to remain silent, anything you say may be used against you at your trial. You have the right . . .'"

Chapter Nineteen

"HOLD ON, EDDIE. HOLD on just a goddamn minute!"

"Do you understand these rights as I have explained them to you?"

"Yeah, I understand them, and you know it. And I know you're supposed to advise the suspect *before* you take his statement, not after."

"That doesn't apply to you, Jack. You weren't a suspect when you came in here with me. Voluntarily. You weren't a suspect when you gave me your statement. Not until just now, when Betty made a liar out of you and shot down your alibi. But I'm glad you understand your rights."

A couple of detectives showed up, the kind you could not mistake for anything else in the world, with cowboy boots and big belt buckles, magnums under their jackets like tent poles. I did not recognize either of them.

"Okay, Eddie," I said. "Let's do this your way. What are you going to charge me with?"

"Murder."

"Why?"

"You had a beef with O'Bannion. You threatened him. You lied about where you were when the murder was committed."

I told myself to keep it calm. I would get nowhere if it came down to a shouting match in front of Eddie's men.

"Okay, so I'm a suspect. But this is not TV, Eddie. This is

not some detective show where all you have to prove is motive, means, and opportunity. You know what it takes to make something like this stick. You gotta prove I did it, right? Not just that I would have liked to."

"I know what I have to do, Jack."

"Okay, Eddie. Let's just look at it for a minute. Let's see what we have, all right?"

"*We* don't have anything, pal."

"I understand that. I'm not asking for anything because you and I have some history. But you and I always took pride in doing the job right, no matter what. That's all I'm saying. If you're right, fine. But let's just look at it."

He let me say that, and waited for the rest.

"On the alibi, it's my word against Betty's. I know you don't have any witnesses who can put me at the Wagon Wheel because I wasn't there. Why would Betty lie? Couple of reasons. Maybe she doesn't want it known that she and I were together, alone at her house, when O'Bannion got it. Maybe she figures whoever did him will come after me next, and this is one way to protect me, get me off the spot. Okay, that part sounds crazy, I know, but this is a crazy deal. For all I know, that's in the back of your mind, too, hang this half-assed rap on me to get me off the street for a while."

"Do you deny threatening O'Bannion?"

"Once, in front of a banquet hall full of people. That's on the record. I won't lie to you. If I had been a little drunker that night I might have taken him out. But only that night. I was hot then, but I cooled. And you know me. If I had decided to do it, I wouldn't have screwed around the way somebody did. Me and him, winner walks. That's my style and you know it."

"I'm listening," he said, chewing his toothpick.

"You were careful at the scene not to let me in before the lab guys finished. I see why now. If you let me go in and they found my prints, I could say I left them when I went in with you. That's good. You took that angle away from me, and I'm glad. So, what's the word? Did my prints turn up or not?"

He did not answer. He wanted me to do the talking.

"It's like the witnesses. I know there aren't any and I know they didn't get my prints, because I wasn't there. So all you have on me is my hard feelings for O'Bannion and Betty's word that I lied about being with her. Think about it, Eddie. If I were going to kill O'Bannion, would I use Betty for my alibi? You know I wouldn't, not without making sure she would come through for me. Give me a little credit. I may not be the most popular guy in town, but I could find somebody to lie for me if my life depended on it, for Christ's sake."

"Is that it?"

"You tell me, Eddie. I'm saying what you've told me won't hold up. If you've got anything else, you tell me."

"You seem pretty sure about the witnesses."

"I am sure."

"And the prints."

"Right."

"You could have worn gloves."

"I could have."

"And I haven't forgotten about Clovis Ringwald."

"Oh, for Christ's sake . . ."

"You killed him with your hands, Jack. Choked him to death."

"He had a gun, Eddie. And there wasn't time to get to mine."

"Yeah, I remember the deal. He was going to shoot your partner. Shot you instead. You got a medal for it. Maybe it's just a coincidence that O'Bannion got his neck squeezed the same way."

"We've been over that part of it, too. Like I said before, thousands of people use that hold. Cops, ex-cops, Latin American security types trained by the U.S. You haven't forgotten about the Hispanic O'Bannion shot, have you?"

"No, I'm trying to keep it all in focus. But I still think it's a hell of a coincidence."

"We're going in circles here. So you have something or not?"

"What if I told you we had a witness, somebody willing to testify that you were at the Wagon Wheel Inn at the time of the murder?"

"I'd say you were playing Perry Mason."

He did not smile. Not even the little curl at the left corner of his mouth that I had seen a hundred times when he was trying to hold back. I was seeing his poker face, all right. Or else he did have something. I remembered that Crandall had known a lot about me, about my hitch in Nam and my disability. I thought about Crandall and his organization for a minute, while everybody in the room, Eddie and his two cowboys and the typist up at the front who was not typing anymore, waited for somebody to make the next move. If Crandall was set up to do wiretaps and tails and all the rest of it, who was to say that he could not or would not plant a witness? I had not noticed before that the air conditioning in the room was on, that there was a chill in the air. Or that my palms were sweating.

"Hey, if you've got a witness, let's see him. Or her. You know the drill. Let's have a lineup. I'm agreeable." I hoped I sounded more confident than I felt. "You're bluffing, Eddie. The whole thing is a con. You don't have a case on me and you know it. So you press me a little, you figure my conscience will do your job for you. You figure I'll flinch, right? Well, no dice. I didn't do it, man. I didn't kill O'Bannion, and the longer we screw around here the less chance we have of finding the people who did."

"There you go with that 'we' crap again."

"Force of habit. But you won't find the killer standing here playing games with me."

Eddie walked up to my chair and leaned in close. I could see flecks in the whites of his eyes, and tiny slivers on his lower lip from the frazzled toothpick he spat at me.

"Jack," he said, taking each word as it came, talking soft

140

and clear. "This is no game. You are the only handle I've got on O'Bannion, both counts. I don't know who the dude was he killed, and I'm not sure who killed him. But you are in it somehow, up to your eyeballs. And it is a serious personal thing with me. It's my job, Jack. My job. Understand?"

I nodded and he stayed there, very close, his breath on me, his eyes on mine as if he had never seen me before. He waited to see if I had anything else to say. When I did not, he moved away. He turned his back to me and motioned for the cowboys. They shuffled over and the three of them talked in whispers while I waited. I thought about making a break for the door.

Eddie finished with the two detectives and they left. Then he pulled up a chair and sat down in front of me. He turned the back of the chair toward me and straddled it. It was a wooden chair with vertical slats in the back, and when he leaned back the way he did, it was as if he were looking through bars at me, as if I were already in jail. It was an old trick; maybe he forgot that I knew it, too.

"Jack, I'll level with you. First, you're not telling me all you know. Second, like I said, you're my only handle. Third, you and I are friends. You know, or you ought to know, that won't mean anything when it comes down to the nut-cutting. But I can't help worrying about you. I don't know whether it matters or not, but I thought you got screwed when they fired you. O'Bannion turned you around and so did Betty. I know you still love her, but I don't pretend to understand why. That's your business. The thing is, you got turned around, right down the line. Your boss, your wife, the Department; probably your partner too, all the people you worked with, if they knew what was going on and kept quiet about it. You know what they call you around here now? Yeah, your name still comes up now and then. You're one of the local legends now, with that stunt you pulled showing up drunk at the awards banquet. They call you 'Turn-around Jack.' That's a hell of a nickname, ain't it?"

I was through trying to figure him out, whether he meant

any of this or was just trying to work on me. I was tired of it, and I did not give any sign when he smiled at me. It looked real, like the old Eddie, but I did not go for it. Maybe I should have, but I did not.

"I'm worried about you, Jack. Better men than you have gone wrong over less. You'd make a hell of a bad guy if you put your mind to it. If it's that . . ."

I tried to interrupt, but he held up his hand to stop me.

"If it's like that, Jack, the best thing you can do is come clean with me. Right now. I know you've heard it before, said it yourself plenty of times. But you know it was true more often than not. It's true now. I'll do what I can for you."

He was through then, at least with that part of it. I did not know what he expected from me, what to say to convince him I had not gone over. The hardest thing to do is act innocent when you really are. So I did not say anything.

"Okay, Jack. I made you the offer. Here's the notice: I am going to nail whoever did O'Bannion. He was an asshole all right, but he was one of ours. I'm going to get to the bottom of this whole deal, one way or the other. Whatever that means to you is your problem, friend or no friend. You got that?"

"I wouldn't have it any other way."

"Good. Now, about the murder charge. . . . What I got and what I don't is none of your business at this point. I can get you in jail, and you can either wait the seventy-two hours or hire a lawyer. What good would that do? Keep you alive a little longer, give you some time to think things over. And . . ." he waved away my interruption again, "if I was to decide that the case was not up to snuff, there's always the material witness angle. I can put you on ice for a while, either way."

"I know that. But I have a suggestion."

"I'm listening."

"We can clear up a lot of your questions in the morning. Put me on the box."

"I didn't think you had much faith in polygraphs."

"I don't. But you do, and you're the one who counts."

"But why in the morning? I can make a call and get you on the box within the hour."

"It has to be voluntary or it's no good."

"Okay. So you spend the rest of the night in jail and we take the box first thing in the morning. It works for me."

"But not for me. Same reason, it has to be voluntary. I'll sign any kind of release you want in the morning at ten o'clock. *If* I spend the time between now and then on the outside. Lock me up and it's no deal."

"Instead of letting myself get good and pissed off, I'll just ask you why."

"If I'm in circulation I may draw somebody out. I may be able to get a line on things. I'm no good to anybody in the can. It may not work my way either, but at least there's a chance."

"This polygraph exam you're going to be so nice and volunteer for—would you have any qualms about which questions my man asked? Are you going to be one of those people who only wants to answer even-numbered questions, or something like that?"

"You pick 'em. Ask me anything."

"Anything?"

"Absolutely."

"You'll sign something right now that obligates you?"

"Yeah, if you need it in writing."

"I do. And screw you if you get your feelings hurt over it. I'm not stupid. I know it won't be legally binding, but if you renege on me, I can use it against you in court. I'll have the girl type something up."

He went to take care of that and I was left to mull over all he had said. "Turnaround Jack." Yeah, that was something.

I signed his paper and the girl notarized it. Eddie offered to make me a copy but I said I had no use for one. That was about all there was to it.

"Okay, Jack," he said. "Go do your deal, whatever it is, and good luck to you. But at ten in the morning, I strap your butt to the box and find out what's really going on. If you don't

143

show, I'll file on you for murder at ten-thirty and I'll come looking for you. Are we straight about that?"

"We're straight."

I walked toward the door, afraid he would change his mind. I was trying so hard to be casual that I felt stiff-legged.

"Jack."

At the sound of his voice I stopped and turned, measuring the distance to the door out of the corner of my eye. But when I looked back at Eddie, he was smiling. It was a tight smile, as if someone had a gun in his back, but I could tell he meant it this time.

"Be careful," he said.

Chapter Twenty

WITHOUT THINKING ABOUT IT, I rode the elevator to the basement and walked out through the Report Section, past the old jail elevator and through the swinging double doors into the ramped drive-through. I was standing on the spot where Ruby shot Oswald before I remembered that I was not supposed to go this way anymore. There were signs everywhere that said POLICE PERSONNEL ONLY. But no one challenged me and I did not care.

Being outside felt damned good, and it looked like a long way to the top of the exit ramp where I could see the blackness that was the night sky above the old gym across Commerce Street. At the top of the ramp, I stopped to draw a deep breath and spotted Della waiting in her little import at the curb.

She saw me coming and pushed the curbside door open with her foot as she scrambled over the console into the passenger's seat.

"Are you okay?" she asked as I slid under the wheel.

"Sure," I lied. "No problem."

I saw a worried look on her face as I gunned the little five-speed away from the curb, heading east on Commerce toward Central. It was after midnight, one of the few times of day you can make decent time on Central Expressway. Two lanes north and two south, it was obsolete the day they cut the ribbon on it back in the fifties, and that was before some meddling fool air-conditioned Dallas and made it livable for Yankees.

The knots in my shoulders and the back of my neck were being treated to a massage by the surprisingly strong fingers of Della's left hand. It felt good, and I looked at her. She was sitting with her legs tucked under her, turned toward me, leaning toward me to rub my neck. The windows were open and there was a breeze. With her right hand she brushed her hair out of her eyes to see me better. She was wearing a white dress shirt, a man's shirt, with button-down collar and the sleeves rolled up. The shirttails hung below her waist and billowed over her upper thighs. The rest of her was legs and bare feet. I wondered who the shirt belonged to.

"I'm sorry to get you out so late," I said.

"Don't be silly."

"Hope I didn't interrupt anything."

She didn't answer, but she made a funny noise. I looked at her and saw she was giggling. If the light had been good, I think I would have seen her blush. The notion reminded me of the way she had looked in my office in her costume, blushing all over.

"What?" I asked, laughing a little myself.

"Stop, Jack."

She covered her face with her hands, as if she thought I could see something there.

"Stop what? I just said I hoped I hadn't interrupted anything. What's gotten into you?"

"Gotten into me?" she squeaked, and then she started giggling even harder.

"I take it you had a good time at the party."

She nodded yes, then looked away, out her window, as if she wanted to stop laughing and she would not be able to stop if she looked at me.

"Stands to reason, with that outfit you were wearing," I said. "So, uh, did you get lucky, or what?"

"Yeah," she said. "I got lucky. Can you believe it?"

"Of course I can. I'd have thought it happens a lot."

"Why do you say that?"

"Jesus, kid, don't you own a mirror?"

"I know how I look, Jack. You're sweet . . ."

"Far be it from me to try to convince you, kid. But I'm telling you, that little body of yours probably saved my life today."

"Really?"

"Damned right. I'd never have been able to handle that guy if you hadn't mesmerized him."

"Wow," was all she said.

"That's exactly what I thought when I saw you in the outfit."

"Gee."

What a kid. I mean, does anybody say "wow" and "gee" anymore?

"So tell me about him."

"Who?"

"The owner of the shirt. What'd you do, leave him at home?"

"Well, he was sleeping, and . . ."

"Exhausted, probably."

"Jack . . ."

"Tell me about him. I want to know. How long have you known him?"

"Not . . . too long."

"Are we talking months or minutes?"

"Jack, I wouldn't . . . you know, I'm not a pick-up person. I wouldn't go to bed with somebody I didn't know."

"Yeah, but for how long?"

"Actually, I'd only met him once before, but he's a friend of a friend. She's known him forever."

"Swell. He's a bum."

"He is not. Why do you say that?"

"Because I'm jealous."

"You are not."

The hell I was not. I thought about some young guy making love to Della while I was having the kind of evening I had

had, and I envied the hell out of him. Her too, for that matter. She was a great-looking kid with a good heart and everything ahead of her. Her life was still simple, she had not screwed it all up yet. I was jealous of both of them.

"He doesn't deserve you," I said, sounding like a father or something.

"Oh, here," she said. "I almost forgot."

With a motion that pulled her shirttails higher up her thighs and made me wonder if she had anything on underneath, she raised up on her knees and reached between the bucket seats for something on the floor behind us. The noise the paper bag made as she lifted it reminded me how long I had been without a drink. Not that long really, but I was sure in the mood for one.

"Here, I brought this for you," she said, tossing the bag out the window and sticking a bottle of Pinch in front of me. "Wait a sec." She opened the bottle and dropped the cap into my pocket. "I thought you might need this."

"God bless you, my child."

I drank from the bottle and offered it to her. I was a little surprised when she took it from me and helped herself. She choked on the whisky and passed the bottle back, coughing and fanning her chest with her hands.

"I didn't think you were a scotch person," I told her.

"It burns," she gasped.

"Yeah, that's the good part."

"Oh," she was still trying to catch her breath.

"Kid, a terrible thing just occurred to me," I said. "You don't keep this stuff around your place, do you?"

"No."

"Meaning that you stopped somewhere and bought this on your way downtown, right?"

"Yep."

"Jesus F. Christ!"

"What's the matter, Jack?"

"Look at you, for heaven's sake. You walked into a liquor store this time of night dressed like that?"

"What's the matter with it?"

"If you don't know, forget it."

I drank some more and she chewed her thumb like she had something to tell me.

"Jack?"

"Yeah."

"It's your fault."

"What is?"

"That I got laid and went into a liquor store and everything."

"How do you figure that?"

"It was all that stuff in the office today, the way you handled that big guy and everything . . . it made me feel . . . I don't know, funny. It . . ."

"I risk life and limb defending your black-laced honor with the pink nipples and everything, and you get so hot watching you go right out and hop in the sack with some bum half my age? Is that what you're telling me?"

"Yep."

She was giggling again.

"Hell of a deal."

"I can't help it. I love that stuff."

"Shut up."

More giggling. I made her take another drink to stop the naughty, throaty little giggle she was making. I liked it better when she coughed.

I pulled up alongside my car at Red's and looked Della over again in the dome light when I opened the car door. Damn.

"Don't forget your bottle," she said, handing it to me.

I took a couple of good slugs and gave it back to her, along with the cap I fished out of my pocket.

"You keep it. I take it your dreamboat is sleeping over?"

"I guess so."

"Fine. Give him this for breakfast in the morning. If he doesn't drink it all, throw the wimp out."

"Really?"

149

"Absolutely. All us real men have a fifth of scotch for breakfast. It's how we separate the men from the boys."

"Okay, thanks."

"Don't mention it. And, hey, leave the cap on until you get home. You don't need to practice with it anymore and try to drive at the same time."

"Yes, sir."

"Listen, kid, I really appreciate your coming down to pick me up. That's twice today you've bailed me out."

"Don't mention it. You know I love it. One thing, though."

"Name it."

"When this case is over, promise you'll tell me all about it."

"Kid, it's too big to . . ."

"Just this once."

"Well, okay. If it means that much."

"Wow, neat!"

"Right."

"Take care of yourself, Jack."

"Don't worry about me, just be careful driving home."

"I will."

"And no stops. Keep your cute little ass in the car until you're home."

"Yes, sir."

"And stop saying that. I'm not your daddy."

"You sound like him."

"Oh, he thinks you have a cute ass too, huh?"

More giggling.

"Good night, kid, thanks again."

She already had her car in reverse and was on her way back to whatshisname when something occurred to her and she stopped with a squeak of the brakes.

"I almost forgot," she said.

"What?"

"There was a message," she said as she bent over and

fumbled through her purse. She tugged a crumpled note out of the bag and handed it to me. "The phone rang again just as I was walking out. I wouldn't have bothered to answer it but I thought it might be you calling back. It was the answering service, said this person had been calling and calling you, big emergency. They thought I might know where to reach you."

On the crinkled paper she had written a name and a phone number. I did not recognize the number. The name was Pilar.

"Thanks, kid."

the phrase it Pat's because that run went in

Chapter Twenty-one

I DID NOT USE the phone at Red's because I did not want to have to worry about being overheard. I wanted a quiet spot to make the call, a place where I could hear everything Pilar had to say, and everything she did not say.

It occurred to me that I might have put Della on the spot by having her pick me up at City Hall. It could work a couple of ways. Eddie Cochran was not above having me tailed. Could be that was where his two cowboys went before Eddie let me leave his office. Could be they were hanging around somewhere when I left to see where I went and who I saw. Eddie did not want to lose me, and I figured there was a fifty-fifty chance the cowboys were out there somewhere keeping tabs on me. The other side of it was Crandall. It stood to reason that I was still in his net from when I showed up at Betty's house. It depended on just how extensive his outfit was, whether he could afford to tie his people up waiting around for me to leave City Hall. They would have had no way of knowing how long I would be. Like I said, it depended on his resources.

Not far from Red's I found a 7-Eleven where the pay phones were around the corner from the front of the store. It was a shady neighborhood where English had been a second or even third language for a long time. The first language changed from time to time as new gaggles of refugees filtered out through the city and settled in the cheap seats. From here you could see, almost hear, the high-tech hum of the downtown sky-scrapers, towers of Babel with lights that never went out. You could see it from here. If you were hungry, maybe you could smell it. But that was it. If the city was an arena, this part of town was the bleachers.

The lights over the pay phones were not working. Odd that they would all burn out like that, at the same time. It was a great place to get mugged, which is not what we call it in Dallas. Here we call it strong-arm robbery. I did all I could about that by standing with my back to the wall while I listened to the phone ring. Usually that is all it takes, putting your back to the wall so you can see what is going on around you. I'm amazed how many people do not know that, who get knocked in the head and robbed because they stick their heads into phone boxes, with their butts out. They always reminded me of ostriches, and I could never work up much sympathy for them.

I lost count of the rings when I spotted a likely threesome coming my way. They appeared from the shadows that ran along the side of the store from the pay phones back toward an alley. No telling where they had come from or how long they had been eyeing me. They said nothing and seemed to pay me little mind, just three young guys going to the store. Maybe I take too dim a view of things, but I was glad I had my back to the wall.

"Yes?" she said.

There was a note of panic in her voice real enough to chill me. I remembered what she was and where she had been. I remembered O'Bannion.

"Pilar, it's me."

"Jack? Jack, where have you been? I've been trying to reach you forever."

"It's a long story. Where are you?"

"What phone is this? Where are you calling from?"

"A pay phone. We can talk, as far as I'm concerned. How about your end? I don't recognize this number you left for me."

"It's all right. I'm in a hotel. It's all right for now. Where have you been?"

"We can catch up on things when I see you. Which hotel?"

"Are you sure you're not being followed, Jack? We must be very careful."

"I may have a tail, maybe not. But I won't have by the time I get there. Where are you?"

I thought I had lost her for a second. She said nothing, but I could hear her breathing.

"The Hilton on Central Expressway. Do you know it?"

"At Mockingbird Lane?"

"Yes. Room two-oh-four. How soon can you be here?"

"Half an hour, allowing time to lose anybody who's following me."

"In half an hour, then."

That was that.

Next I called Betty at her house but got no answer. I did not have enough change for the other call I wanted to make, so I went inside the store and bought a pack of cigarettes to break a five and asked for a couple of dollars in quarters. Paris was long distance.

Pop answered. He recognized my voice. Yes, they had heard about O'Bannion. I did not ask what else they had heard.

"How's . . . the boy?" I did not know what to call the kid, whether they still called him Little Jack or if they were humoring Betty now and calling him John.

"He's asleep."

"I thought y'all might have left already headed over here."

"Betty said let him sleep, said tomorrow would be soon enough."

"Yeah, I guess she's right. Is he . . . is he okay?"

"I told you, he's asleep."

"Would you mind looking in on him for me?"

"What's going on over there, Jack? What's the matter?"

"Nothing to worry about. Just go along with me, okay? Go take a look and make sure the boy's all right."

Pop laid the phone down with a clunk on the dark-stained oak dresser beside his bed and I heard Mom questioning him.

He answered her with something about people who go off to live in the city. In less than a minute he was back.

"Like I said, Jack, he's asleep."

"You're sure. I mean, it's not just pillows under the covers or anything like that?"

"Good Lord, Jack. You know the boy throws his covers off in his sleep. He's fine. What's this all about?"

"Nothing, Pop. Sorry I bothered you."

Trust me, she had said.

I was in East Dallas, between Red's and Central. The Hilton was not more than a couple of miles away. But I had a stop to make first. I climbed back into my car and wondered if there was another transmitter underneath it, to take the place of the one I had found before. But I did not take the time to check. If the notion that had been bumping around in my mind so lightly, so tentatively that I was not even sure when it had started, was anything more than paranoia, there was not likely to be a transmitter. But not finding one would not prove the hunch was right, anymore than finding one would prove it wrong. That was the killing thing about this whole deal: There did not seem to be anything I could nail down once and for all. But I had it in mind to change all that. There was one key to the deal, one item that was more substance than shadow, that was there every time the story was told. The drop was the key. One transmitter more or less did not matter anymore.

For openers I ran through ten or fifteen minutes of the usual maneuvers, figure-eights and double-backs, stuff you do to lose somebody or to get a look at them. The cowboys were easy, they showed themselves without even knowing they had. There were a couple of possibles besides them, nothing definite. When I had done all I could to be sure of things, I saw to it that Cochran's cowboys picked me up again.

When I knew they were onto me, I drove in a more or less direct line to a hotel on Central Expressway, out about five miles past the Hilton. I left my car in a parking space in the rear and went in through a door that opened into a guest-wing corridor. It should have been locked from the inside for security, but I knew it would not be. I had been there before.

Moving quickly, I made my way forward toward the lobby, taking care not to show myself in any windows where I might be seen from the parking lot. From a safe distance to one side of the desk I spotted the man I needed. I did not know him, but I knew a lot of guys like him. He was wearing the uniform of a security officer, but I happened to know he did double duty and the hotel paid him minimum wage. I waved at him and he came over.

"Yessir, can I help you?"

"Yeah, you can. You drive the van that makes the airport runs, right?"

"Yessir, on the hour, except this time of night. Next run's not scheduled for a while yet."

"Well, let's make an unscheduled run. How about it?"

I showed him a twenty and he looked like the idea appealed to him.

"You bet. My van's right out front."

"Great. Here's what you do. Pull it around to the service bay. Find something in there you can toss into the van, some boxes or something. I'll meet you around there. Got it?"

"I guess so."

I showed him another twenty, and he got more definite about it. He took the two bills and slipped me a key off the ring on his belt.

"You'll need this," he said. "It'll get you into the service bay from this side. You know where it is?"

I did. In Vice I had worked a case or two in this hotel, and most of the others in town. I took the key and the guy gave me a wink.

The guy really got into it. He found more junk to throw into the back of the van than we needed, so much that when I climbed inside there was barely enough room for me in the rear baggage section. I had to tell him to stop. I was satisfied that we could not be seen in the bay. If anybody checked the van when we pulled out, it would look empty, like the guy was on his way to the airport to pick up a late arrival. Happens all the time. Or maybe he was just running an errand to another hotel. The junk in the back was for me to hide under in case anybody stopped us and looked inside. Nobody did. My guess was that Cochran's cowboys would be settled down nice and cozy in their car out back somewhere keeping an eye on my car. It would probably be daylight before those two got suspicious.

My man dropped me off in a good spot at the Hilton, and I made him a proposition. How did he feel about making a dry run out to DFW International, just for the hell of it? Luke-warm, really, but he did appreciate the forty bucks.

"That's for what you've done so far. If you make the run, there's another twenty in it for you."

"Well, hell. In that case, you bet."

"And a little extra to keep your mouth shut."

All told, I had made him happy eighty dollars' worth.

"If anybody asks, you got a call from the airport to pick somebody up. When you got there, he just wasn't there. Maybe he got tired of waiting and caught a cab. You got it?"

"I got it," he said. "Listen, though . . ."

"What?"

"Not that I really give a crap, but you ain't up to anything illegal, are you?"

"Have you seen me break any laws?"

"Nope."

"Well, there you are. But I don't mind letting you in on it to ease your mind. It's what they call an affair of the heart. You can understand that, can't you?"

"I guess so."

He was fat and fifty, and did not look like he had been young a day in his life. I wondered what he knew about affairs of the heart.

"It's a long story," I said. "And too sad to tell, but the crux of it is I've got ex-wife trouble, get me? I just can't take any chances, if you know what I mean."

"Hey, I know something about ex-wives, all right."

He liked my story and drove away a happy man. Buy the illusion, Crandall had said, or something like that. I had given the man way too much money, but it was Crandall's anyway.

Inside the Hilton I took the stairs to 204 without being any more visible than I had to be. The room was just off the mezzanine, around a corner from all the conference rooms. I looked the layout over for a minute before I knocked on the door. There were maybe a dozen rooms that opened off this corridor before it turned to the right and ran on into the south wing. There was an exit door at the corner that led to a flight of stairs that would put you in the parking lot in the rear of the hotel. South of the parking lot was commercial property, a railroad, and a park beyond that. Places to hide if you made it that far. I remembered finding a missing kid in that park my first month out of the academy. No big deal, he had just wandered off from home to go play on the swings. That is how your mind works sometimes, running off like that for no reason when you need to be paying attention to business.

From where I stood in the hallway outside 204 I could shout and make myself heard by the clerks at the lobby desk below, maybe even by the telephone operator in the office behind the desk. Pilar had done a good job of picking her hideout. Or her trap. I thought about O'Bannion again, and it occurred to me that, whatever Pilar had in mind for me, she had picked a hell of a lot nicer place than the Wagon Wheel Inn for it. I knocked on the door, careful to stand to one side. There was no answer.

I heard a door open behind me. I turned and there she was. Pilar's face, the half I could see, loomed like a mask in the darkness of room 203, across the hall from 204. From my angle, the door chain looked like a necklace across her throat.

Nice touch, I thought, at the same time that I thought that if it was a trap it was off to a good start, with her at my back. I turned to face her, my eyes searching the shadows below her eye for the muzzle of a gun.

"You are alone?" she whispered.

"Yeah, open up."

The door closed and I heard the chain work in the hasp. The door opened. Room 203 was dark, and Pilar was not in sight.

"Come in," she said. "Hurry."

"Turn on a light."

"Don't be a fool. Come in."

"Turn on the goddamn light and step out where I can see you."

I heard her call me something terrible in Spanish, still whispering. But the lamp on the dresser in the room came on, and I could see her in the mirror. She was away from the door, standing between the two beds.

I went in.

Chapter Twenty-two

SHE LOOKED BEYOND ME at the doorway as I stepped into the room. She was afraid I had someone with me. Who, I did not know. Maybe I would find that out later, when we got to the question-and-answer period. First, I wanted to put my own mind at ease. I had my right hand jammed into my jacket pocket to give her something else to worry about.

I pulled the door closed behind me, and she started to move toward it. But when I slipped the chain into place, she caught herself. She might have been wearing the same clothes as when I met her at the Wine Press, a white silk blouse and a plain but expensive skirt. The blouse was wrinkled.

Without saying anything I moved into the bathroom to satisfy myself that it was empty. It was. So was the closet. No clothes, no bags.

"Traveling light," I said.

"Where have you been, Jack?"

I had not come to answer questions.

"Before we settle down for a chat, there's some old business to be taken care of."

"Old business?"

"You owe me a pistol and some ID papers, remember? I told you I wanted the gun and the stuff you took off the guy O'Bannion shot before we went any further."

If she wanted to argue, she thought better of it. She turned from the waist and reached for her purse on the bed behind her. I had not seen the purse until I looked where her left hand was going.

"Wait," I said, keeping my voice flat. She looked at me with a question in her eyes, first at my face, then at my hand in my pocket. "Don't bother taking anything out. Just hand me the purse."

It was a little purse, what I guess they call a clutch. She laid it into my left hand easy, and I could feel the weight of the pistol inside. While she was in the mood to do as she was told, I thought I would make the most of it.

"Sit down on the bed. Keep your hands in your lap."

That went all right. She minded well, her eyes on mine the whole time. I didn't know whether she was scared or just watching me, waiting for an opening.

I had the edge on two counts. First, she did not know where I had been or what I knew. Second, she did not know what I had in my pocket or what I intended to do with it. If I knew anything, it was how worrisome it was to be in the dark. Of course, all I had in my pocket was my hand, but I was going to remedy that.

There was not much inside the purse except for the pistol and a Santa Rosan passport that belonged to a guy by the name of Guzman. It was full of stamps and seals, and looked official as hell. The gun was an Iver-Johnson .22 automatic, small enough to hide in my palm. It felt good in my hand, cool and heavier than it looked.

She said nothing, watching.

There was a safety switch on the left side of the pistol, in the rearward position. I thumbed it forward to expose the red dot that meant it was ready to fire. The hammer was down. Holding the gun in my right hand, I used my left thumb and forefinger to ease back the slide. The slide came back stiff against the spring, and I saw the casing of a chambered round. I eased the slide forward and milked the trigger, very gently. It was tight; about an eighth of an inch back, the hammer began

162

to rise. I stopped there and let the trigger ride forward to rest; the hammer returned. Then I worked the release at the base of the butt and removed the magazine. Through the confetti-sized holes in the side of the clip I counted five rounds.

"You know about guns," she said.

"First Iver-Johnson like this I've seen. Looks like a Walther."

I looked at the first bullet in the clip. It was a hollow point, .22 long rifle. I put the clip back in and worked the slide to kick out the round that was there and chamber another. The ejected round fell to the floor and I scooped it up. Same thing. The primer looked good.

"What are you doing?" she asked.

"Checking for blanks."

I popped the clip out again and fed the round I had extracted into it. Five in the clip, one in the chamber. That was six more tries than I had before. Of course, I could not be sure about the firing mechanism. Everything looked okay, but it is hard to tell with an automatic just by looking.

When I knew all I needed to know about the gun for the time being, I dropped it into my jacket pocket. I left the hammer down and the safety off. It was double action on the first shot. If I needed it, I did not want to have to screw around with a safety before I used it. Trigger pull on the thing was stiff enough that I was not worried about it going off before I meant for it to.

With that out of the way, I felt a little better about Pilar. She might have plans for me, but it did not figure to be anything immediate. I put the passport in an inside pocket and dumped what was left in the purse onto the bed.

There was a couple hundred dollars in cash, a pair of handrolled cigarettes I assumed were joints without taking time to make sure, and half a dozen black pills that could have been anything. Interesting.

She was waiting for me to get around to her, but it was not easy for her. If she had gnawed her lip much more, it would have bled. But I was in no hurry. Without offering her one, I fumbled a cigarette out of the new pack and lit it.

"They make me nervous," she said.

"Cigarettes, you mean?"

"No. Guns."

"Why?"

"For good reasons, Jack. Can we talk now?"

"Feel free. As a matter of fact, I insist."

"What is wrong with you? Why are you looking at me that way?"

"If you're going to talk, talk. Cut out the bullshit."

"Where were you when I called, Jack? Where have you been? How much . . ." She was talking too fast, but she caught herself.

"How much do I know? Is that what's got you wound up so tight? Or are those pills really what they look like?"

"We need each other, Jack. We must be honest with each other."

"Okay, you've convinced me." I moved around the room a little, smoking my cigarette. I did not mind if taking my time made her expect one thing when she was about to get another. "Tell me something, honestly."

"What?"

"Your limp. It's from a wound you got in the war in Santa Rosa, right?"

"You know that."

"It was a bad wound, took a long time to heal?"

"Months. But what has this to do . . ."

"I was just thinking on my way over here about a kid I knew in High School back in Paris. Paris, Texas, of course. I don't think they have high schools in Paris, France. Anyway, this friend of mine was in a car wreck our sophomore year. Screwed up one of his legs real bad."

"Jack . . ."

"In a way, that wreck was the best thing that ever happened to him. Know why?"

164

"Of course not."

"It made him the arm wrestling champ of the whole school. The crutches did it, dragging himself around by his arms. He didn't look that different, but he was strong as hell in his arms. I won more beer than I could drink that year betting on that little guy. He wasn't much bigger than you. I guess you were on crutches for a long time."

"Yes, but I don't see what that has to do with anything."

"I'll bet that little guy I went to school with could have choked a man twice his size to death, especially if the big guy trusted him. Trusted him enough to let the little man get behind him, up close."

"What?"

"'Poor baby, had a rough day? Let me rub your neck and make you feel all better.' Yeah, O'Bannion would fall for that, coming from you. Is that how it was?"

She was at me like a cat, her eyes afire. I did not hit her hard, but it was a punch, not a slap. She spilled backward across the bed, full of rage and pain. With one hand on her wounded cheek, she turned her face to me.

"Is that how it was?"

"What are you saying, Jack?"

"That you killed O'Bannion. And now I'm going to kill you."

Chapter Twenty-three

SHE BELIEVED IT. NOBODY is that good an actress.

Her eyes were full of tears.

"What are you saying?" She said it again. Maybe she could not think of anything else.

With my left hand I grabbed her and yanked her off the bed. I held her close, bending her head to my chest, and shoved my face against her neck. I smelled her.

"What . . . you're hurting me!"

"Not yet I'm not. I was there at the dump where you killed him. I smelled you on the bed. Your perfume is hard to forget."

"No, no, Jack. No!"

I held her that way and let her squirm.

"Bastard."

"So scream," I said. "What's stopping you?"

She did not stop cursing me, but her voice was not loud.

"Scream your head off. You know as well as I do they'd probably hear you down at the desk. That's one reason you picked this room in the first place. If the desk clerks didn't hear you, some of our neighbors would. They might not be good samaritan enough to come in here, but they'd call down and raise hell about the racket. So scream."

Instead, she stopped making any sounds at all, just lay there.

I smoked another cigarette and let her stew for a while.

When I was ready I stubbed out the butt and moved in on her again.

"O'Bannion was making trouble, wasn't he? He wanted a bigger cut, or did he just want to know what the hell was really going on? Did he threaten to go to the Department? Is that why you killed him?"

"All right. All right, Jack. I was there. You're right, I was there."

"Where?"

"At the motel."

"And you killed him."

"No. I was there, you're right. O'Bannion called me. He wanted to meet with me, said it was important."

"What was it about?"

"He wouldn't say on the phone, just that he had to see me. I told him it would be dangerous, that I might be followed . . ."

"What difference did that make? O'Bannion was being tailed himself, wasn't he?"

"I don't know. I mean, I suppose he was."

"Was he being followed or not?"

"I swear I don't know. I don't think so."

"Go on."

I did not think so either.

"I left early so I'd have time to lose anyone following me. Still, I got there before O'Bannion. He had told me the cabin number. It wasn't locked. I went in, but there was no one there. I waited on the bed for him. That's why you smelled me . . . my perfume . . . on the bed."

"Then what?"

"A car pulled up outside. I thought it was O'Bannion at first. But it wasn't."

"Who was it? Don't make me drag it out of you."

"It was Crandall. He got out of the car with a bag in his hand. Then Mario drove away in the car. I couldn't see where he went."

"What kind of bag?"

"Like a doctor's. So I went out the back way as quickly and quietly as I could. I had left my car some distance away. I hid behind the cabin for I don't know how long. I hoped I could warn O'Bannion somehow, but I was afraid. I didn't know where Mario was, and I was afraid they would get me, too."

"That's it? You saw Crandall get out of the car in front and you slipped out the back. That's all you did?"

"Yes, why?"

"You didn't get dressed?"

"What do you mean?"

"You didn't put your clothes back on before you sneaked out? What did you do about your clothes?"

Questions popped into her eyes like cataracts. How much did I know? She was afraid to lie.

"I took them with me, grabbed them off the chair and took them in a bundle under my arm. I didn't have time to get everything. I suppose Crandall found whatever I left behind. I hid in the shrubs. It was cold. I put my clothes on in the dark."

"I know," I said.

It was a bluff, but it was working. She could not be sure I had not been there, hiding somewhere. I was on a roll. What I did not tell her was that I knew how a woman like her would keep a man like O'Bannion in line. She would make him forget any qualms he had, and she would not be dressed when she did it. I thought about her in the ratty little cabin lying naked on the bed, waiting for O'Bannion. About Betty.

"Okay," I said, lighting another cigarette and trying to look as if I already knew the answer. "Then what?"

"I hid in some shrubs."

"Getting dressed while you waited."

"That's right."

"And then O'Bannion drove up," I offered.

"Yes. Not long after Crandall went inside. He . . ."

"Where did O'Bannion leave his car?"

"He parked right in front of the cabin, in front of the door. I remember thinking that was careless of him."

"And you warned him, right? You yelled at him to get out of there, that Crandall was waiting inside to kill him. Is that what you did?"

"No," she whispered, and dropped her head. She was chewing her lip again. "I didn't do anything."

"You didn't feel anything for him, did you?"

"Not enough to risk dying for him."

"You've never cared very much for anybody, have you?"

"May I have a cigarette? Please, Jack?"

"No. Answer me."

When she did not see anything for her in my eyes, she turned away and put both hands over her face. She let the leg she had arched so gracefully go slack, and it slid down onto the bed. Her skirt had ridden up, and I could see a lot of bare thigh. It did not move me. Her face turned toward me as if it were the only part of her still alive.

"There was someone I would have died for," she said. "A long time ago. But that is none of your business."

"I've got time. Talk about it."

"If you push me too far, you'll have to kill me, Jack. I'm no use to you dead."

"You're no particular use to me alive."

"You don't know everything."

"Talking to you isn't changing that. Tell me something I don't know."

"What do you want to know?"

"For one thing, why you were so afraid of Crandall all of a sudden? You've been sharing a house with him."

"He had reasons to keep me around. But not now that he knows I was a witness to murder."

"You knew Crandall would kill O'Bannion. You sat there in the bushes and watched the big oaf park his car right at the front door and go blundering inside, expecting to find you warm and waiting. And you knew all the time that Crandall was going to kill him."

170

"Yes."

"So you let O'Bannion die, and you made a run for it while Crandall was busy. Where did you go?"

"When Mario drove back to the cabin for Crandall I made a run for my car. I got out of there as fast as I could. As soon as I was sure I was not being followed, I went straight to a pay phone to warn you."

She looked at me to see if I was buying it. I did not feel one way or the other about it. If she had meant to warn me, it was only because she needed me. "I called and called, but you were not there."

She wanted to ask me again where I had been, but she had caught on by then that I was not in an answering mood, so she let it go.

"Then you came here?" I asked. She nodded. "You took both rooms, this one and the one across the hall?" Another nod.

A couple of things were kicking around in my mind. One was whether or not I should take Pilar somewhere else. What I had in mind might take a while. Crandall would be looking for her, and Cochran for me. There was the chance that this place, this whole thing, was a trap. For all I knew, the place was wired and Art Crandall was listening next door, but doubted that for a couple of reasons. And I did not like the idea of moving the girl.

"Give me the keys," I said.

There was no argument. She put her left hand inside her blouse. Through the material I saw her fingers fumbling with something, and I brought the little automatic most of the way out of my pocket. No sense ruining a jacket shooting through the material. But her hand came out with just a couple of room keys. She held them out to me while I studied her breasts. They looked natural, as if there was nothing under the silk but her. I had not thought she could hide anything there. She would have to be searched, I decided. I took the keys from her and eased the pistol back where it had been.

"Tell me about the drop, Pilar."

171

"You know about that already."

"Yeah, all except the who, what, when, where, and how. I've got your word for the why."

She stretched and I watched a little shiver run the length of her, like she was having a chill.

I could see she was not inclined to talk anymore, but that was all right. I was through asking questions for a while.

"Get up."

She raised herself on her right elbow, facing me.

"I said get up. On your feet."

"Why?"

I gave her a hard look and she thought better of asking questions. She pushed herself off the bed and onto her feet.

"Shake your hair out. Run your fingers through it," I told her. "Again, backward and forward, all over your head."

She watched me as she did as I said. Her hair was a mess, but it was full and black, and it did not look too bad as it swung this way and that. Maybe she thought she was having an effect on me, getting my mind off business. I did not mind what she thought as long as I could be sure there was not something dangerous pinned in her hair, a razor blade or a needle of some kind. That was why I had her doing this, letting her run her own fingers through it first.

"Like this?" she asked, her head tilted forward, looking up at me through her lashes the way she had not bothered to do when I lit her cigarette that time at the Wine Press.

I nodded, showing her a little smile.

"You like this, Jack?"

She was swinging her hair back and forth, using her hands to pull it this way and that. I did not answer, but I noticed that she shifted her weight subtly onto one leg, enough to make a nice line with her hip for me.

"My hair looks awful now, I know."

"Your hair is fine. Take off your skirt."

One of her eyebrows cocked a quarter of an inch and dimples at the corners of her mouth told me she was hiding a

172

smirk. She really thought she was getting to me, I guessed. She did as I said, but her fingers were shaking and she fumbled with the button. Before she got it undone she had to stop once and wipe the back of her hand across the tip of her nose, and she sniffled. Like she was coming down with a cold. Finally she got the skirt undone and let it slide down her legs. She stepped out of it and I saw she was not wearing anything under it. I had to admit she looked damn good from where I stood. She stood on one leg and cocked the other a little toward me with her heel raised an inch or two, so I would be sure to notice.

"The blouse."

More trouble with buttons. She had enough of it after four and ripped the blouse open, tearing off the top two buttons. Her breasts surprised me. They were bigger than I expected, firm with brown nipples upstanding like pencil erasers. That is not a very romantic way to put it, but it was what I thought when I saw them. I was not in a romantic mood. Her body was shiny with a film of sweat but she could not help holding her arms tightly across her belly and she could not help shivering a little.

"Turn around," I said.

She did, and I saw the scar that went with her limp, the limp she had not been able to hide at the Wine Press. It was not pretty, a long and dark snake of a thing running down from the point of her hip around behind and ending at the back of her thigh. It was fairly old, had done all the healing it was going to do. It had the look of the kind of work a surgeon does when he is more concerned with saving the leg than the looks of the thing.

"Jack," she said softly. "We are in this together. I could be good for you."

"You were not so good for O'Bannion."

"He was a fool. Oh!"

"So am I," I said.

I left the pistol in my pocket and reached out to touch her hair with my right hand. When she felt my hand there, she

173

arched her neck to make it easier for me. There was nothing gentle about the way I searched her hair, but she did not complain. I found no pins or blades in her hair or anything else. When I was through there, I brought my hand down along her spine. Her skin was cool and clammy, her muscles tight. I had found what I was looking for. I stepped away from her.

She looked over her shoulder at me, questioning without words.

"Lie down."

She looked relieved to get back onto the bed. Her body sank into the bed and nothing about her moved except her eyes. It was a long time before she said anything.

"I'm cold," she said, and pulled the bed cover up from one side to cover her. I did not object. Her left hand rubbed back and forth across her nose. "If I tell you about the drop, what do you need me for then?"

"If you don't tell me, what the hell do I need you for now?"

"Men have found uses for me."

"I can imagine," I assured her. But her heart was not in it, the seductive femme fatale thing. Not at the moment, because she was feeling pretty rough.

Her eyes were hot and wet and she was having chills again. She drew her knees up against her belly and turned on her side to draw the bedspread tighter around her. She might have been coming down with the flu, but she was not. I knew what she was coming down with, and I knew I had the whip hand. It was only a matter of time.

"Jack, I don't feel so good."

"I can tell."

"I need my medicine, in my purse. Okay?"

"You mean this?" I scooped up some of the black pills and offered them to her.

"Yes."

"What is the matter with you?"

"Malaria," she lied. "From when I was with the rebels. Jack, I need to go to the bathroom, I'm going to be sick."

174

"The pills will help?"

"Yes, I told you."

She pulled the bedspread back and rolled over to the side of the bed to get up.

"I'll get some water," I offered. "You can take your pills right there."

"No, just give them to me and let me go to the bathroom. I don't want you to see me like this. Just give me a minute in the bathroom and I'll be all right, I'll be better. You looked in there already, you know there's nothing in there. Don't be afraid of me, tough guy."

She stopped, still sitting on the edge of the bed, and both hands went to her stomach. Her eyes squinted shut and she clenched her teeth shut hard, all of which told me that her cramps had started.

I stripped the bed farthest from the door down to the springs. When I had looked through them at the floor and knew nothing was hidden there, I threw the bed back together again.

"Come here," I said.

"I'm sick, Jack. For God's sake . . ."

"Come on."

She shook her head no, so I grabbed her and put her on the other bed.

"I think I'm going to die," she whimpered.

"You'll feel better in a little while," I assured her. "Of course, after that you're going to feel a hell of a lot worse."

"You bastard," she hissed, afraid that I had guessed what was really wrong with her.

I rolled her onto her stomach and spread her cheeks with one hand. With the other I found the string I had felt there when I searched her. I pulled the thing out. Gun or no gun, she would have killed me with her bare hands when she felt it leave her, but I threw myself down on top of her and smothered her. I forced her face into the bedding until she thought only about breathing. Then I let her breathe and the fight was out of her. She cried.

I looked at the thing I had taken out of her. It was a condom, its open end tied off and the whole thing slimy with K-Y jelly. I untied the knot and was not surprised at what was inside. I had seen it before.

"When was the last time?" I asked her.

"What?"

"You heard me. When?"

"A long time ago."

"A couple of hours can be a long time when you're needy. When?"

"Early this morning."

"You mean yesterday morning?"

"Yes."

"Good."

So it had been almost twenty-four hours. I knew she would tell me everything. How long it would take depended on her habit, how much and how often she had been getting it. But it would happen. I had known my share of junkies, and I never met one who would not trade a secret for a fix when it came right down to it.

Chapter Twenty-four

SHE CRIED THEN, FOR a long time. I got the feeling it was good for her, to let go and cry like that and to stop pretending to be something she was not. I let her go. Maybe it was some release she got or just not having to hold herself together anymore, but she melted into a puddle of sobbing on the bed until I almost could not tell she was human anymore, just a jerky thing tangled in the sheets making noises.

I figured it might be a while before I could get anything more out of her, so I smoked a couple of cigarettes and looked the place over more carefully than I had taken time to when I first came in. Pilar had wanted me to let her go into the bathroom when she got sick. If she wanted to be alone there, it figured that was where she had stashed her works, the needle and all the rest. There was nothing in any of the drawers that did not belong there, but I had not expected anything. The stuff had been in the shower-curtain rod, not a very original place. It was all there, her hypo, a rubber tube for tying off with, a spoon with a curved handle, all the hardware she needed. No dope, though. All she had was what I had taken from her. That figured. If she had to leave in a hurry, there might not be time to retrieve her kit from the shower rod. But that was no big deal, she could replace all that stuff easily enough. She wanted to be sure the dope stayed with her wherever she went.

I did not stop looking when I found the stuff. I went over the rest of the bathroom and everything else pretty good, but did not find anything else of interest. When I was satisfied, I settled into one of the chairs by the table on the side of the room away from the door. I was close enough to the bed where Pilar lay to put my feet up on it. I did, and made myself comfortable. Getting my feet up eased the nagging pain in my back. My back always hurt when I was tired. Pilar had stopped crying.

She raised her head. She was lying on her stomach more or less diagonally across the bed, with her head toward me and her backside toward the door. That could not hurt. If somebody with bad intentions barged in, the first thing he would see would be Pilar's butt. Maybe it would distract him, the way Della's outfit had done with Mario.

"Now you know," she said. At least that is what it sounded like. She sounded about like she looked, and I had to strain to make her out.

"Here," I said, offering her the cigarette I had just lit. She opened her mouth and I put it there. She inhaled hungrily. I took an ashtray off the table and put it on the bed between us. "Feeling a little better?"

She nodded, taking the cigarette from her mouth between two fingers. With her other hand she took a stab at pushing her hair out of her face. It did not work.

"What happens now?"

"You mean what do you have to do to get your fix? Is that what you mean?"

She nodded, drawing on the cigarette.

"What do you usually do? What's the going rate with a man like Crandall?"

She turned herself over a little so I could see her breasts, and smiled. She was feeling a little better now. She finished the cigarette and stubbed it out in the ashtray.

"Come here," she said, "and I will show you."

"Get serious. You're a junkie, Pilar, and you look like one. Your goddamn eyes look like cigar butts."

The muscles along her jaws tightened, but she did not argue. A couple of things passed across her eyes, like clouds across the sun. But she knew she was in no shape to try anything. "What then?" she asked.

"Tell me about the drop."

She flopped back down on the bed and buried her face. She shook her head from side to side to tell me no.

"I know," I said. "The drop is your life insurance. If you tell me what I need to know, I won't need you anymore. The thing is, you are going to have to trust me before this deal is done, one way or the other. Look, you feel pretty rough now, but not as bad as you're going to in a couple of hours. And you and I both know that's just the start of it. If your plan is to kick your habit, that's fine with me. You know better than I do what your chances are. But if that's what you have in mind, I want you to know that I'll do my part to help you out, by not letting you have the stuff. No matter how much you beg for it."

She cried again. I did not imagine she thought that would move me, so maybe she just felt like it. Maybe she had already started feeling bad again.

"How did you get on this stuff anyway?" I asked. Not that I really cared, but I wanted to get her talking.

"You don't care," she said.

"I might," I lied. "If I thought I could believe you."

"It was in the war," she started. "Everything was in the war. Everything in the world died in the war, and everything else was born in the goddamn war."

She seemed to want to talk, for reasons of her own. She wanted to sort things out, or she hoped that talking would help her to live through what was coming. Either way, she decided to tell me the story of her life, and I settled down to listen.

There was a lot at the first of it that I did not bother to listen to, crap about her old man and the way life had been growing up as a rich kid in Santa Rosa. Then daddy sent her off to some artsy fartsy girls' school in the States, I did not catch the name. That was about the time the revolution was revving up back at home, but Pilar did not know about such things then. She met a boy at school. I was not clear on whether he belonged at the girls' school or if he went to a boys' school down the road. Anyway, this kid did something for her in the romance department. She had been pretty sheltered growing up, and he was her first. They got to be quite an item around the campus. Only he was a radical, the way a lot of rich American kids were back in those days. He knew more about things in Santa Rosa than she did, and he took it upon himself to educate her. He told her about how tough the peasants had it and how the oligarchs screwed everybody over and raped the land and plundered the treasury and all that. I guess it was news to her. Of course, she was not buying it, because the kid was talking about her daddy and his friends. Papa was the Minister of the Interior, the guy who ran the state police.

I was not clear on the time frame of all this, partly because I had other things on my mind and partly because Pilar was not talking too clearly. Whenever it was, she went back home to daddy and the good life after school. Only now she was not so sure about things. There was some fighting in the countryside by then, and daddy was pretty busy. Then one day she hears from her college sweetheart. He is in Santa Rosa now, and he wants to see her. Turns out he is down there fighting with the rebels. Only that would be giving the kid too much credit. According to Pilar, the boy was a klutz with hardware, and had even managed to wound himself trying to learn how to put together a satchel charge. So now he was a water boy or a medic or something. Being a young girl and still in love with him, she slipped out of the house and spent some time with the guy. He showed her around and convinced her that things really were like he had told her back at school. I got the impression that that was the first time Pilar had ever seen any real peasants. The servants at her daddy's big house did not count. Anyway, lover boy turns her into some kind of revolutionary herself, although it was not clear from listening to her whether she was full of social fervor or just caught up in the romance of the thing. Naturally, there were some problems.

For one thing, the commandante, the Santa Rosan in charge of her sweetheart's outfit, is not sure she can be trusted. He knows her dad from way back, and has no use for him, to say the least. There is a squabble and a half, to hear her tell it, and a couple of all-night committee meetings. Finally, the rebels decide to give her a try. Only, who needs her out in the bush lugging a rifle, right? They decide that everybody should do whatever he is best at, serve in the way he or she is best-suited to serve. The thing is, they decide that her best use would be as a spy. They order her to bed down with some particular colonel on the army staff. This guy likes the ladies too much for his own good, and he is known to talk more than he should in the sack. She is shocked by the notion, but her boyfriend convinces her that it is her duty. I tried to remember a time when I ever believed in anything that much. I could not. So she goes back to town and turns out a whore for the revolution. Not long after that, she met Arthur Crandall.

When Crandall's name came up, I started listening better. He was one of the many American businessmen in Santa Rosa, she said. Which I guessed was his CIA cover. One night at a fancy ball her daddy gave for all his friends, Crandall danced with her and made her a proposition. He was a businessman, he said, and he wanted to hedge his bets making getting on the good side of the rebels, just in case they won. That way, maybe they would let him stay in business after the war. He said he knew that Pilar was a rebel spy, but not to worry about how he knew, said he made it his business to stay on top of things like that. In fact, he could put her people onto a couple of truckloads of stuff they needed, arms and ammo.

Pilar said she did not trust Crandall at first, but she passed his tip along anyway, and it paid off. There was more after that, information that Crandall gave her and she passed to her friend the commandante. Always the information proved to be good, and El Commandante began to think that Pilar was okay after all.

Naturally, it was all a scam. Once he had wormed his way into their confidence, Crandall set the rebels up for a trap. The way things worked out, Pilar was in the bush visiting her lover when the hammer fell. When the smoke cleared, her lover was dead and most of his comrades were either killed or captured. The commandante was shot up pretty bad, but he managed to slip away. Pilar was wounded, too. A grenade. She woke up a long time later in a private hospital.

"What did your father say when he found out you'd been shot up in a raid on a rebel camp?"

It was the first time I had stopped her to ask a question, and she looked up at me, a little surprised, as if she had forgotten I was there.

"He never knew. Crandall saw to that. He staged a phony rebel ambush in which my friend the talkative colonel was killed. Crandall told my father that I had been with the colonel and was wounded. He assured my father that I was getting the best of American care in a hospital run by his company, a private place where he could look after me personally. My father was very grateful to Crandall for that. He visited me when he could, but he was terribly busy then."

"And that is where you picked up your habit," I said.

"There was a lot of morphine at first, for the pain. I can remember Crandall and the doctors talking. They gave me what he told them to give me."

"Nice guy. So he made sure you came out of it addicted to the hard stuff. Why?"

"I was of use to him. As long as he could be sure of complete control over me, I was what he called an asset. Since I had also been wounded in the attack on the camp, he thought the rebels might still trust me. When I was able to walk again, he ordered me to renew my contacts with El Commandante."

"How did that work out?"

"There wasn't time to find out. The rebels were in the capital and the war was over in a matter of days. It was all we could do to get out of the country, my father and I."

"That must have told your commandante something right there."

"Crandall thought of that. He had me tell El Commandante that I was going with my father to spy on him, in case he tried to organize a counter-revolution from the States."

"And the commandante bought that?"

"He seemed to. In these things, you never know. That is the worst part . . . you never know anything . . . for sure."

"You're telling me," I said. "So you and Daddy skipped out to Miami with all the money you could haul. What about Crandall?"

"My father left Santa Rosa with nothing. He was not . . . like the others."

"Crandall?"

"He stayed behind at first, but it wasn't long before he showed up in Miami and looked us up. We were shuffling from one Santa Rosan exile group to another, like beggars. They admired my father, they said. They felt sorry for us."

"What did Crandall want with you?"

"He had something big to discuss with my father . . . that is how we ended up in Dallas. That is where the whole thing with the trade commission got started."

"The drop was Crandall's idea, his deal?"

"Yes. Jack . . . I don't . . . I'm getting sick again. Please . . ."

"You know what you have to do, Pilar." I was tired of waiting for her to get smart, and there was not time to wait for her to get really sick. It was very late, and I had a big day coming up. I needed some rest, too. "Tell me about your habit. How much, how often?"

"As much as he'll give me, and as often. He almost never gives me enough to go all day. Sometimes he will, depends on how he wants me to be."

"Jesus, kid. Why do you stay? He's not the only connection in the world."

She gave me a look I would never forget, her eyes boring into mine as if she were willing me to understand and believe because this time she meant what she said, no matter what.

"I loved my father," she said. "If I had tried to leave Crandall, he would have told my father the truth about the goddamn war."

Crandall's double hold on her. Dope and information. The guy took no chances. Funny kid, I thought, to do what she had done and to have gone through so much and still to care about her old man like that. After her father died, Crandall made sure he managed the dope to keep her around as long as he needed her, which after all was only for a few days. He would have kept her on a short leash, small doses, just enough so she could function without really feeding her need. That would mean she could not go long without coming to him for another fix, less than a day away from withdrawal, probably.

Moving quickly to get it done before she put up a fight about it, I tore the sheets from the bed we were not using into strips, wide enough for what I had in mind. Then I wrapped her in the bedspread she was lying on and tied her up snugly with the strips. I gagged her, too, because I could not trust her to keep from screaming, not completely. I needed her out of action so I could close my eyes, get a little rest, and think. She did not make much of a protest.

Crandall was a great one for hedging his bets. He had Pilar's father in his pocket and that covered him with the counterrevolutionaries. He had Pilar, his link to the other side. If he had been an agent in Santa Rosa, it stood to reason he had at one time run a network down there. That was how he kept on top of things, how he got onto Pilar's connection with the rebels in the first place. Maybe his old network, at least part of it, was still in place. That part did not concern me as much as the other thing, the thing with O'Bannion. I still was not sure exactly why Crandall needed him, why he sent Pilar to lure O'Bannion into the deal. Or did he? What if Pilar was really working on her own with O'Bannion? That made sense. From her angle, it made a lot of sense.

With what she had to offer plus whatever big payoff she promised, she could be sure of the big man. Lieutenant of Narcotics. Maybe she had found herself another connection after all. It was something to think about.

It would be daylight soon and I had to sleep. I called the desk and asked for an eight o'clock wakeup call, then took off my jacket and shoes. I checked the door to be sure the chain was on, and settled into my chair for a nap.

It can be dangerous to leave a person gagged. I hoped that if she started to choke to death she would make enough noise to wake me. If not . . . either way, I had to get some sleep.

I had read a magazine article or a story somewhere where this guy said that going cold turkey off of hard drugs had been over-dramatized, that it was really not much worse than a bad case of the flu. The tricky part was supposed to be mental. I wondered about that, about whether the guy who wrote that had ever gone through it himself.

Chapter Twenty-five

IT WAS A BERTRAM 28 with sea drives. Not so nice a day this time, though, swells running against me and a low cloud cover. The boat rode well, it handled nicely. I was on the bench at the helm. Somehow I knew that the kid was not there this time. I looked forward and the woman, the blonde, was not there either, on the foredeck where she always lay sunning herself. Then why was I there? Where was I going? I looked aft and saw the marlin tackle laid out. Okay, I told myself, this time it's just a fishing trip. That is when I saw her, the woman, making her way back along the freeboard. She was working one hand along the rail to keep her balance and carrying something in the other hand. I could not make out what she was carrying, and I could not see her face either, or her hair. She was wearing a hat.

"Not much sun today, huh?" I called to her.

She did not seem to hear me. I yelled it again, but still she did not answer, did not give any sign that she had heard me. She disappeared from my view as she made her way down into the cockpit behind and below me. I turned to look at her, but I could see only the top of her hat. It was a straw job with a scarf underneath, a red scarf. I could not remember Betty ever wearing a hat before.

"Bad day for a tan," I said, as I turned back to my steering.

Still she said nothing, but she was climbing the ladder behind me. I sensed rather than heard her, except that there was a bump as she made her way up, something metallic clanging against the ladder. Sure I was taking the swells at the angle I wanted, I felt like turning to watch her come up.

Her hat brim snapped down in the wind as her head appeared, covering the top half of her face. I could see only her lips. Her mouth was round and hard steel, blue-black, with a hole in the center. There was a twist to the inner wall of it, a throat like a railroad tunnel. I slammed the helm over hard to throw her off, but I knew it would not work. I knew it was too late.

I awoke to a sound like the gurgling of a cut throat. It was like part of the dream at first, for longer than I could be sure of. Almost too long for Pilar. She was choking, on the gag and her own vomit. I cut her loose and dragged her into the bathroom.

"Please . . . God, please . . ."

That was all she said, all I could make out of what she was trying to say. She coughed and spat and thrashed around so much that I was afraid she would hurt herself. Trying to hold her so she would not bang her head on the wall or the side of the tub, I lowered her over the side and laid her on the plastic nonskid decals the hotel put in the tub so no guest would slip and fall taking a shower. I held her by her hair and turned on the shower, hot. She did not like it at first, but I held her under the stream until her face was clean. I pounded on her back and bent her forward at the waist to make sure her airpipe was clear. When she could curse me clearly I knew that she could breathe, and I worked the jet of steaming hot water over her to wash away the mess. When she was clean, I let the water run for a while over her back and shoulders until they did not feel clenched any more. Once she got accustomed to the water she stopped cursing and only moaned.

I ran cool tap water in the sink and unwrapped a drinking glass. I made her drink as much water as she could, most of it pouring over her chin down onto her breasts.

It was like lugging a corpse, lifting her out of the tub. I had her perched on one hip on the rim of the damn thing when she slipped and I grabbed her to keep her from falling. My back snapped so loudly I thought I had been shot, until the old finger of pain I knew so well flicked from the base of my spine down my leg to my knee. For all my worrying about Pilar, I was the first of us to scream. There was nothing I could do about it except hope that the people in the next room were sound sleepers. Maybe they would mistake my pain for passion.

Pilar and I ended up on the floor in a heap. It was several minutes before I could maneuver myself into a position that did not hurt more than I could stand, which happened to be on my hands and knees. It usually is when my back goes out like that.

She was shivering, from lying wet on the cool tile floor. I crawled as near to the towel rack as I could and managed to pull a couple of bath towels down for her. That hurt. It was not so bad rubbing her dry, as long as I was careful how I moved. When that was done, I draped the dry towel over her and lay down in a fetal position to wait.

There was no way to know how long it would be before my back eased. What I needed was a scalding-hot whirlpool bath and a massage, to be followed by several tall scotches and bed rest. But that would have to wait. When I thought I could move without screaming again, I went to work at getting to my feet. That only took about three minutes. I could live with it as long as I did not try to straighten up. Bent over like an old man, I hobbled back to the beds. There was nothing I wanted more than to lie down, but I knew if I did I might never get up. The phone rang.

"Good morning, sir. It's eight A.M."

"Thank you," I said, before I realized it was one of those computerized deals with a recorded message.

Later than I thought. Two hours before I was due to take Cochran's polygraph.

"Pilar!" I called. I could hear her making noises on the bathroom floor, but none of it meant anything.

I put up with the pain it cost to get a cigarette and light it. While I was fumbling with my jacket, I took the little automatic out of the pocket. With the gun stuck in the waistband of my pants, I felt less like a cripple.

Pilar had not gone far while I was away. Now she was the one in a fetal position, curled tightly on the floor and murmuring about being cold.

"Hey. Hey, kid, can you hear me?"

If she could I could not tell it. Dragging her to one of the beds was out of the question. I did not even feel up to dragging her off the bathroom tiles onto the carpet. So I did the next best thing—I lay on top of her to warm her. It seemed to help. I had not been there long before she was curled up against me, and the murmuring had become a low and throaty moan. It was like holding a cat, a kitten in from the rain. It did not feel bad, and maybe I was feeling something for her.

I knew when her troubles eased the next time because I could feel it in her, as she relaxed and came to.

"You're doing fine," I told her. "You've made it this far. You can kick it, kid."

"Fuck you, I'm dying."

"When's the drop?"

"Today."

"I figured that," I said. "What time?"

"An hour after I make a call."

"Where?"

"Downtown."

"Could you narrow it down a little for me?"

"I want my stuff first."

"Not yet," I said.

"Bastard."

"Don't fight like that, you'll just wear yourself out more."

"You promised."

"You still haven't told me much. But answer one more question and you've got a deal."

"I don't believe you. You're killing me."

"It's a truth check. I'll ask you one more question, and I already know the answer. So I'll know if you're lying, understand?"

"You are only torturing me. You're worse than Crandall."

"Here's the question: How many people does Crandall have? Remember, I already know the answer."

She craned her neck to look at me, and I could see her fighting to make sense of me, of what I was saying.

"If you know already . . ."

"Like I said, it's a truth check. If you lie to me about this, I can't believe you about the drop. If I can't believe you, you don't get the dope. Understand?"

"Yes."

"So let's have it. How many players on Crandall's team?"

Sometimes you can tell what a person is thinking. Pilar on a good day, no way. But this was not a good day. Everything left in her world was riding on this. She might lie, probably would, if she thought I was bluffing. What I saw in her face now was her trying as hard as she could to decide to call me. But, God, the stakes were high. Too high. She needed what I had taken from her so badly that she could not risk it.

"One," she said.

"One. That would be the guy Crandall calls his chauffeur, Mario, right?"

"Yes. One. Now? Now will you give it to me?"

"Okay, kid. Hold on a second."

Like a fool, I had left the dope on the table all the way back across the room. I did not want Pilar to see what bad shape I was in with my back. So I did the best job I could of getting back to my feet and fetching the nasty rubber for her. When I got back to her, she had gotten herself into a sitting position on one hip, bracing herself with one hand on the floor. I had put her works, the needle and spoon and everything, in a drawer under the sink. I dropped them and the tied-off rubber onto the floor in front of her.

Until she saw the rubber, she had been holding one of the towels around her to cover her breasts. But when she caught sight of the dope, she forgot about the towel and everything else except getting the stuff into her veins. She went to work getting everything ready, with more energy than I would have thought she had left.

"Help me, please," she said.

"You can do it," I answered, disgusted with myself. "It's bad enough I give this shit back to you."

"You think . . ." She laughed as she went to work. "You think I should kick it, don't you? That's all you know, Mister Whitebread. You got any idea how many junkies kick this shit? One per cent, maybe two. And that's . . ."

"That's what?" I asked. She had lost her train of thought as she tied the rubber tube off around her arm and hunted for a vein that was still good.

"That's bullshit from the cure farms. I don't think nobody ever put this shit down once they got the taste for it. So don't feel bad about not saving me, okay?"

Our eyes met, and I saw something in the look she gave me that made me wish I was a better man.

"Really, Jack. If you had flushed this stuff or kept it from me much longer, all you would have done is kill me. I swear it. I'll never get off of it." A little moistness in her eyes made me think she knew what she was saying and meant it. "It's not your fault."

I did not say anything else, and neither did she. When she was ready, I lent her my lighter to melt the stuff down into a liquid so she could load her spike. I did not watch the rest of it. Partly I did not want to see her do it to herself, partly I had something on my mind. She had not lied about the size of Crandall's "team." I had been bluffing about knowing that, of course, but she had not dared to call me. Still, I was sure of the number. It fit the notion that had been nibbling at me lately.

Mario was a cripple, thanks to me and Della's little lace costume. But even with two good legs, it did not figure that Mario had done very much surveillance work. Crandall had to sleep sometime, and he had a bad back, too. Mario would have his hands full just keeping an eye on things, Pilar and this and that. Crandall might know how to do a tap, but not necessarily. If he did, somebody had a fulltime monitoring them, or at least a regular job running by to pick up tapes. So who told Crandall that I came to see O'Bannion the day his picture was in the paper? Or that O'Bannion had a date with Pilar at the Wagon Wheel Inn? If Pilar was working with Crandall, she could have told him about her tryst with O'Bannion. But that did not compute, for two reasons. First, it queered her play to have O'Bannion step in as a dope connection, either to replace Crandall or to supplement him. Second, if she was in on it with Crandall, why had she run from him, hidden out here at the hotel? Or called me, for that matter? It could be she was in with Crandall and all the rest was for my benefit. That was always a possibility in a deal like this. But I did not think so. I thought I knew how Crandall kept tabs on O'Bannion, but I did not like it. If I was right, it was the dirtiest part of this whole deal, even worse than the pretty woman on the bathroom floor with the needle in her arm.

Chapter Twenty-six

SHE WAS WELL IN a matter of minutes, she was happy again. She did not say much at first, just sat there on the bathroom floor wearing an idiot smile. She was not even mad at me anymore. She sat there nodding and grinning, not worrying yet about where she would get her next fix. That would come later.

It would be a while before she was up to making her call to set up the drop, and that was all right with me. I had a call of my own to make.

Lieutenant Cochran was in, the nice lady on the phone told me. I said I would not mind holding.

"Cochran."

"Kyle. Good morning."

"Good morning yourself, smartass. My guys told me what a cute dude you were last night."

"Sorry about giving them the slip, Eddie. But listen, you gotta see about getting yourself some better hired hands. Maybe the cowboys could go to a school or something."

"They're not too smooth, are they?"

"Wouldn't make a patch on their old lieutenant."

"So enough chitchat, Jack. I assume you're calling to confirm your ten o'clock appointment."

"Kinda. I wanted to let you know I may be running a little late. I didn't want you to think I ran out on you."

"How late?"

"It's hard to say. There's something I have to do first."

"Well, I'm glad you called, Jack, because it's good to know you made it through the night. I mean that."

"Thanks, I appreciate it."

"And I mean what I said last night, too. You have your butt in my office per our agreement or I'll file on you for the murder of Brendan O'Bannion. Do you understand me?"

"Nothing could be fairer. Don't suppose I could talk you into holding off for a couple of hours?"

"No, but I will do you one favor."

"What's that?"

"I'll tell you what I found out about your playmate Arthur Crandall. Only because I hope you'll have enough sense to pull up when you find out who you're screwing around with."

"Sounds ominous."

"Couldn't be much worse. Here's the deal: There wasn't time to go through channels, so I just called a friend of mine to see if there was anything he could tell me."

I knew Eddie had done some kind of intelligence work in the war, and he had good contacts. I was ready to listen.

"And?"

"Crandall's name was like saying the magic word, Jack. I mean, I expected a duck to come down on a string or something. The man is very hot in the intelligence community."

"What does that mean exactly?"

"For one thing, that the Agency is real nervous about what he might be up to these days. They want it known that the man is no longer on the payroll. My friends asked me more questions about Crandall than I asked them—where he was, everything I knew about the guy."

"Which is nothing. Are you dead sure it's the same guy? There wasn't time for you to get the photos up there to them."

"Up where? They saw the pictures. It's definite."

"How?"

"Don't worry about that."

I was not worried about it, just curious. I had assumed the

Agency people Eddie was talking about where in Washington. To get the pictures to them that fast, Eddie had to have connections I would not have thought he had. Or maybe he just borrowed the telefax machine at the local FBI office. That was probably it. The other way it could be was that his Agency friends were in town. That was what I was wondering about. Eddie might be an even more interesting guy than I knew.

"Okay, Jack, this is what I got. Crandall is his real name, or as close as we'll ever get. CIA for a long time. First posted to Santa Rosa back in the good old days. Southeast Asia after that. Worked the Golden Triangle, doing nobody knows or will say what. Then in-country, Vietnam, probably connected with Phoenix. Impressed so far?"

I was. The Golden Triangle was a part of Indo-China. It was to opium and heroin what China would be to rice if they had their marketing and distribution act together. Operation Phoenix was still secret as far as I knew, but the unofficial word was it had involved what spooks call "wet work." Vietnamese locals who did not love their Uncle Sam had a way of turning up missing when Phoenix teams were in the neighborhood. It all sounded plenty big league enough for me. There was more.

"After we pulled out of Nam," Eddie went on, "Crandall asked to be sent back to Santa Rosa, where he still had friends. The brass obliged him. He was tight with the Minister of Justice there. Of course, the good guys lost that one, too."

"I hear it depends on your point of view."

"The goddamn commies won, Jack. Anyway, your man Crandall was a member in good standing up to that point. But when the dust settled and the paperwork got done, they sacked him. Seems he had been playing dirty."

"How dirty?"

"As dirty as it gets. Interrogation with torture and drugs, war crimes, if you drag out the books. The word is he's probably killed about as many people as ride buses in Dallas, or had it done. You get the picture."

"What's his style?"

"Whatever it takes."

"Does he work with an organization or is he a loner?"

"Lone wolf, I'd say. He was so out-of-channels when he was with the Agency that nobody really had a handle on what he was up to. That's probably why he lasted as long as he did. He used what they call indigenous nets, locals not connected. Overlapping networks, checking up on the other side and each other at the same time. Very compartmentalized, need-to-know only. The guy trusts nobody."

"He'd hedge his bets, cover both sides."

"Very much so. He uses disposable people. Recruit'em for a reason, lose'em when the job is done."

"What else?"

"Jesus, Jack, ain't that enough?"

"Did my name come up when you were talking to your friends?"

"Nah, you're an anonymous source. You've got enough trouble already."

"I appreciate that."

"I doubt it. But it works both ways. If I get any blowback on this, any hint that you passed on what I just told you, a murder rap will not seem like a big problem anymore. Clear?"

"Clear."

"That's it, then. You're here at ten sharp or you're a wanted man."

"You don't mean that."

"The hell I don't. I'm tired of screwing around with you."

"I'll do my best."

"Just be here."

A loner. That fit. Crandall would not bring an army with him, a big organization. He would hire and fire whatever talent he needed locally. Feed them whatever line worked and keep them around as long as he needed them, or until they became problems. That explained O'Bannion. Pilar's father too, probably.

When I put down the phone I spotted the passport sticking

out of my jacket pocket on the back of a chair. I thumbed through it, looking at the stamps of entries and exits. The owner, a man named Guzman, who looked in his photo like a character who belonged in this kind of a deal, had done some traveling. A couple of long stays in Cuba. Mexico several times, Costa Rica, and Nicaragua. And the States. His second trip to America had been his last.

"Who was this guy Guzman?" I asked her.

"What?"

She was still in the bathroom, and I noticed then the sound of water running. My back was not much better, but I made my way over to check on her. I did not like having her out of my sight for very long.

She was scrubbing her face. I watched without high expectations. I had seen her at her worst and she had no makeup to patch things with. But it was a good sign that she felt like trying.

"Guzman," I said again. "The guy with the passport, the man O'Bannion zipped. Who was he?"

"El Commandante." She looked up from the sink, her hands cupped almost daintily beneath her chin. She had tucked a towel around her breasts to cover herself. Her hair was wet and pulled back from her face. She looked better than I had expected. "When I was with the rebels. Guzman was commander of my cell."

"The one who got shot up in Crandall's trap but managed to escape?"

"Yes."

"The one Crandall sent you back to after you had recovered from your wound?"

"Yes."

"And you said he still trusted you, because you had been wounded in the ambush too. He welcomed you back."

"They are two different things, you know. He did welcome me back, but there is no way to know if he trusted me or not. He had sworn to murder my father. I know that."

"Because . . ."

"Because my father ordered that all of the rebels captured by Crandall were to be shot. After Crandall was finished interrogating them. The interrogation was . . ."

"I have a pretty good idea what it was. Jesus, this whole deal is like a ball of snakes!"

"What do you mean?"

"A gang of reptiles all balled up, screwing each other blind. This whole thing is just turning out to be incredibly tight, everybody tied in with everybody else. How did Guzman happen to be in Dallas?"

"He was doing the advance for the trade delegation."

"Security?"

"Same thing, counterintelligence. He'd have been a brigadier except for the trap that Crandall tricked him into. His assignment to counterintelligence was the leadership's way of saying that he should have been more security conscious, or such a thing would not have happened."

"And I'd heard commies had no sense of humor."

If she saw humor in any of this, she showed no sign of it. When I did not ask anything more of her, she went back to washing her face. I did not move away from the door.

Chapter Twenty-seven

PILAR MADE THE CALL. She swapped Spanish with a voice on the other end of the line, a voice that sounded the way I felt, tired and scared. I had not let on to any of the people in this deal that I spoke a little Spanish. As Crandall would say, none of them had a need to know.

What I got from the call sounded straight enough. The deal was on, as arranged. There was a little bit I could not make out so well, that sounded like lines from a poem. That would be a sign and countersign, I hoped, so that each could let the other know that all was well. It could have been a signal the other way, but I decided not to worry about that. Either way, I knew I had to make the pickup, and it figured that was the way Pilar needed it, too. No point borrowing trouble.

I lent Pilar my comb to do what she could with her hair. It helped a little. She sat in front of the mirror opposite the beds and combed her hair. I watched her, and thought again that this was one of the sexiest things a woman does. She was at a point in her addiction where the stuff had not begun to eat away at her yet. Her body was good, lean, and tight, but with soft curves where you would want them in a woman.

She looked different. It was not just that she had got her fix and was not sick anymore. It was the way I looked at her, too. She did not look like a siren, like the kind of woman who . . . like some kind of a femme fatale. She looked younger, more like a kid. Like a young girl who had been through too much.

"Tell me about the arrangements," I said.

"Are you a Sidekicks fan?" she asked.

"Not particularly."

All I knew about the Sidekicks, or soccer generally, was that they were not allowed to pick the ball up and run with it, and that they had a guy on the team named Tatu who took his shirt off and threw it into the crowd when he scored.

"You will be today," she said, turning to smile at me over her shoulder. "The drop is set for the game. The Santa Rosa trade delegation will be there. The Americans are treating them to their first indoor soccer."

"Okay. How is it going to be?"

She worked on her hair without answering for a minute or two.

"Don't think about it that much, Pilar. Just tell me the truth."

"It will take two of us to do it," she said. "To make sure it goes off without any trouble."

"I'd expect you to say that. Why?"

"The man knows me. He will only make the drop with me."

"The hell you say."

"It has to be that way."

"And what am I supposed to do?"

"What O'Bannion hired you for in the first place, back me up. Protect me."

"No problem," I said.

No problem at all, unless Guzman's pals in Santa Rosan counterintelligence had their eye on the man who was going to make the drop. Or Cochran and his cowboys got onto the deal somehow and showed up looking for me on a murder rap. Or Cochran's CIA contacts really were in Dallas, not Washington. That could be interesting. And then there was Crandall. He had to be looking everywhere for Pilar, knowing she could make the drop herself and cut him out of the action. The whole thing with the drop was shaping up like one of those free-for-all wrestling matches with half a dozen tag teams in the ring at the same time.

"How long are you good for now?" I asked.

She knew what I meant, but there was a hurt look in her eyes when she put down the comb and turned toward me.

"Long enough. I won't be sick again until tonight sometime. Late tonight, if I'm lucky."

"And then what? Where does the next fix come from?"

"I don't know, unless . . ."

"Unless what?" I asked, knowing all the time what she had in mind. As a matter of fact, I had been thinking about it myself.

It was either a brilliant move or one of the dumbest things I had done in my life. You could make a case either way. Pilar needed her dope and I might or might not need Pilar after the Sidekicks soccer game. She had run away from Crandall and it stood to reason he was looking everywhere for her. So maybe the last place he would look was at her father's house.

On Crandall's team there was only him and Mario, the chauffeur with the bum knee. If Crandall knew Pilar's only source of heroin was his stash, the house could be a trap. But if he thought O'Bannion was taking care of her, then he could not afford to sit around there waiting on the off chance. . . . It was a crap shoot any way you looked at it.

Pilar took only a couple of seconds to slip into her blouse and skirt, and looked considerably better dressed than I had expected, given the night she had been through. We left DO NOT DISTURB signs on both her rooms at the hotel, hoping we would not have to come back to them.

She led me down the stairs from the hallway into the underground parking garage and slid behind the wheel of a chocolate-brown Mercedes. In a matter of minutes we were on our way.

"Don't worry," she told me.

"You've got to be kidding."

"I mean about all the alarms, all the security at the house. It's only a front."

"Like everything else," I said, and spent the rest of the drive looking over my shoulder to see if anyone was following us and trying to remember how I had gotten mixed up in this whole *magillah* to begin with.

Chapter Twenty-eight

PILAR WOULD HAVE PULLED right into the driveway but I made her make a couple of passes first. Everything looked all right, but I had a nervous feeling about it. The house looked as much like a bunker in the daylight as it had the first time I saw it, the night I noticed the high-intensity lights reflecting off the broken shards of glass on the tops of the high walls. The van was still parked out front, but Pilar assured me it was empty.

Finally there was nothing left to do but to go in and find out. She opened the driveway gate with an electronic gadget that was clipped to the sun visor of her car and we went in.

We left the car in the drive and she closed the gate behind us. We walked up the curving walk that led us past a big window that showed us our reflections. We could not see inside the house.

"Stop worrying," she said as she unlocked the front door. "Crandall is out looking for me."

"And Mario?"

"Him, too," she laughed. She really did not look scared at all. Not even nervous. "Come on."

It occurred to me that she was not scared because this meant a hell of a lot more to her than it did to me. It was her dope we had come for, and she had plenty of reason to convince herself it was safe. All I had was a feeling we were being watched.

The inside of the big house was a surprise. It was empty. No furniture in the cavernous den, nothing on the walls. I followed Pilar to the left past a formal dining room that was empty except for a chandelier and a kitchen with fast-food wrappers and Chinese take-out cartons strewn from one end of a long counter to the other.

Down a long and thickly carpeted hall she led me past a couple of closed doors before she tried the knob of a door that looked odd until I realized that it was the only one along the hall that had a peep hole in it. The knob did not turn when she twisted it, and she turned to me with a hungry look.

"Open it," she whispered tightly.

"It's locked," I said.

"I know that, goddamnit. Break it down!"

Okay, so this was the room with the dope in it. Crandall's room, probably. A couple of things came to mind. First, that he might have taken the time to move the dope, might have it with him wherever he was. Second, that he might be behind the door, watching us through the peephole. So I took the little automatic out of my jacket pocket, held it waist high in a line directly below the peep hole and fired a round into the door.

The little gun made a hell of a racket in the close quarters of the hallway and splinters from the door flew like shrapnel from a hand grenade.

Pilar spun away from me down the hall, cursing in Spanish for all she was worth. I took a close look at the bullet hole in the door, amazed to see that the slug had gone all the way through; it was not much of a door. I stepped back to the wall opposite the door to get some leverage and kicked hard, aiming for the edge of the door just above the knob. The door burst open with a bang and I went in right behind it with my little automatic ready. No one was there.

There was a bed and a telephone, some books and magazines in a sloppy pile. The bed had been much slept in and never changed. To the right of the door a closet stood open, empty except for one suit hanging and some dirty shirts in a pile on the floor.

Pilar was past me like a shot and dashed into the bathroom. I heard her slamming metal doors and throwing things around. When I stepped into the doorway behind her she had the lid off the back of the toilet and was pulling something out of the water tank. I saw that it was a tightly wrapped bundle with a plastic cover. She started to scream when I reached over her shoulder and took the bundle away from her. But I only wanted to make sure it was not a gun. I squeezed it and knew what it was. I let her have it and, after I had made sure there were no weapons hidden in the room, I went for a look around the house.

As I looked through the other rooms in the house I tried to think things over. The soccer game was at three. Thank God it was an afternoon game. I would have hated to wait with Pilar on my hands for an eight P.M. kick-off. Or whatever it is in soccer. It was almost eleven. I wanted to get to Reunion Arena where the game was to be played early enough to look things over, make a couple of arrangements. But not so early we stood out, so early we could be spotted. There might be others who knew about the drop. They might be looking the place over, too. I thought the house we were in might not be a bad place to kill an hour or two. I could not remember if Cochran had any way of knowing about this house. I had not told him anything about Pilar. We could lay low here for a while, I thought, because my bad feelings about the house were easing away as I finished looking through it.

Pilar seemed to have been right about the big house being a front. Her father must have rented it for appearances, to impress somebody. On the inside it looked like a dump. This was not a place anybody lived in. It was a hideout for professionals on a job.

I had seen closed-circuit TV cameras outside, but there did not seem to be any monitors inside for watching what the cameras saw. Maybe they were dummies.

When I had convinced myself that we were alone in the house, I went back to the room where I had left Pilar.

I stopped in the doorway when I saw her sitting on the

bed. Her precious plastic-wrapped bag of heroin was on the bed beside her. She sat with her hands in her lap, looking at me.

It is the little things that make all the difference, tiny things that you see but they don't register. You don't snap. Like the look on Pilar's face. I had not seen exactly that look before, and I moved toward her with that look on my mind, wondering what it meant. It meant something serious enough that I closed my right hand around the butt of the .22 in my jacket pocket, checking to be sure the safety was off.

Behind the broken door on my right was the closet. I had looked into it when I searched the room and I was not thinking about it as I moved toward Pilar on the bed with the strange new look on her face. I should have been thinking about it. That was where it came from.

Right off the bat it broke my right arm, this thing, whatever it was, that came at me. It hit me so hard from my right side that it broke my arm above the elbow and drove me into the wall on my left, hard enough to make my rib cage pop. All the air in my body left in a gush and I puked. It went slowly from there, the way it does when you are dying.

We could have been under water, the way things looked and sounded to me. Everything was moving at once, but slowly, and the sounds we were making were like that, too. When he moved to hit me again the noises his feet made scraping across the carpet sounded like those you hear at the bottom of a pool at the deep end when somebody jumps in not far away, echoey and muffled. My right hand was out of my pocket for some reason, but I could not do anything about that. It was not mine anymore, that hand. It looked too white, and flopped up in front of my face all on its own like a hooked fish on a boat deck. I looked past it toward the closet. There was a false wall in the closet that made a hiding place that I had not found. It was standing open now.

He did not want to kill me yet, or the next blow would have been to my head. Or the first one, for that matter. But it was not, it was down across the small of my back. I screamed, and then it was over for a while.

It was bad being out because it felt like my head was stuffed into a bag of ticking packed so tightly that I could not breathe, with sparks jazzing around in front of my eyelids. That was bad, but coming to was worse. My back hurt so bad I forgot my arm was broken.

There was no way for me to know how long it took, but I finally managed to turn myself in a way that let me breathe again. It was good that my legs were not numb because that would have meant my back was broken. It was not broken. But pain worse than any I had ever known before stabbed across my waist and down my left leg. Some of the noise I heard in the room was me whimpering. I tried to stop.

My vision began to clear. I saw two feet moving away from me, one black and one white. Another of the sounds I heard was the white foot dragging across the carpet. To me it sounded like a nail drawn across a blackboard. There was a voice, too.

It was Mario, Crandall's chauffeur. When I got my good arm under me so I could raise my head off the floor, I saw that Mario was using a crutch under his left arm. His left leg was in a cast from the thigh down. Good, I had crippled him. From his right hand swung what I took to be a lead-filled pipe about three feet long. For such a big man coming out of a cramped place like that closet, he had really gotten good leverage on me with the pipe.

Mario seemed to be finished with me for the time being. He was moving toward Pilar on the bed. No hurry, she was not going anywhere. She was talking to him in Spanish. She threw Crandall's name at him a couple of times. I did not have any trouble understanding the tone of her voice, and now the look in her eyes made sense, too. She was scared, the way a snared bird would be scared of a cat. As he moved within reach of her, she squirmed away. She wriggled away from him on the bed. She put up as much fight as she could, but he was too much for her.

It was not easy for him with his crutch to manhandle her. He had to lay his pipe on the floor to do it. But he got it done, with a fistful of hair and a string of curses. She squealed, but not very loudly. We both knew screaming would do no good.

He had her on the bed now, pinned on her back beneath him. His intentions were obvious and he acted like a man who had been thinking about doing what he was going to do now for a long time. He had her wrists gathered above her head in one of his big hands and was pulling her blouse off by the time I finally worked my left hand around to my jacket pocket. I could tell the pistol was still there by dragging my busted arm across it.

Mario lifted himself to get at Pilar's skirt and she kicked him, aiming for his bad knee. I did not have the pistol out yet but I could feel it with my good hand. Mario went down to his good knee and scooped up the pipe. She tried to roll out of the way but he was quick with it. It caromed off her hip and she screamed. She was through fighting him then. She started talking again, pleading, reasoning, saying anything she could think of to say. She never looked at me, never turned her face or even her eyes toward me. Neither did Mario, and by his heavy breathing and the hump of his back as he moved over her I knew he was thinking only of her.

I did not want him on top of her, did not want him on the bed at all, because I did not think I could raise the gun high enough or hold it steady enough to hit him there. I did not want them together because I might hit her. I would shoot anyway, take whatever shot I could get, but I wanted him with at least one foot on the floor. I was almost ready. The gun was in my left hand, just clear of the pocket, when he moved his hand between her thighs and laughed.

"Hey, Romeo," I said. I did not have the wind for anything witty.

It was enough. His head spun toward me at the sound of my voice with a look of amazement as if he had already killed me once. That was the last I saw of his face for a while. After that I just looked at his foot. Not the one in the cast. Too hard to tell where the bones were. I wanted the other one, his good one. He moved off the bed toward me and I saw the black foot, the one in the tassle loafer, come down on the carpet maybe eight feet away from my left hand. I was stretched out on the floor, my left arm extended in a straight line toward the foot of the bed, toward the black shoe. If he sidestepped, I would never be able to bring the gun around in time. But he did not, he was too strong and mad for that. I could tell by looking at his good foot that he was coming straight on, pivoting to get leverage with the pipe. This time he would aim at my head.

The little gun made a hell of a noise. So did Mario. He yelled horribly and the foot jerked up from the floor. His bad leg did not hold him, and he came crashing to his knees. His crutch shot out from under him and broke a lamp.

I raised my sights a bit by cocking my wrist as Mario started for me on his hands and knees, screaming. The second slug whacked into his crotch about three inches below his belt buckle and he doubled over, face down, his butt in the air, and howled like a banshee.

The last one was easiest. His face was buried in the carpet, the top of his head now only a foot or so away. That one opened the roof of his skull with a little pop like a vacuum jar being opened, and he was dead. He shuddered and spasmed a time or two, but it was over.

Chapter Twenty-nine

PILAR GOT OFF THE bed and came to me. I saw that she stepped wide around the dead man, afraid he still might hurt her somehow. She made a hell of a fuss over me, but I kept a tight grip on the little gun because I did not trust her either.

"My God, Jack," was what she was saying when she had calmed down enough to quit talking Spanish so fast I could not make anything out. "My God, Jack." She said it over and over until I asked her to stop.

"Are you all right?" she asked then.

"Shut up and get me some whisky."

I did not want her hovering over me. Everything hurt. As she left, I looked at the bed to make sure she had left the heroin behind. She had. That was as far as I trusted her, as far as I could keep my eye on her dope.

By the time she got back with a fresh bottle of scotch I was sitting up. I had rolled myself over and propped my back against the wall. My legs still worked, but not my right arm. I did not feel like moving anymore for a while.

Pilar handed me the scotch and I made a face at her. She had not opened it, and I only had one hand left. I was not about to turn loose of the gun to open the bottle. She saw what I meant and opened it for me.

"Is there anything I can do?" she asked, sounding like she meant it.

"Yeah. See if you can find something clean for a sling in this dump. Tear off part of a sheet or something."

She left again and I used my left hand to pull my right up from the floor. I laid the right hand in my lap and took a good slug of whisky against the pain I got for my trouble.

Pilar was back fast with a real sling, something she had taken out of a first-aid kit somewhere nearby. She folded the white linen square and ran it under my bad arm, then tied it neatly behind my neck. She did a good job and my broken arm was held snug against my ribs. It did not stop the pain but it made it more constant, dependable. I thought I could live with it for a while.

"Search him," I told her.

She did not want to, but she did not argue about it, either. She turned Mario over and went through his pockets. When I insisted, she ran her hands around his waist as well, and came up with a pistol. She held it gingerly between her thumb and index finger and looked at me.

"I'll take that," I said.

She stepped over the corpse and handed me the gun. It was a 9 millimeter, one of the Latin American knock-off copies of a Colt government model. Single action, with a thumb safety. It was not easy, but I managed to get the magazine out and counted six rounds. There was one in the chamber as well. Mario had been carrying it cocked and locked, like a good boy. The idiot. He had been too interested in working me over to just shoot me. That would have been the professional thing to do, the smart thing. But he wanted to pay me back for that business with his knee. That was stupid. Even dumber, he'd forgotten that I had a gun, too. If he had been hiding in the closet when I shot through the door, he sure as hell knew I had something. But he wanted to screw around with me. He probably figured I was down for the count, gun or no gun. He thought he had plenty of time to settle things with me after he had his fun with the girl. He was too dumb to live.

But it was the dumb ones who always manage to hurt you.

And the big man had done a job on me. I put his gun in my hip pocket and the .22 in my left jacket pocket. Then, with the bottle in my hand holding my broken arm tight against me, I got to my feet. It hurt like hell and must have sounded like it, too, because Pilar looked up from her search of the body as if she thought I was dying.

"What have you got?" I asked, to keep my mind off the pain.

"Some money. His passport."

"Let me have the money," I said. "Leave everything else."

She handed over the money, several hundred dollars. She stood waiting for me to tell her what to do next. I looked at her. The long-suffering blouse was in tatters around her, her breasts and shoulders bare. I told her to get dressed.

I followed her out the door and down the hall to her own room. She left the door open when she went in so I could follow her. I was not making very good time, my leg shot through with pain that felt like lightning.

She was standing in front of her closet when I made it to her door. Her room looked about like Crandall's, like some kind of camp.

As she peeled off the ruined blouse and her skirt, I noticed her scar again and decided something.

"Where is your passport?" I asked her.

"Crandall has it."

"Figures."

"But," she said, smiling at me. "I have another."

"Smart."

She smiled a little.

"Do you have a telephone in here somewhere?"

"No. There's one in Crandall's room and another in the kitchen. That's all."

No phone. I looked at the door to her room and noticed the locks. There were two that worked with keys. Both were on the outside of the door. There were no locks on the inside.

215

"One more time," I said. "Tell what this drop is all about."

"Names. You know that. A list of names. Assets in place . . ."

It is probably dangerous to ever think you can tell when a woman is lying.

"You're lying," I said.

"Jack . . ."

"Save it. It's not about politics at all, or intelligence, or any of that crap. You know why?"

"Why?" she asked, finishing her change of clothes.

"Because you don't care anymore. Not about all of that. No more than I do."

"You're wrong."

"Probably. But not about the thing we're after. It's not a list of names."

"What then?"

"I think you and I both know. But in case you don't, I'll like it better if you're left wondering."

She had nothing to say to that, but the way she did not say anything made me sure I was right. I told her to get her things together, that I had a phone call to make.

I used the phone in Crandall's room because it was closer and I could watch her put the dope into a big purse she brought from her room.

I called Betty O'Bannion. This thing was coming to a head in a couple of hours and I wanted to talk to her before it was too late. Imagine my surprise when Crandall answered the phone at Betty's house.

"Let me talk to Betty," I said.

"If you let me speak with Pilar. Fair's fair, Jack."

"If you've done anything to her . . ."

"You'll kill me, I understand. Is Pilar with you?"

"Yes."

"Then may I speak with her, please?"

I gave the phone to Pilar and all she needed to know was

in my eyes. She spoke Spanish with Crandall, still not knowing I could make most of it out. She told him where we were, what had happened with Mario, that Mario had not hurt me, and a couple of other lies. He must have asked her if we had the thing yet, if we had already made the drop, because she looked at me as if she needed advice. I took the phone from her.

"Enough, already," I said. "Put Betty on."

"Jack?" It was Betty's voice, and she sounded scared. "Please, Jack . . . he came here, and . . . I'm sorry, Jack, about everything. Please, just give him what he wants. He . . ."

That was all she got to say. Crandall came back on the line.

"You are to be commended, Jack."

"What for?"

"For killing Mario, of course."

"Oh," I said. "She told you about that, did she?"

Pilar did not seem to know what to do or say. She watched me closely for some kind of a sign.

"Yes. Are you all right?" Crandall asked, making his voice sound as if he was concerned about my health in a different way from the way he really was.

"Never better, nice of you to ask. And you?"

"As well as can be expected, Jack. My back is troubling me, always does in cold weather. I know you understand how that can be."

I laughed a little, knowing Crandall had made a point of telling Mario about my back. And of course Mario had made a point of laying his pipe across my back.

"You should take better care of yourself," I told him. "Do your stretching exercises twice a day, like a good scout."

"You're right, of course, Jack."

"So what else is on your mind? A little woman-swapping?"

"Don't be silly. You haven't anything to swap. Pilar means nothing to me."

"What, then?"

"A slightly different swap. You give me the thing I want and I give you dear little Betty."

"Sounds fair."

"I knew you'd think so. Do you have it yet?"

"How the hell would I know? All you people've been so goddamned secretive . . ."

"Don't be silly, Jack. If you have it, say so and we can do business. If not . . ."

"Not yet."

"When?"

"Soon. A couple of hours."

"Where?"

"That's my problem. I'll tell you where we're going to make our little swap."

"You'll tell me where the drop is set or I'll kill this . . ."

"Won't work. Shut up and listen. Listen. Trinity River, on the downtown side, south from the Commerce Street viaduct. Follow the road to the railroad overpass. I'll meet you there. You can see me coming."

"When?"

"That's not so easy. Say between three-thirty and four. But don't freak if I'm a little late. This is a complicated deal."

"If you're not there by four . . ."

"No deadlines. Be professional about this. I'll be there if I can, as near the time as I can. If something happens and I can't make it, we'll have to arrange the swap some other time, some other . . ."

"Bullshit! Today, at your place and time, or Betty dies. I don't have the time or the inclination to screw around with you on this. Got it?"

Pilar had left the room when I took the phone and now she was back, and she was excited. She pointed toward the front of the house and I nodded.

"I'll do the best I can," I told Crandall. "See that nothing happens to Betty."

Before he could say anything else, I hung up the phone and Pilar whispered to tell me there were men outside.

218

Chapter Thirty

I DID NOT LOOK to see how many there were, but I did hear some kind of machinery being applied to the locks on the front door.

"Who are they?" I asked Pilar in a whisper.

"I don't know," she answered.

"How about the back of the house?"

"They are there, too," she said.

"You got a look at them, didn't you?" I insisted. "Are they the Santa Rosans?"

"I don't know. I didn't recognize any of them. Maybe they're contractors. Come with me."

She reached for my good hand to lead me back down the hall, but I snatched my hand away from her. I wanted no hang-ups if I had to use it. She hurried away down the hall like she had a plan, but I lagged behind long enough to take a peek through a crack in the curtains at the front window, reminding myself that the men outside could not see in. I was hoping it was Cochran's men; I would not have minded a murder rap, the way I was feeling and the way Betty had sounded on the phone. But I did not know any of the men working on the front door. There were three of them, and they looked more than serious enough for me. I managed to get the cap back on the bottle of scotch and dropped it into a jacket pocket hobbled off down the hall the way Pilar had gone as fast as I could.

She was waiting for me at the end of the hall and led me through an open window into a narrow path between the wall of the garage on our left and a tall dense hedge on our right. I made too much noise getting through the window, but that could not be helped. We scrambled along for fifty or sixty feet between the wall and the hedge and then she turned to her right just as we came to the corner of this hedge and the other one, the one that ran along the high wall toward the front of the house. When I caught up with her, I looked where she pointed and saw there was a hole in the wall that stood on the other side of the hedge we had been following. Looking through it, I saw that there were bushes on the outside of the wall, too, covering the hole. The hole in the wall was pretty new; someone had pick-axed enough bricks out to make this escape hatch without worrying about how it looked.

I went first and managed to get into a crouch outside the wall without exposing myself beyond the bushes that covered us. I could see well enough to spot the two men who were standing watch in the alley behind the house. They were a good distance away, opposite the main part of the house. They were not looking in our direction.

"Great," I whispered to Pilar. "Now what?"

She motioned me to follow her and I did the best I could. Lugging her big purse with the heroin inside, she dashed across the alley and angled across the unfenced yard of the house beyond. I followed her and thought I heard footsteps behind me.

Pilar reached the street beyond the houses that backed up to her father's house and turned to her left, really running now. I had no hope of keeping up with her. My back and my leg insisted that I stop, that I lie down and let them rest. At the street I gave up the chase and turned to look back the way I had come. I heard footsteps again, coming closer. Half a block up the street I saw Pilar drop to her knees beside a car parked in the driveway of a house with a FOR SALE sign in the yard. What was she doing?

Footsteps and muffled voices, coming up the alley toward the fenceless yard where we had cut across from the escape hole: The two men in the alley had seen us after all, then. I didn't know who they were but there would likely be no time for introductions. They weren't cops and cops were the only game not in season as far as I was concerned. I was in no condition to run, fight, or put up with a lot of rough questions. I was glad I had Mario's gun now. It would make for a better show than just the .22. I tossed the whisky bottle aside and moved closer to the house that belonged to the front yard where I was squatting, with the idea that I would cut down the angle as much as I could and get a shot or two at the guys chasing me before the lights went out.

I was still thinking along that line when I heard Pilar call my name. I looked up to see her at the wheel of the car from the driveway down the street. Then it made sense. If you go to the trouble of hacking an escape hole in the back wall of your house, it follows that you would have a getaway car stashed nearby. In the driveway of a vacant house up for sale would be as good a place as any. There must have been a set of keys hidden underneath the car somewhere.

"Get in!" she said, reaching behind her to hold open the rear door on the driver's side.

In I went, with all the speed I could muster. As she roared away down the street, I looked back at the two men who ran out onto the sidewalk behind us. They did not yell or shake their fists or anything, like in the movies. One of them seemed to be talking into his hand. The other picked up my discarded bottle of scotch and I cursed him.

On our way back to Preston Road, which was the only way to go to get onto a main road and make any time, we passed a young man sitting in a parked car. Like the man we had left behind us, he was talking into his hand, too. He was blond, with dark glasses and a mustache, in a bronze Dodge Diplomat. I did not like it, it smelled like the government to me. The little microphones they strap to their thumbs to go with their earpieces, like the Secret Service, the car, everything. I was very glad Pilar had come back for me before any shooting started.

I did not know how much she knew about not letting someone follow her, but I was not taking any chances. I told her where to go and how fast to drive, now fast, now slow, the usual stuff plus about 50 percent. We killed the better part of two hours that way, and when we were through I was less than sure we had lost them.

We ended up in a shopping center at Lovers Lane and Inwood. Inwood would take us down to Stemmons or Hines and that way to Reunion Arena on the west end of downtown where the Sidekicks played, and the Dallas Mavericks, too. We eased past the Inwood Theater and I noticed that a Fassbinder film was playing. I wished my last few days had been a film, but there was no future in thinking that way. I told Pilar to park in front of a drugstore.

"We need some things before we go to the game," I told her.

"Can I get something for you, for the pain?" she asked. She had not made a peep about all the driving around we had done. She did not want a tail, either.

"A bottle of aspirin or something. Mainly, I want you to get me a tape recorder, with tapes and batteries. One of those real little ones, you know what I mean?"

"I understand."

"On second thought, make it two of them. Yeah, get me two of those little recorders. As small as you can get them, but I want good ones. Don't try to save your money, buy some good ones."

"All right, Jack, for Christ's sake, I understand. Is that all?"

"Yeah, that's it for this place. Get some cigarettes. We'll stop down the road somewhere and get something to eat. We'll feel a little more human with a meal in us. Maybe some more whisky. I think I'll need some whisky courage before we're through. Can you think of anything else?"

"I'll see if anything comes to me. I'll be right back."

"I know you will, but leave the keys anyway, just in case."

She did not ask any questions, not about the keys or the tape recorders or anything else. I guess she was used to taking orders. She killed the car when she went inside and left the keys dangling from the ignition. I was pretty well-chilled by the time she got back. It was a cold day and getting colder, the sky turning from a sleety gray to a threatening dark blue. The wind was up, too. It looked like a storm might be coming. I was glad we were on our way to a nice warm arena for the drop. My business after the game with Crandall would be different. That would be outdoors and nasty. If I lived that long.

We ate without either of us making any cracks about a last meal and then stopped at a little package store just before Harry Hines Boulevard and bought another bottle of scotch. I hit the bottle pretty good and Pilar had a drink, too. She said she was cold.

It was not a sell-out crowd for the Sidekicks, but a pretty good one. Plenty of people to get lost in. I was following her lead now, and I did not mention to her—as we bought our tickets and made our way into the stands—that I thought I had seen our blond friend with the mustache lounging in front of a souvenir stand. She had enough on her mind, and I was not sure it was him.

Chapter Thirty-one

I WAS NOT VERY well-suited for blending in with the crowd, and my job was to cover Pilar from the sidelines. Being conspicuous was not part of it. So I told her to wait for me while I went into a men's room and did what I could about it. I took off the sling and it did not hurt as much as I had expected. She had picked up an elastic bandage at the drugstore. I slipped off my shirt and wrapped the arm as best I could to keep everything inside from moving around. Then I got back into my shirt and my sportscoat and took a look at myself in the mirror. The arm looked all right but my face did not. I needed a shave, bad. Fortunately, Pilar had thought of that, too. She had picked up shaving stuff, a small can of cream and a disposable razor, and I used that to scrape my face clean. It was not easy doing it with my left hand, but I looked better after than before. That was it. I was ready. My right arm was wrapped and hung loose at my side. I did not think it was obvious there was anything wrong with it. I had the .22 in my left jacket pocket and I stepped into a stall to switch Mario's 9 millimeter from my hip pocket to my belt under my jacket. I knew I was not that good a left-handed pistol shooter, and I wanted both guns handy in case I needed them.

When I stepped out of the men's room into the walkway Pilar was not there, but somehow I did not worry about it. I was beginning to think I could trust her, at least until we got our hands on the thing everybody wanted.

I had just tossed the sling and the drugstore sack with the shaving stuff into a trash barrel when she showed up, walking toward me from the direction of the nearest souvenir stand. She was carrying a pennant that must have been the visiting team's. It was not a Sidekick's—that was all I knew about it.

"You look better," she said.

"Thanks, wish I felt better. What now?"

"We watch the first quarter."

"Okay. What's the deal with the souvenir? You a fan?"

"Not particularly. It's for the signal."

"What signal? I thought the guy knew you—that was the whole idea about you being the one that made the pickup."

"The signal to tell him it's all right. A *go* signal."

"And if everything's not all right?"

"Then I hold the pennant upside down."

"Wow, just like in the movies. Where are our seats?"

She looked at our tickets and figured it out. I did not mind the idea of sitting down for a while. My arm felt swollen and the fingers of my right hand were numb. I wondered if you could get gangrene from a broken arm.

We settled into a couple of seats while the teams were being introduced. We were upstairs, in the cheap section, and the tiers of seats looked almost vertical, like I would fall all the way to the playing field if I was not careful. She had brought the whisky in past the guards at the gate, the pint bottle tucked into her waist under her jacket. I asked her for it and she passed it over. I took a long drink to get the warm feeling back into my chest, another to wash down a couple of aspirins.

"Is the pain worse?" she asked.

"Nah, I'm all right," I lied.

The game started and the crowd was enthusiastic. I curled up inside my jacket beside Pilar in the warmth and closeness of the noisy crowd and tried to keep an eye out for anyone who looked like a threat.

The thing is, soccer is big in Mexico, all over Latin America. And Dallas has a hell of a lot of Hispanic people living here, one way or another. If I had the idea that I could spot a couple of Santa Rosan spooks in this crowd, I just was not thinking. It stood to reason they would have to be dumb lucky to make us, too, with the crowd and everybody jumping up every time something happened and everything. So I thought I might as well get some rest before the main event.

I awoke with a start when Pilar nudged my arm. I did not know how long I had been asleep, but it had been long enough for my back to stiffen up and now my left foot was asleep, along with my right hand. I was in a hell of a shape.

"It's time," Pilar said to me. "Come on."

Mostly I watched my step as we worked our way down with the crowd toward the aisle that would take us out into the part of the stadium where the refreshment stands and restrooms were. I watched my step because, like I said, the rows of seats were almost vertical and the steps were a lot steeper than I would have liked, nursing my bum leg and trying to let my bad arm hang so it would look natural.

"I looked it over on the way in," Pilar said. "I've got a place spotted for you."

"Good," I said. I hurt all over and did not mind letting somebody else do my thinking for me.

"There," she said, pointing.

I ambled over to the spot, a corner where a ramp leading up crossed one leading down and a column stood holding up the roof. I put my back to the column so it would not be easy for anybody to sneak up on my blind side, and watched Pilar go to work.

She did a pretty good job of looking natural as she made her way through the rest of the crowd toward one of the refreshment stands, her little pennant in her hand.

This could have been the part of the conversation she had over the phone in the hotel that I did not understand, the part where the guy on the other end told her which refreshment stand to go to. I get confused easily with numbers and letters in Spanish.

The mezzanine or whatever it was, this level we were on above the ground floor, was full of people. There was some kind of a break in the soccer action, a half or a quarter or something. I did not know how long they had been playing because I had taken that nap, but I probably would not have known if I had watched the whole thing. I don't know much more about soccer than I do cricket, which is nothing at all.

My left hand was on the little gun in my pocket as I watched Pilar move away from me. I was more likely to hit something with Mario's big gun, but there was no way to get my hand on it without looking suspicious as hell. This crowd was going to make shooting a pretty bad idea, anyway. I hoped the guys on the other side saw things that way, too.

She was about twenty-five yards away now, just getting into a long line for hot dogs. There were four lines and I was curious how she picked the one she did, the third one from the left. There was a woman with a couple of kids directly in front of Pilar, a teenaged couple behind her. The four lines snaked around from the middle of the mezzanine to the counter, and now and then Pilar was screened from me.

Up and down the length of the curving walkway I looked, hoping I had been wrong about the blond kid with the mustache. Pilar's head appeared now, between the heads of two men in the line next to her, between her and where I was standing, and then she was gone again. It occurred to me that this was why she was in that particular line. She was in the third one from the left, meaning she was screened by the first and fourth lines from anybody trying to watch her, me included. The second line from the left would have the same advantage. I decided the man she was going to meet was in the second line. After that I paid more attention to that line and I thought maybe I made the guy.

The one I picked for the courier was a little man with glasses and a nervous air about him. He was wearing the kind of short-sleeved shirt with pockets and trim that you see in Mexico, the kind made to be worn with the shirttail outside the pants. He was not the only man in the place dressed that way, but he was in the second line from the left and I picked him.

The little man took no notice of Pilar that I could see, but that did not mean anything.

It was going fine, as far as I knew. When I could see Pilar every now and then as the lines moved, I could see the pennant and it was still rightside up. We had not talked about it after she explained the drop signal, but I had it in mind that if anything went wrong she would use the same signal to let me know.

He walked right past me. There was no doubt in my mind this time. It was the same blond kid from the bronze Dodge, the one with the radio in his hand. He walked within ten feet of me, but I was in a good place with my back to the column and he did not see me. He was walking toward Pilar, but not directly toward her, not as if he had spotted her. I checked the little automatic for the hundredth time to be sure the safety was off and watched the spook walk on.

If Pilar saw the guy, she did not show any sign that she made him. She was still just a soccer fan waiting in line for a hot dog. And blondie did not see her either, as far as I could tell, because he moved right on past the four lines and around the bend in the walkway without breaking his stride.

My guy, the little nervous man in the Mexican shirt, got to the head of his line before Pilar made it to hers. I saw him pay for a hot dog and a soft drink and turn to leave. Stretching on tiptoes, I spotted Pilar's head in the line to the little man's right. She was two or three places back from the head of her line and still not paying the little man any attention. He took his hot dog and drink and excused himself as he sidled his way back into the walkway and turned toward me. Maybe I guessed wrong, maybe this was not the courier.

I knew I had been right about him the instant the two Latins showed up. I was not sure where they came from, from the crowd milling around or from one of the waiting concession lines. I had not noticed them before. But there they were anyway, one on either side of the little man. I knew I was right about him from the look of the two men, but especially from the look on his face when one of the men leaned over and spoke into his ear. The little man was a corpse and he knew it. I knew it, too, but there was nothing for me to do about it. My job was to cover Pilar. I hoped the swap had already been made, somewhere there in the two lines where it would have been hard to spot. That was what I hoped, as I tried not to be obvious about watching the two guys very quietly and efficiently murder the little man with the hog dog.

Chapter Thirty-two

THEY WERE SLICK AS could be, these two. They killed him right there in front of me, in front of a couple hundred soccer fans, and I was the only one who saw it. Everybody else in the place thought the little man had a heart attack or a stroke or something, because that is what the two killers told them.

He never had a chance. When the two showed up alongside him, he knew it like a rat knows it when he feels the hot breath of a hawk's wings at his back. He had the soda pop in one hand, the hot dog in the other. The man on his right leaned over and said something to him and the little guy turned his head toward that one. He was shaking his head, "No, no," and saying something with a really earnest look on his face when the man on his right slipped him the blade. The killer had one hand on the little man's arm and he raised it, raised the little guy's arm a little with one hand and slipped the thin blade into his ribs with the other hand. It was a very thin blade, maybe even an ice pick, because there was no blood showing but the little guy crumpled right there on the spot. The Coke fell and spilled across the floor, the hot dog dropped, and the other guy, not the one with the blade, starting yelling.

"Get a doctor!" he yelled. "Somebody get a doctor. This guy's having a heart attack!"

They let him down easy onto the floor and yelled some more about doctors and heart attacks. The milling crowd first surged away from them, from the spilling Coke and the dying man and the murderers screaming for somebody to get a doctor. Then, when all the spilling was over and there was no more mess, the crowd got curious and closed in around them. And that was when the two killers melted away. They were smooth.

I could not see where Pilar was anymore for the crowd gathering around the murdered man. I slipped from my place in the corner into the crowd and worked my way toward the concession stand. There was some jostling and my arm hurt. No Pilar.

Moving as fast as I could, I shuffled past the concession stand and craned my neck this way and that trying to catch sight of her. Nothing.

Back the way I had come, hoping I had missed her in the crowd. Nothing.

Double cross. That was what was running through my mind when I finally did spot her. She was on the ramp that led down to the ground level and the exits. She was trying to run out on me. I shoved my way through the crowd to the head of the ramp and started after her.

I was closing on her and she had just left the foot of the ramp onto the ground level when I noticed her pennant. It was hanging from her hand, upside down. When I saw that, I slowed down.

There was a woman walking almost beside Pilar, to one side of her and a step back. She had her hands in the pockets of a smart tweed jacket and did not look Spanish at all. Was it her? There were other people around, but the crowd was thinning out now because the game had started again. I had my eye on a man walking directly behind Pilar, but he turned off at the foot of the ramp and hurried back toward the stands. Pilar kept walking toward the nearest exit and the woman in the tweed jacket stayed one step to her left and one step back. It was her.

I fell in behind them, hoping the woman walking Pilar out of the arena would be so worried about Pilar that she would not spot me behind her. I stayed a little to her left, so she would not pick me up in her peripheral vision. We were getting close to an exit, it was only twenty-five or thirty yards away, the exit nearest the gate where Pilar and I had come in. Pilar's getaway car was parked within a couple hundred yards of the exit. There was not much time now before they were at the exit gate, just a few more steps, past the column coming up on the left and then the gate. I broke into a run as Pilar came abreast of the column, not caring now if the woman in the tweed jacket knew I was behind her.

She heard the sound of my running behind her and started to turn. I could see her head swiveling toward me, the raised brow arching above her right eye as she turned to look over her right shoulder so she could keep Pilar in her field of vision at the same time she looked to see what was coming up behind her so hard and so fast. I saw her right hand start up out of her jacket pocket, saw a glint of blue steel between her thumb and the strap of her hand.

But that was as far as she got with the gun. I hit her from behind at full tilt and she flew forward into the column. It was a concrete column and she was out like a light.

I did not bother to call for a doctor or to say anything about the woman fainting, I just turned as quickly as I could and grabbed Pilar by the arm. We started to run, but she held me back and I knew she was right. We could not afford to attract any attention.

There was a cop at the gate and I told him there was a lady on the ground back there by the column, did not know what was the matter with her. He said he would look into it and started that way. If anybody saw me slam her, they were not making a fuss about it. Pilar and I walked out the exit gate toward her getaway car.

"Did you get it?" I asked.

"What?"

"Don't start that dumb act again, goddamnit, and don't make me pull another body search. Did you get it or not?"

"Yes. Did you see him?"

"The little guy with the glasses? I saw him."

"He is an old friend of my father," she said.

"Was."

"What do you mean?"

"I mean he didn't get to eat his hot dog. Two men took him out right in front of me."

"I didn't hear anything . . ."

"They used a knife. They were very slick."

"It never stops, does it?"

"We can hope. Where is it?"

"I have it."

"No shit. Show it to me."

"Not now. We're not out of it yet."

"Look . . ."

I stopped and grabbed her again, turned her toward me to tell her I wanted whatever the hell all this fuss was about, but when I did I saw the two men trotting along after us and I suddenly had other things on my mind.

"Uh-oh," I said. "Company's coming."

She turned and saw them.

"They're the ones who killed your dad's friend."

"I know them."

"Santa Rosans?"

"Yes, they are Guzman's men."

"Great." I looked around, hoping there would be a uniform we could run to. "Never a cop around when you need one."

"Let's go!" she said and took off like a deer in the direction of the car.

To tell the truth, my arm and my back hurt so bad I felt more like dying than doing anymore running. Screw them, I thought, and dug the 9 millimeter out of my belt.

"¡Alto, por favor!" I called out to the two men. They both grinned at my bad Spanish, their teeth big and white in their brown faces. They stopped trotting my way, all right, they broke into a dead run.

I was pretty well-hidden from them by a row of parked cars, so all they could see were my head and shoulders. So maybe they did not see the gun in my hand. Or maybe it did not matter to them. Either way, they came on, running and grinning. I waited for them to get closer, until they were within a couple of cars of me before I made a move. Then I stepped back between two cars and laid my left arm across the trunk lid of an Oldsmobile. That steadied the gun, and I stooped down to line up the sights. They stopped grinning then, but it was too late for one of them. They both tried to stop, their shoes sliding on the gravel like cartoon characters skidding around a corner. They were scrambling like crazy to keep their feet under them and change direction when the gun boomed. I had a pretty good sight picture on the one nearest me when I squeezed off the first round, and I touched off a couple more for effect.

I slipped along the side of the Oldsmobile into the next row and took off at the best lope I could manage, to put distance between me and them. But I could not resist looking back. Beneath the Oldsmobile I saw one of the men down. He was not moving and I did not hear anything but the noises I was making dragging my bad leg. One down, one to go. Plus the blond kid.

Pilar had the thing everybody wanted and she was gone. I had a short lead on a killer who was quick on his feet and good with a knife, and a broken arm that hurt like hell when I tried to run. My back hurt. I took a couple of seconds to kneel behind a car and jam my right hand into my belt so the bad arm would not give me so much trouble. Bending from the waist to stretch my back, I looked beneath the car to see if I could see the Santa Rosan, any movement that might give me an idea which way he was moving. Nothing. No sounds either except the distant roar of the crowd inside the arena. Guess the home team scored.

Knowing it all depended on whether she thought she still needed me, I shoved off again, moving in the direction Pilar had gone, toward her car. There was no way of knowing what her plans were now. To get the hell out of town and do whatever it was you did with the thing she got from the dead man at the drop, of course. But I did not know what that involved. She had her passport, she could hop into her car and be at the airport in twenty minutes. I had all the money, though, and she had no credit cards. Unless she had hidden money or something in the car. It did not figure she would wait around for me, but it was the only thing I had going. I did not care to double back toward the arena and try to hail a cop. The Santa Rosan was between me and the arena. Probably. And I was not ready to bring the cops into it yet, not as long as Crandall had Betty. I thought about Betty and the thing I would need to get her back, the thing Pilar had.

My mind was working too fast and I was trying to keep my head up, keep my eyes moving so I could spot the Santa Rosan if he showed himself. I was so busy trying to see everything and think things out that when I saw the pennant lying on the ground it did not register at first. It was a visiting team flag and I slowed down enough to scoop it up with my left hand, holding it with my thumb and little finger, the cloth snugged around the butt of Mario's pistol. She must have dropped it, I thought.

Fifteen or twenty yards beyond the place where I found the pennant I stopped again. Running bent over to use parked cars for cover was killing my back. I thought I was pretty close to the place where Pilar had parked the car, but I could not be sure exactly. What the hell, one place's as good as another. She's long gone anyway, I told myself.

When I had settled in between a station wagon and a pickup truck with a camper on the back to wait for the Santa Rosan to show himself, not thinking anymore about what came after that so I could focus all my attention on listening and watching for him, a car went by. I heard it stop, back up. When it stopped again, at a right angle to my hiding place, a door opened. I looked in and saw Pilar at the wheel. She was looking over her shoulder toward the arena and maybe toward the Santa Rosan, if she could see him. Or maybe there was something else. She motioned for me to get in. I waited a second, to check her hands. One was on the steering wheel, the other open, beckoning me.

I got in and she spun away down the lane between parked cars toward an exit. But she did not exit, she spun into a hard left turn instead, and we were racing along the perimeter of the lot, toward a corner a quarter of a mile away where it was not likely anyone would see us or interfere with whatever happened next. I did not ask any of my questions, just relaxed and slumped down in the plush upholstered seat to let my back rest, and waited for the throbbing in my arm to stop. Whatever she had in mind, I still had Mario's gun in my left hand and I made sure the safety was off.

That did not matter. I felt him before I heard him, as he uncoiled from behind me, behind the seat where he had lain waiting for me to get in the car beside her. It was no use, but I would have tried him anyway, would have rocked the gun back over my shoulder and done as much shooting as I had time for before he killed me, but he was too quick. His hand closed on the gun before I could do it and I felt the cool heavy friend taken from me.

"Very good, Pilar," he said. His voice was deep, with a trace of an accent. A Spanish accent, naturally.

Chapter Thirty-three

PILAR DID NOT LOOK at me for a long time. When she did, she did not look me in the eye. She was about to say something, to explain something, when something she saw, something about me, brought her up short. Her eyebrow arched the way I had learned it did when she sensed danger, the way an animal's ears prick up at the sound or scent of a predator.

That look made me feel better about things. I thought I knew what it meant and what she saw that spooked her when she looked at me. I was slumped toward the door in the seat beside her, my right hand still tucked into my belt, my empty left hand open, palm up, on the seat. The pennant was where I had put it, tucked into the jacket pocket on my left side, only the stick showing. I liked what I saw on her face—the little signal she tried not to send she tried to call back too late.

But I did not like what I was hearing. The man's voice from behind me was speaking to Pilar in Spanish and I could make out that he wanted what they all wanted, the thing that Pilar had got from the dead man inside the arena. He was talking softly, but he sounded like a very serious man. I turned to look at him but all I saw was the gun in his hand and a pair of very dark sunglasses before he told me in English to face the front. I did.

They talked as if I were not there and I began to wonder what had become of the second Santa Rosan, to wonder whether he had seen me get into the car, whether he had a car somewhere on the lot, where was he now. It would have suited me much better if they had done their talking in traffic, put a little distance between us and all the action here. But I was not being consulted, so I just sat there and listened without letting them know I understood what they were saying.

There was a lot of politics in it, the man in back talking about current events as if they really mattered. He sounded a lot like Crandall, I thought, without the whimsy. He was talking global stuff at first, East and West with capital letters. Pilar did not have much to say about that. Then he got down to Santa Rosa, which he kept calling "the motherland" or the Spanish equivalent. He did not think much of Pilar's patriotism and I got the impression he had been on the other side in the war, was still on the other side. I looked over my shoulder toward him as far as I could without moving my head and attracting his attention. I could see far enough to see the bore of his pistol was leveled at my head. He was talking to Pilar, but he had not forgotten about me.

Pilar began to argue with him and they got pretty heated, accusing each other of being traitors and murderers, each counting the dead and wounded on one side or the other. If she was trying to get on his good side, I thought she was playing it pretty tough. Her father's name came up and she began to cry, but she did not let that get in the way of standing up to this man with the gun at my head. She told him how much she loved her father, that she was through with the revolution because the junta had betrayed the people, that she was working with her father and his memory to give Santa Rosa back to the people. It sounded convincing as hell to me, and I remembered how she had talked about her father in the hotel room the night before, when I had been so hard on her and she had been so sick from her need for the dope. I believed her. The guy in the back, I did not think he was buying it.

Things would have to be different this time, Pilar was telling him. Not the way they had been before the war, when so few had so much and so many had starved.

I noticed cars moving around the lot, here and there people leaving the arena. The game was winding down and pretty soon this would be a public place again. Whatever the man in back had in mind, it would happen soon. Pilar was really going now, talking humanity and rights and dignity and a lot of other stuff I had no problem with except that time was running out.

"If I could put in a word here," I said, "I'd appreciate it if you two would give me a couple of subtitles or something. What the hell is going on here?"

"He is with the counterrevolution . . ."

"You needn't speak for me, Pilar," the man interjected. "My name is . . ."

"Who cares?" I cut in. "I'm not going to vote for any of you. Just tell me what's the deal."

"I don't know how much she's told you, Mister Kyle, but I am here to see that the right thing is done."

"Fine, then you don't need me," I said, moving my left hand toward the door handle. He tapped me smartly on the head with his pistol and I let my hand drop into my lap. "Or maybe you do. I'm listening."

"She has something I need, we need. Something that belongs to us. I am here to make sure she delivers it to the right party. That's all."

"The right party being you, I guess."

"Exactly."

"Makes sense," I said, looking at Pilar. "Give it to him."

"Don't be ridiculous, Jack," she said, fixing me with a look I thought meant I was not to say too much.

"Why the hell not? Am I just confused, or aren't you two on the same side?"

"That is the question," the man nodded. "The problem is, we do not trust her."

"Neither do I," I agreed. "But than that's just the way I am. You've got to work that out for yourself. But I would like to point out that I killed a guy back there a few minutes ago, at least I'm pretty sure I killed him. As you may not have noticed, people are beginning to leave the game, and it's only a matter of time until a fan trips over the body. That's going to bring the cops and this parking lot is going to be too crowded for comfort."

More Spanish, the man sounding excited, interrogating Pilar about the man I had shot and everything that went on inside the arena. I got the impression they had discussed this before, in the car when the man first got the drop on Pilar, before they picked me up.

"There were two of them, did she tell you that?" I offered. "Maybe the one who's left took the time to pick up his pal. Maybe he's out here somewhere now, cruising the lot in his car with his buddy in the trunk looking for us. I don't know, just thought you'd like to consider it."

"You're right," the man said.

"Damn right I am," I spat, turning in the seat to get a better look at him. He eased back away from me when I moved, which was a good idea because it would make it harder for me to get to him. Impossible maybe. "So why don't we either settle this thing right now and go our separate ways or else all get the hell out of here before things get sticky. What do you say?"

"You're right," he said again.

"So what's the deal?" I demanded of them both. "Look, bitch, either give him the damn thing or don't. You, wise guy, either shoot us or don't. But enough of this goddamn talking."

"Drive," the man said.

Pilar obeyed, turning the car in a semicircle that brought us around the way we had come, driving toward the nearest exit from the lot.

Everything happened fast. I was still turned to my left toward the man with the gun behind me. Pilar was driving, her eye on the rearview mirror to watch him, too. I saw it in the man's face before I heard the roar of the engine, before the car barreled into us on the right side and drove us into a car parked on the left of us. It felt like an explosion, and I was thrown by the impact across the seat against Pilar. She screamed. I saw the man in back brace himself and raise his gun. He was firing even as the metal screamed and the tires wailed, as the two cars careened together across the lot. His gun roared and echoed inside the car, flame scorching the air with the smell of cordite, the empty brass rattling against the windows and landing hot on the seat in front of me, in the floor. He was shooting fast, a twisted grin showing his teeth.

Glass popping in the other car. I turned to see the windshield dancing alive with the slugs whacking through into the car.

Before the two cars came to rest the man in the back turned and tried to open the door behind Pilar. But it would not work; we were pinned against another car on that side. Looking over his shoulder at the car that had rammed us, he twisted in the seat and raised his foot. Heel first, he kicked and the window shattered. Quicker than he could have rolled the window down, he was out through the shards of glass onto the hood of the car on our left. As he went, I saw that he had the gun he had taken from me, Mario's gun, in his left hand, his own gun in his right. From the hood of the car he fired twice more, then dropped to the ground and out of sight behind us.

From the car that had rammed us, more shooting. I got low and pulled Pilar down with me.

"Drive," I told her.

"What?"

"Drive. Get the hell out of here."

"But . . ."

She was thinking about the man, but I had other problems. I had Betty O'Bannion and Crandall on my mind. Besides, I was not equipped to be of much help. The little .22 in my jacket pocket was not up to the competition.

"Go, goddamnit," I hissed at her.

She drove, not raising her head to look through the windshield. There was a terrible scraping as the car tugged away from the cars on either side, peeling metal and chrome as it worked free. When we were in the clear, I looked back to see the end of it. Our guy was standing at the driver's window of the ramming car, firing with both hands. There was movement in the car, but I could not make it out. As Pilar turned a corner, I saw the standing man stagger back and drop to one knee. Maybe they had killed each other.

She headed for the nearest exit, driving too fast. I made her slow down and then I made her change direction. People were running in the lot now, generally moving away from the shooting. Here and there I saw uniformed cops trotting toward the sound of the shooting. One was talking on a handheld radio. It would soon be raining cops. She knew it, too, and did not want to go the way I showed her, but she did.

I made her pull up at the curb near the main arena gate where there was a souvenir vendor hawking his wares. Only he was not doing much hawking. He was standing near cover at the gate, craning his neck to see what all the excitement was about out on the lot. I took the keys out of the ignition and left Pilar in the car while I hustled over to the vendor. I peeled a couple of twenties off my roll and he let me take two pennants. The visiting team's.

Pilar had a look in her eyes when I got back into the car that told me I had guessed right.

"Drive," I told her.

Chapter Thirty-four

I HAD PICKED THE place for my meeting with Crandall because it was close to Reunion Arena and secluded enough that maybe we would not be interrupted. Now I wished that I could change it. I had not expected so much excitement at the arena, for the neighborhood to be swarming with police cars. But there was nothing I could do about that now, I had no way of getting in touch with Crandall, and I knew anyway that he would balk at any last-minute moves.

The poor stolen car that looked like I felt was as safe as I could make it, stashed in a parking lot behind a bar on Industrial Boulevard, about midway between the arena and the place where I was to meet Crandall.

After I left the car, I hiked back under Stemmons Freeway toward the arena. I got as close as I wanted to, close enough to see the lights and the crime scene guys working around the wrecked car that the Santa Rosan had rammed us with. There were enough uniforms in the area for a parade, and I could make out some plainclothesmen huddled to one side. Eddie Cochran would be there, I knew, or at least somebody who could find him pretty quick.

There was no shortage of spectators. I estimated that about half of the people who had seen the soccer game were loitering around the parking lot, not wanting to leave until they had seen a body. The ambulance was standing by until the medical

245

examiner's people finished with the corpses. I knew that there were not likely to be any survivors at the scene. Anybody who lived through the firefight would have left one way or another. It occurred to me that the way things had worked out had left me damn near in the clear. The man in the back seat had taken Mario's gun with him. That left him to answer for the guy I shot with it in the parking lot. Killing Mario, that was self-defense. If I lived through the day, I would have the X rays to prove it. That only left the O'Bannion murder.

What I needed now was a messenger and I let several prospects pass before I picked one. Not too young, not too old, prosperous-looking enough to make me think he would insist if he had to, make me feel sure he would get the message delivered. I did not explain anything to him, just handed him my business card with the note addressed to Lieutenant Cochran I had written on the back and told him it was very important. He looked me over pretty good and I think he believed me. I think I looked like I was serious. He left me headed in the right direction and that was all I could do. Except that naturally I picked a second messenger a couple of minutes later and gave him the same message on another card with the same instructions. What is it the technical types call that, redundancy? I believed in it.

And then there was nothing left to do except to go see Mr. Crandall. I turned my back on the arena and started walking. On the way, I thought things through one last time and went over my plans, such as they were, to make sure I had not left anything out. When I was in a place where I was not likely to be seen, I rigged up the little gun and turned up the collar of my jacket against the wind. It had turned colder suddenly. Or maybe it was just me. I snuggled my gloves inside my jacket sleeves to keep the wind off my wrists and dismissed as a bad idea an urge to buy another bottle of whisky. I would need a clear head more than courage.

If things had worked out the way I had planned for them to, I would have driven to the meet, turning off of Commerce at the east end of the Trinity River bridge and nosing down onto the levee road heading south toward the railroad bridge. Then down off the levee to the little road that runs under the railroad bridge between the big pilings, where sometimes cops working late nights take their girlfriends or take naps if their off-duty jobs have worn them out. I thought, as I hiked up from the ditch behind a liquor store that fronted on Industrial Boulevard and backed up to the river levee, about how times had changed. Women cops now. I wondered if they brought their boyfriends to the river bottoms.

If I had wanted to be cute, I could have approached the meeting place another way, taken a chance I might have caught Crandall off guard. But I did not want to be cute. Until I knew where Betty was and what shape she was in, I wanted to play it absolutely straight. So I dragged myself up one side of the levee and down the other, coming down onto the road a hundred yards north of the railroad bridge. I wanted Crandall to see me coming, to see that I was alone. I did not want to spook him.

Limping along the road toward the railroad bridge, I worked my eyes back and forth among the pilings, trying to make him out. He was there, all right. But I could not see him. Damn, it was cold. Bad weather to lie on the ground waiting for help to come, if it came to that.

To my surprise, I found myself among the pilings, standing in the little road directly beneath the railroad bridge, still with no sign of Crandall or Betty, or even a car. I started to worry that something had happened to them.

"Good afternoon."

I still had not seen him, but he was close, off to my right somewhere.

"I said, good afternoon. Aren't you speaking?"

"I don't like talking to myself," I answered.

"Understandable. Would you feel more conversational if I materialized?"

"It might help. You wouldn't mind, would you?"

"Of course not," he said, in a different-sounding voice, as he stepped from his hiding place into the road behind me and on my left.

"Nice touch," I said, and I meant it. I turned to face him. "Are you a ventriloquist on top of everything else?"

"Don't be silly. Just a little speaker and a microphone. Effective though, isn't it?"

"Where's Betty?"

"You'll never learn, will you, Jack? No feel for amenities, always business, strictly business."

"It's a little chilly to stand on ceremony. I hope you haven't left her tied to a tree someplace where she'll catch pneumonia."

"Of course not. I know how much she means to you. I assure you, she's well. As comfortable as circumstances permit."

"Where?"

"Not far. And your part of our bargain? Did you bring it with you?"

"It's nearby, too," I said, and probably saved my life. If he knew I had it on me, there would be no more reason to talk.

"Excellent. Then we can proceed."

"Suits me."

"Of course it does. This way."

He ushered me between two pilings toward the brush at the foot of the levee and then I saw the van, almost hidden by tall weeds.

He unlocked the van and we both got in, eyeing each other like cats in heat. He made a nervous move when I put my gloved hand into my jacket pocket, but I showed him I was only going for my little flashlight and he eased up. I checked out the inside of the van, expecting to see Betty trussed up in the back. But it was clean. Not just empty, clean. It might have just rolled off a showroom floor.

In the light, I noticed he had a pair of binoculars around his neck. They were oversize, and I remembered seeing some like them before, with infrared lenses for night vision.

"Guess you used the night glass to see if I brought company."

"Naturally, and you didn't. I hope you're not offended that I took the precaution anyway."

"Business is business."

"Good man."

"Where to?" I asked.

"To your dear Betty, of course. Isn't that what you want?"

"I want to get this over with."

"As do I. Shall I take you somewhere first? Do you need to pick up anything?"

"No, but that doesn't mean you could find what you're looking for if anything happened to me. Or that I can't produce it once you keep your part of the deal."

"Of course you would say that. I wish I could believe you."

I tugged a pennant out of my pocket and handed it to him. His face gave him away a little when he spotted it, then settled back into his mask when he realized that it was not what he had thought.

"Look here . . ." he sputtered.

"That's just to show you that I have it. And you know what's missing and how small it can be. So you know how easy it would be to hide and how hard to find. Satisfied?"

"I hope you understand that you are screwing around with vital national security information. That the lives of thousands are at stake."

"You never quit, do you, Crandall?"

"Quitters never win, do they?"

He cranked the van and pulled out of his warren in the weeds, turned south and drove beyond the railroad bridge along the foot of the levee. I saw that he was scanning for a tail as he drove, and did not waste a lot of effort answering the questions he asked about the shootings at the arena. He did not care very much who shot whom, and we both knew it.

We drove south beneath a couple of freeway overpasses and another bridge until we were about opposite the dead end of Industrial at Corinth, where the levee disappeared into heavy brush and scrubby woods. I did not like that he had left Betty in a place like that.

Finally, after he had driven down a deeply rutted trail past a couple of lean-tos thrown together out of trash by persons unknown and since gone, he stopped the van off to one side of the trail. There was a stand of trees in front of us and as I climbed down from the van I caught a whiff of smoke. Crandall motioned for me to precede him but I declined. Side by side, we walked into the grove of trees where I saw in a clearing what was left of a rusty oil drum with a fire in it, tree limbs and trash piled to one side to keep it going. There was a crate of some kind standing in front of the barrel.

"Okay," I said. "Where is she?"

"By all rights I should insist on your producing your part of the bargain first, Jack, but I understand your feelings. I'm a romantic at heart. If you will excuse me."

He left me standing by the fire, which was going pretty good and giving off enough warmth to make a difference. But I did not make myself comfortable as I watched him walk to the edge of the undergrowth. Instead, I tried to use the uncooperative fingers of my right hand to loosen the fingers of my left glove. I had the .22 jammed into the left glove, its barrel run snugly down the index finger. I could shoot it from there, but not very well. My index finger was curled back to rest on the trigger. I did not mind the gathering gloom of the storm coming up or the shadows beneath the trees, the flickering light of the fire. In good light, Crandall might have noticed the odd look of my left hand. The right hand was not working at all now, and I let it go. What I had would just have to do. I let my broken arm hang as naturally as it could at my side. He knew I was right-handed, and had no way of knowing that Mario had broken that arm. So it stood to reason he would be watching my right hand for a sign that the show was starting. That would give me a little edge. I would need one to offset his advantage. Not only did he have two good hands, but we were on his turf.

He had had plenty of time to pick this spot and rig things his way. And I had no way of knowing exactly what he had in mind, except that he intended to walk away from our little conference with a couple of million bucks in his pocket and a corpse or two on the ground.

I watched Crandall at the edge of the brush. He was moving things, pieces of plywood and a scrap of sheet metal. When he was through, he knelt and I saw Betty lying on the ground wrapped in a blanket. With his eye on me all the time, Crandall untied her ankles and helped her to her feet. He was smiling at me when he unwrapped the blanket and let it fall, stepping behind her at the same time.

She was gagged and her hair was a mess, most of it down across her face. Her hands were tied behind her and she was wearing the same robe she had worn the night before to seduce me. She was shivering.

"You see, Jack. Safe and unharmed."

"A little underdressed," I said, keeping everything I was feeling out of my voice.

Her robe was torn down the front and one side was off her shoulder down to her elbow, exposing a breast and the curve of her waist. The slit up the side that had done so much for me the night before, in front of O'Bannion's fire, was much higher and wider now.

"Don't concern yourself about that. We'll make her more comfortable in a moment. First, I must ask you: What has become of Pilar?"

"What do you care, as long as I didn't bring her with me?"

"You're right, I know. Humor me."

He was holding Betty not more than fifteen feet away now, close enough that I could see the panicky light in her eyes as she shook her hair back from her face and looked at me. Close enough to see the strain of the muscles in her neck and shoulders, the swing of her breasts as she pulled against him, trying to come to me.

"Cover her and we'll talk," I said.

"No. But here, how's this?"

He moved her, still in front of him, toward the fire. I saw in her face that she felt the heat of it. I wondered if she was also remembering the night before, the other fire.

"Now tell me, Jack. Where is Pilar?"

"In hell, I imagine. I killed her about an hour ago."

Chapter Thirty-five

"NO!" HE SAID, SMILING indulgently as if his nephew had just told a whopper.

"Yeah," I answered. "The body's in the trunk of her car, the Mercedes. Want to see it?"

"I don't believe you," he insisted.

"Who cares?"

"It's not like you, Jack."

"It's like you," I said. "I'm learning."

"I suppose so."

"So let's hop back into your van and run over on Industrial to the bar where I ditched the car, if you've got so goddamn much time to kill."

"No, of course not. But I have to tell you, Jack, if you're not lying about this, you are coming along. I mean that, you're really catching on to things."

"So maybe you and I should go into business," I said.

"I think so. Not on this current project, you understand. It's late in the game to bring in new partners on this one. But down the line, I think that would be a very interesting idea. You'll be available?"

"Yeah, I'm in the yellow pages."

All our bullshit was really starting to stink up the place. We both knew that one of us was going to kill the other in a matter of minutes, but each of us wanted the other off balance when he started. I had Betty, in a manner of speaking. At least I knew she was alive and I had my eye on her. He had good reason to believe that I had what he wanted, but he could not be sure yet whether I really had it on me or what I intended to do with it. Advantage me. I could start the ball rolling whenever I wanted, if you looked at it one way. I had what I wanted and what he wanted; I did not need him anymore. Crandall, on the other hand, could not afford to kill me yet, unless he was willing to gamble that I had the thing on me and he could find it. So, figuring the odds, he was not ready for the shooting to start just yet, not if he could help it. That was why he was doing all that yakking, making a fuss about what a good boy was I for whacking Pilar, like it was a big deal. Me, I would have loved to put one between his eyes, but he was standing a little too far away and a little too close to Betty for me to risk it with my left-handed inside-the-glove trick shot. I would try it if he made me, but I would rather wait for a better chance. One reason I thought I could afford to wait was the way he kept eyeing my empty dangling right hand. I liked that. I wanted him to watch that hand right all along; I wanted him to be looking at that hand when I shot him with the other one.

He went on about Pilar, about what a poor thing she was, how he had done so much for her and all that crap, about how I had done the right thing, put her out of her misery, really. He was trying to give me a lot to think about, about Betty half naked and shivering, about poor Pilar. He knew thinking about things like that would get in my way.

I looked at him as if I were listening, but I was only thinking of Eddie Cochran. He would be there now, at the railroad bridge, with a man or two he thought he could trust. I hoped it was not his cowboys, or that they were better at this kind of thing than they were at tailing. Eddie would be getting antsy as hell, wondering if I had put him on a wild-goose chase. That was a good move by Crandall, keeping Betty away from the meeting place. Gave him an ace in the hole if I had brought help.

"But enough about that," Crandall said. "Down to business."

When he reached inside his coat, he did it so gently, careful to show me the pocket where the hand was going, that I knew he was not going for a gun. I thought it would be a good time to take my shot, but he must have thought the same, because he moved half a step to his left, putting Betty between us, until he had the little tape recorder out in his hand.

"There," he said. "So you'll know, I have you on tape confessing to the murder of Pilar Maldonado."

I moved just as carefully with my left hand and produced my own recorder. He did not try anything either.

"Fair's fair, Arthur. Let's talk about Pilar's father."

"Why not? The truest friends are two men who can hang each other. I gave the old man to Guzman. Guzman was a fanatic. When we spotted him running security for the trade delegation, I knew he was a risk we couldn't afford. And Maldonado had already served his purpose once the drop was arranged. It wasn't necessary for the old man to make the drop personally. Pilar would do for that, it was agreed all round."

"Then you used Pilar to set up O'Bannion. He took care of Guzman for you. You couldn't afford to have Guzman put out the word with the counterrevolutionaries that you had sold the old man out. O'Bannion takes the heat on the Guzman killing and that keeps you out of the limelight. Once he brought me in, you didn't need him anymore. That about it?"

I looked at Betty. She was watching me, not Crandall. The fire was close beside her, and it made her torn gown almost invisible. She was a flickering vision, a naked ghost rising from the flames like smoke.

"Exactly. O'Bannion was willing to hold the bag until the drop because Pilar had convinced him the payoff would be worth it."

"Yeah, it would have been money with O'Bannion. For me it was military secrets, the struggle to free her people, like that. I guess she told O'Bannion it was about drugs."

"Approaches tailor-made. No two the same."

"And a bonus too, for O'Bannion. I mean, Pilar gave him her . . . personal touch, didn't she?"

"Of course. So you see how much trouble you made for me, coming between me and Pilar. I still needed her for the drop. It's your fault I've had to resort to using Mrs. O'Bannion this way."

"Guess I've made a real mess of things," I said. I tried to look as if I were lost in thought and shuffled to my right, nearer Betty, to improve the angle. But Crandall caught it without seeming to and adjusted for it. It would still be a tricky shot. "Yeah," I said, stalling. "I have to hand it to you. Tell me, how did you find out so much about me?"

"Really, Jack, you can't say I've been anything but patient with you, but enough is enough. We have business. The sooner we're done, the sooner you can make Betty here comfortable."

That was supposed to make me look at Betty, but I did not go for it.

"She's all right," I said. "And don't get nervous. I've got what you want right here."

I put my recorder down on the crate beside the fire barrel and he put his beside mine. Then I tugged the pennant I had showed him earlier out of my pocket, showed it to him again, and tossed it into the fire.

"Jack!" he said, a catch in his voice.

"Take it easy. Here's the one you want."

I held up another pennant in my left hand, between my thumb and the hidden barrel of the little automatic in my glove. Crandall jumped a little when he saw the pennant. He finally knew I was for real, and he was already counting the millions.

I saw the movement out of the corner of my eye. Betty was doing something, but I did not look away from Crandall to see what it was. I should have. Crandall hesitated for a heartbeat, then he did take his eyes off me, turning his head to his left toward Betty. That was my chance. My left hand was extended toward him, holding the pennant for him to see. I let the little flag go and it fluttered toward the ground at an angle. I was bringing my left hand the rest of the way up, a couple more inches, for a shot. It was almost at eye level when Betty threw herself against my right side.

She screamed through the gag.

It hurt like hell and the weight of her body staggered me. She had worked her hands free somehow. My left leg buckled under me and I went down. Crandall and I fired within a split second of each other, and both of us scored.

It did not hurt at first and I could not take time to worry about how bad I was hit. The little automatic had fired all right, but the slide had jammed, binding on the lining of my glove. My left hand hurt more than the bullet in my gut from the flash burn and the pinch of metal.

Betty was on top of me, on top of my right arm, but it was useless anyway. I used my teeth to yank the glove off my left hand and the gun fell loose from the glove, onto the ground. Betty was screaming. I scooped up the gun and kicked her off of me.

He should have been shooting while I was busy, he should have finished me off. But he had not, because the updraft of the fire in the oil drum had drawn the pennant toward the flames. Crandall was on his knees at the drum, trying to pluck the flag away from the fire. He was having trouble doing that, though, because I had shot him in the face. He was bleeding like I had chopped off his head, and having trouble seeing. He was trying to hold his jaw shut with one hand and save the pennant with the other. I shot him again, in the right ear this time, and he toppled over, dragging the fire barrel with him. The fire spilled out in a shower of sparks and trash, and I saw the smoldering pennant flutter safely away from him to come to rest on the ground beyond his outstretched hand.

Betty was hysterical for several minutes after that. I did not have a good hand to slap her with, so I let her get it out of her system.

While she did that I took inventory. Crandall's gun was lying on the ground not far away, a short-barreled Smith & Wesson .357. I decided the reason I was still operational must have been his choice of ammunition. He was used to thinking like a professional, thinking that everybody who is anybody these days wears some kind of body armor. Which is why a pro will either shoot you in the head or load up with some hot-jacketed rounds to make sure he gets through the vest at you. The thing was, not being much of a pro myself, I was not wearing anything harder than my tweed jacket. He had hit me in a pretty good spot, considering everything, but the slug had been so hot and hard that it was in and out without expanding. The entrance wound was pretty low, by the way I was bleeding, just to the left of my navel. Since I could work my arms and legs, I told myself the bullet had not hit any important bones, like my spinal cord, for instance. But it was going to burn like hell when the shock wore off and this and that started leaking around in there.

Betty was down to quiet sobbing by the time I lurched to my feet. She looked up at me and screamed again. She had gotten rid of the gag.

"I thought you were dead," she said.

"Damn near it."

I was in no shape to jog up the road for help. I might have been able to drive the van, but there were still a couple of things to take care of right where I was. It hurt when I did it, but I managed to drag a pretty good-size limb out of the fire barrel and wrestle it over to the van. It hurt worse when I slung the damn thing up on top of the van, but I figured it could be seen from a long way off from there. It was going pretty good and I found some smaller stuff to pile on top of it. People might not mind a little shooting, but a fire always gets attention.

I turned back to Betty and the dead man beside the spilled fire.

"Are you going to die?" she asked.

"Probably."

"I'll go for help."

"It's on the way."

"You need a doctor."

"It's taken care of."

She had not seemed to notice what I had done with the van, and I knew what had distracted her.

She studied me as if she really cared. But I could see the old machinery behind her eyes.

"Jack, really, I'd better take the van and go for help."

"You can't."

"Why?"

"For one thing, the van is on fire. For another, if you try to walk out of here I'll kill you."

Chapter Thirty-six

"WHAT DID YOU DO with it?" I asked her.

"What?"

"The pennant. The little flag."

"What are you talking about, Jack?"

She moved toward me.

"Funny he did such a sloppy job of tying you that you got loose like that. He struck me as a pretty thorough kind of guy."

"Jack, listen to me," she said softly. "People will be here soon. We have to get out of here."

I fought back a spinning, sick feeling and eased myself down to the ground. She knelt beside me.

"Give me the pennant," I said.

"Jack . . ."

"Either give it to me or tell me what it's for, what all this is about."

"I don't know anything about it."

"Then it's no use to you. Give it to me."

"Jack, listen to me. There isn't much time."

"I'm listening."

"This," she said, producing the singed pennant from inside the gathered waist of her robe while I watched her breasts rise and fall, "is worth a lot of money. Millions, Jack. Millions."

"I'm listening."

"So let's make the most of it. Who's more entitled, after all we've been through?"

261

"What did you have in mind?" I asked.

"Well . . . you're in no shape to travel, obviously."

"Obviously."

"So the logical thing is for me to leave with this. I'll send for you and we'll meet later, when you're well."

We looked into each other's eyes and for an instant it was as if none of it had happened, as if it all had been a dream. I looked beyond her, beyond the signal fire atop the van, at the darkling sky. And then at Betty again. She was ravishing.

"You know, baby," I said, "the sad thing is, until today I would have believed you."

"Jack!"

She moved closer, lifting herself to me, still kneeling, letting the robe slide off her shoulders as she came, smoke and fire in her eyes. She kissed me.

"Forget today," she whispered. "Remember last night. You wanted me, Jack, you want me now. It can be the way it was, baby."

She covered my mouth with hers before I could answer, and our little place in the woods was silent except for our breathing as she worked me over in her special way. She was killing me, making all my wounds hurt, but I did not want her to stop. When she did stop finally, there was blood on her, my blood on her gown and her breasts and there was a light in her eyes like a star twinkling to show me the way home.

She tried to help me up but I could not get my feet under me again.

"Darling," she said. "I don't want to leave you. Can you make it?"

"You know me."

She hurried to the van and slapped at the burning tree limb with her bare hands and then with a stick she found until all the fire was gone. She went to Crandall's body and went through his pockets for his keys. Then she knelt beside me again.

"Come on, Jack. Lean on me. We'll take the van to my house and get my car. I'll grab some things there."

"And then what?"

"What do you mean? We catch a plane and get out of here."

"And go where?"

She did not answer me, and I knew why.

"See," I said, making my voice as gentle and full of her as I could. "It won't work, will it? You can't have it both ways. If you didn't know what was going on, how can you know where to go, what to do with the pennant that'll make it worth over two million dollars? Were you going to tell me Crandall told you all about it after he kidnapped you?"

"It occurred to me," she said.

"Don't."

"Jack . . ."

"Don't. I don't give a shit, one way or the other. I'm just tired of being lied to."

She said nothing.

"Let me make it easy for you, Betty. You were in on it all along. That's how Crandall kept tabs on O'Bannion. We thought it was wiretaps, an army of guys tailing us, but there was only Mario and Pilar to do the dirty work. And it was all Mario could do to keep up with Pilar. Crandall didn't tell you Pilar was an addict, did he? That he made her one? No, you wouldn't need to know that. He was stingy with information, and that's why there's no way on God's earth he would have told you anything if you were his prisoner. His partner, that's a different matter."

"Jack, you mustn't . . ."

"Blame you? I know what O'Bannion was, don't forget."

I stroked her hair and she snuggled against me.

"He was going to leave me."

I did not have anything to say to that.

"I had to think of the boy. You see that, don't you, Jack? I know you see that. I had to think of the boy."

"Of course," I said.

"Crandall came to see me. He had photos of them together, Brendan and Pilar. He said they had to be stopped."

"And there was money in it, did he tell you that?"

"Not at first. That came later. Jack, it's almost three million dollars. Imagine, baby, just imagine! My god, at ten percent we'd have three hundred thousand a year for life and never even touch the principal."

"What did you do for Crandall?"

"You know already. I spied on Brendan for him."

"When he went to the Wagon Wheel Inn to meet Pilar, did he tell you where he was going?"

She nodded.

"Of course he did, the poor bastard."

"Jack . . ."

"O'Bannion was no friend of mine, baby. But he loved you."

"Then why the hell . . ."

"You don't get it, do you? He wasn't double-crossing you for Pilar. It was the other way around. That's why Crandall killed him."

"You mean Brendan was going to . . ."

"He was going for his big score. He saw you and him and the kid, set for life somewhere on the other side of the world. If you'd played him fair, it might have worked out that way."

"Why didn't he tell me?" she asked, and I could see it all spinning around in her head.

"Bad business, in case Crandall tried to get something out of you. Ain't that a laugh."

"Why did he bring you into it?"

"To end up holding the bag for him. Again."

"And you were only in it to protect me, poor darling. Poor darling."

She kissed me again, and I let her. But my heart was not in it anymore, not even for old-time's sake.

"You told Crandall O'Bannion was going to the Wagon Wheel to meet Pilar. You knew Crandall was going to have him killed. You knew about the money by that time, you knew the whole thing."

"Yeah, I knew all about it. I wanted O'Bannion dead."

"So last night I showed up at your door and you invited me in. And while we were reliving old times, you knew O'Bannion was being murdered. At the same time. That must have really made you feel good."

"Baby . . ."

"And it made you my only alibi. Couldn't have been better if you'd planned it."

Before she could answer, we both heard the siren. Up on Industrial Boulevard somewhere, but coming our way. It started to rain. She kissed me quickly and stood up, pulling her robe together against the cold drizzle.

"Time to go," she said.

"I'm ready."

She stepped around Crandall's body and retrieved the blanket from the place where Crandall had hidden her, and drew it around her shoulders like a cloak.

"It's too late."

"What do you mean?" I asked.

"You'd slow me down, probably die on me. I'm in a hurry."

"No need to be. You've got the pennant. You're a kidnap victim, not a suspect."

"Until the cops talk to you."

"Talk's cheap. I'm their prime suspect on O'Bannion and I don't have any evidence. I couldn't hurt you if I wanted to. Sit down and wait for the cops. You can be on the first plane out in the morning."

"I can't take the chance, Jack. Besides, there's nothing to say that this flag is the only place in the world to find the magic numbers. Somebody else could be on their way to the Bahamas to make a withdrawal right now. I'm too close to take any chances."

"What about me?"

"What about you? I told you, I'll let you know where I am and you can meet me."

"And the kid?"

"Sure, him too."

"Why don't I believe you?"

"If you love me, you'll believe me, Jack."

"Got me there."

"And if you love me you'll let me go." She smiled at me with a sureness that would break your heart. "'Bye, baby."

"You're right," I said. The pain was coming alive in me now and I was getting weaker as my blood pumped out. I was dying and I knew it. "I won't really shoot you. But there is one thing you ought to know . . ."

"I know, Jack. You love me."

"Besides that. You ought to know that pennant you have is worthless. Unless you want a souvenir of all this."

"What?"

"It's not the one with the account number of the Bahamian bank on it. It's just an extra one I picked up at the game. It's funny . . ." Things were happening to me on the inside, and I had to catch my breath to keep from throwing up. "That was the drop, Pilar swapped her pennant somehow for the one with the numbers on it, swapped with the little dead guy with the hot dog . . ."

"You're delirious," Betty snapped, at the same time turning the pennant she had this way and that looking for the numbers that were not there. She ran to the van and turned on its lights, still looking. She finally convinced herself it was not there, and stalked back through the cold drizzle to stand over me with her hands on her hips. "Where is it?"

"Pilar has it."

"You . . . you . . . stupid . . . sonofabitch! You didn't! You couldn't!"

"I did."

"Why?"

"I figured she had it coming. I hope she spends some of it getting well. She'll probably put it all in her arm, but I can't help that. At least, she promised not to buy any goddamn guns with it."

"You gave three million dollars to that junkie whore? What about me? You love me! Don't you think I have anything coming to me?"

"As a matter of fact, I do," I said.

"I just . . . cannot . . . *believe* . . . this," she moaned, sagging to the ground between me and Crandall. "I swear, you dumb sonofabitch . . . you're lying. You've got it. You've got it somewhere . . ."

I saw her hand fall to the ground beside her, to the place where I knew Crandall's revolver lay. I wondered if she would really do it, knowing she could get away with it if she had a little time. It might be a near thing, though. The siren was still coming and not far away now. But sounds are tricky, it might not be coming for us at all.

I was about used up, and it was getting harder and harder to see clearly. Her hand moved a little, and I wondered . . .

Eddie Cochran stepped quickly and quietly from the cover of the van with his gun in his hand. He swept the place with his eyes, sized up my condition, spotted the gun on the ground beside Betty, and kept his eyes moving until he had seen everything.

"Hold it," was all he said.

Betty moved away from the gun, as if she were afraid Eddie could read her mind.

"It's all right, Eddie," I said.

"You look like hell, Jack," Eddie said. "Who's the stiff?"

"Arthur Crandall."

"I guess it'll be self-defense and she's your witness."

"Wouldn't count on her," I said, struggling to my knees and reaching for my tape recorder on the crate beside the smoldering fire barrel.

But Betty saw what I was doing and remembered at last that everything we had said was on tape. With one quick motion she swept up my recorder and Crandall's and threw them into the fire. Eddie grabbed her, but he was a step too late to save the evidence. There was still enough life in the fire to do the job.

Two more figures appeared beside the van and I turned to see Eddie's cowboys. They smelled blood and gunpowder and they looked disappointed that I was the one left upright.

Betty glowered at me, full of hate and triumph.

"One more thing," she hissed, "before you die." She reached out with her finger, leaning over me, and would have jabbed her finger into my wound if Eddie had not stopped her. "The kid is not yours. Do you hear me? Your precious little Jack isn't even yours, he's Brendan O'Bannion's son! You stupid jerk!"

Eddie took her away and gave her to the cowboys. I heard him tell one of them to call an ambulance for me, code three. He also ordered Crime Scene Search and the M.E. He knew how bad off I was, and he took off his raincoat and laid it over me.

"I'd love to know what was on those tapes she burned," he said.

"Same as on this one," I said, and tried to pull my backup recorder out of my righthand jacket pocket. I could not manage it, though, and Eddie got it out for me. When he pulled it out of my pocket, it tugged loose the lapel microphone I had clipped in place.

"Don't tell her about this," I told Eddie. "She's had a rough day."

"Right," he said, smiling. "I'll at least wait until she's given us a statement before I play it for her. Should be interesting."

"I think so."

"I promise you, man, I'll put her ass away if I can," Eddie said. He sounded like he was telling me good-bye.

"Whatever."

Eddie talked some more after that, but he had begun to sound distant by then. I looked toward the van and saw everything being done. One of the cowboys had brought up their unmarked car and Betty was in the back seat, wrapped in her blanket, telling them her story. There was someone else too, a

268

man standing on the edge of things. I could not be sure, but it looked like Blondie, the guy with the radio in his hand. Must be a friend of Eddie's, I thought.

Eddie laid me on my side and snugged his raincoat around me to make me warm. I looked up at the blackening sky and thought it looked like the ocean with a storm brewing. I felt myself being drawn out into the dark deep sea, the waves reaching out for me, closing over me . . .

And then at the very last I thought about the kid.

Chapter Thirty-seven

I LOST A LOT of blood in spite of everything Eddie could do before the paramedics came, and it got to the point that dying was optional, I could have died if I had wanted to. It can get that close, so close that if you fight you stay and if you let go, it is over for you.

They kept me in the hospital a couple of weeks and pumped enough new blood into me to put the color back into my cheeks. Eddie Cochran was waiting for me when I got out.

"You're looking pretty good," he said to me in the lobby of the hospital. "How do you feel?"

"I'll live. What are you doing here?"

"You need a ride home, don't you?"

"Yeah," I said. "I thought maybe you and I had business."

"Nah, you're in the clear. Everything checked out."

"What about Betty?"

"Believe it or not, the DA's going to prosecute. Conspiracy to murder."

"The tape came out all right, huh?"

"It was good," Eddie said. "Clear and incriminating as hell, especially after she had given us a statement saying she didn't know nothing from nothing. She did not hold up very well in front of the grand jury."

"What do you think the odds are?" I asked.

"For conviction?"

"Yeah."

"Sixty-forty, if you make a good witness. And if it goes to trial."

"Why wouldn't it?"

"Her lawyer's talking plea bargain."

"That's okay, too."

Eddie helped me into his unmarked car and we drove away. But we did not drive toward my office or Red's bar either, which I would have preferred. He drove me to White Rock Lake instead.

"What's the deal?" I asked.

"Somebody wanted to see you for a minute."

"Who?"

"You'll see."

Eddie drove down Lawther on the east side of the lake to the place where sailboats were moored in stalls along wooden docks and here and there lay anchored off by themselves. No one was sailing today. The sky was blue and clear and there was a wind, but it was biting cold.

The car parked in the little lot by the sailboat dock was a clean blue Olds with a PARIS HIGH SCHOOL WILDCATS bumper sticker. Betty's mom and dad had bought it a couple of years ago, new, after driving old cars and pickup trucks all their lives. It was the nearest thing to a luxury they had ever allowed themselves.

Mom and Pop turned away from the lake to look at us as we drove up. Neither of them waved. She had a scarf pulled tight over her head and her arms were crossed to keep her hands warm. He stood square and flat-footed like a tree, with his hands in his pockets and his cap pulled low.

"What is this?" I asked, looking at Eddie.

"A conspiracy. Get out and visit. I'll be back in a couple of minutes to pick you up."

I got out, and probably looked like an old man doing it. My middle was still taped and I was sore as hell. My back had gotten better, but it stiffened in the cold. The tires on Eddie's car crunched gravel as he drove away behind me.

"Hello, Jack," Mom said, and she came to me and hugged me lightly. When she kissed me on the cheek I caught a scent of lilac. "How are you feeling?"

"I'm okay," I said.

Pop did not move, just looked at me with his head cocked to one side.

"Good to see you," I said, covering the distance to him and pushing my hand toward him. He took my hand in his and his grip was as firm as ever.

"Glad you're up and about," he said. "Look like you're still pretty sore."

"It's not bad."

Then I saw the boy. He was out on the dock, hunkered down and looking out toward the nearest boat.

They did not say anything more, so I asked about Betty. They said she was doing all right, considering.

"I'm sorry for the way things worked out," I said to both of them. "All of it."

"We know that," Mom said. The tears might have been from the cold. "Pop and I know that. It wasn't your fault."

There did not seem to be anything else to say, and I wondered why we were all there in the cold bright winter sunlight by the lake. I turned my collar up and swiveled my head around. The car was still there, parked half-hidden behind cedars and underbrush in a parking lot up the hill overlooking us. It had been behind us when Eddie and I came into the lake grounds, maybe before that. I could not tell if there was anyone in it now, but I thought I knew whose it was.

"We're going to take the boy back home with us to stay for a while. He'll be better off out of the way until things get settled down over here."

Mom's voice turned me around to face them and I saw the boy again, still a crumpled red pile that might have been just a raincoat left on the dock.

"That's good," I said. Mom and Pop were good people, the kind of straight and calm people who hold the world together. The kid would be better off with them than with anyone else in

273

the world, on their place with the horses and cows. With Queen, the mixed-breed bitch who had adopted them and only now and then went away to run with the coyotes who lived in the woods along the creek that fed the lake where the fishing was good. If he got to be too much for old Mom and Pop, the kid had an aunt and uncle up the road with kids of their own. They were good people and it was a good place for the kid. None better. I envied him.

"We don't know how long it'll be," Mom added. "Maybe through the summer . . ."

"Until all this is settled," Pop put in, and that was that. I looked at Pop and he did not look away.

"The boy wanted to see you before we left," Pop said.

"I didn't know if I'd ever get to see him again."

"You're his daddy," Pop said, as if that covered it all.

"I don't know how much Betty has told you . . ."

"I expect she's told us everything we need to know." Pop cut me off, not wanting me to finish.

I did not know if Betty had told them what she had told me, that the kid was not mine. And I could not find the words to ask. I did not want to hurt them.

"Daddy!"

He was charging up the dock toward me, his arms outstretched and the hood of his red parka riding down over his eyes so that I was afraid he could not see and might tumble off the dock into the cold water. But he made land and careened over the gravel toward us, reaching up with his hands once to push the hood away from his eyes and almost falling.

"Daddy!"

His grin was bigger than the puckered hole in the hood that Mom had drawn tight against the cold. There was just his little red nose and the middle third of a big grin showing when he threw himself at me over the last three feet and landed in my arms.

"Careful, son," Pop cautioned him gently. "Your daddy's kinda stove up."

"It's okay," I said. "It's okay."

And it was. I hugged the bundled little bugger to me until I thought all my stitches would burst. But it was okay. It was fine.

"Daddy, see the boats!"

"I see, I see. You like them, huh?"

He nodded a big yes and grabbed me around the neck to squeeze me as hard as he could. Everything hurt, but I did not care. Not about the pain or what his mother had said or what she had done or any of it.

When we had hugged enough to suit him, he hopped down and dragged me by the hand out onto the dock to show me the boat he wanted. He had a thing about boats, this kid. He got that from me, I guess.

We looked at the boats until my nose and fingers were numb from the cold, and then Mom and Pop came out to take him away and put him in their warm car and take him to their place for who knew how long.

I stood on the dock and waved to him and he waved back as they drove away. He kept waving until they were out of sight, and I knew he kept waving after that.

Even as cold as it was out there, it was still a bright and sunny day, and I could look out across the lake and sense the water moving under me and make myself believe that I was at the helm of a boat. My boat, and the lake was the Gulf of Mexico, and the sun was near and warm and a big fish, a tarpon, was waiting just ahead. The land in the distance, the brown-and-gray barren winter hills with the smoke stack of an old power plant rising, was the hot green coast of Santa Rosa. There was peace there now and fishing was good again, I told myself.

When the car ground to a stop on the gravel behind me, I did not turn around. I was still dreaming of my boat and my son and thinking how good I had felt when Pop had said he would like me to come see the boy as often as I could.

I did not turn around when the car door opened and

closed, when the sound of footsteps moved toward my back along the dock.

When I felt her just behind me, hesitating, I spoke.

"Hi, Della. What are you doing here?"

"I brought you this," she said, moving close beside me and offering a bottle of Pinch, which I took gratefully. "I thought you might need it."

FOR THE BEST IN PAPERBACKS, LOOK FOR THE

In every corner of the world, on every subject under the sun, Penguin represents quality and variety—the very best in publishing today.

For complete information about books available from Penguin—including Pelicans, Puffins, Peregrines, and Penguin Classics—and how to order them, write to us at the appropriate address below. Please note that for copyright reasons the selection of books varies from country to country.

In the United Kingdom: For a complete list of books available from Penguin in the U.K., please write to *Dept E.P., Penguin Books Ltd, Harmondsworth, Middlesex, UB7 0DA.*

In the United States: For a complete list of books available from Penguin in the U.S., please write to *Dept BA, Penguin, Box 999, Bergenfield, New Jersey 07621-0999.*

In Canada: For a complete list of books available from Penguin in Canada, please write to *Penguin Books Canada Ltd, 2801 John Street, Markham, Ontario L3R 1B4.*

In Australia: For a complete list of books available from Penguin in Australia, please write to the *Marketing Department, Penguin Books Australia Ltd, P.O. Box 257, Ringwood, Victoria 3134.*

In New Zealand: For a complete list of books available from Penguin in New Zealand, please write to the *Marketing Department, Penguin Books (NZ) Ltd, Private Bag, Takapuna, Auckland 9.*

In India: For a complete list of books available from Penguin, please write to *Penguin Overseas Ltd, 706 Eros Apartments, 56 Nehru Place, New Delhi, 110019.*

In Holland: For a complete list of books available from Penguin in Holland, please write to *Penguin Books Nederland B.V., Postbus 195, NL–1380AD Weesp, Netherlands.*

In Germany: For a complete list of books available from Penguin, please write to *Penguin Books Ltd, Friedrichstrasse 10–12, D–6000 Frankfurt Main 1, Federal Republic of Germany.*

In Spain: For a complete list of books available from Penguin in Spain, please write to *Longman Penguin España, Calle San Nicolas 15, E–28013 Madrid, Spain.*

In Japan: For a complete list of books available from Penguin in Japan, please write to *Longman Penguin Japan Co Ltd, Yamaguchi Building, 2-12-9 Kanda Jimbocho, Chiyuoda-Ku, Tokyo 101, Japan.*

FOR THE BEST IN MYSTERY, LOOK FOR THE

☐ A CRIMINAL COMEDY
Julian Symons

From Julian Symons, the master of crime fiction, this is "the best of his best" (*The New Yorker*). What starts as a nasty little scandal centering on two partners in a British travel agency escalates into smuggling and murder in Italy.
220 pages   ISBN: 0-14-009621-3 $3.50

☐ GOOD AND DEAD
Jane Langton

Something sinister is emptying the pews at the Old West Church, and parishioner Homer Kelly knows it isn't a loss of faith. When he investigates, Homer discovers that the ways of a small New England town can be just as mysterious as the ways of God.   *256 pages   ISBN: 0-14-778217-1 $3.95*

☐ THE SHORTEST WAY TO HADES
Sarah Caudwell

Five young barristers and a wealthy family with a five-million-pound estate find the stakes are raised when one member of the family meets a suspicious death.
208 pages   ISBN: 0-14-008488-6 $3.50

☐ RUMPOLE OF THE BAILEY
John Mortimer

The hero of John Mortimer's mysteries is Horace Rumpole, barrister at law, sixty-eight next birthday, with an unsurpassed knowledge of blood and typewriters, a penchant for quoting poetry, and a habit of referring to his judge as "the old darling."   *208 pages   ISBN: 0-14-004670-4 $3.95*

FOR THE BEST IN MYSTERY, LOOK FOR THE

FOR THE BEST LITERATURE, LOOK FOR THE

☐ THE BOOK AND THE BROTHERHOOD
Iris Murdoch

Many years ago Gerard Hernshaw and his friends banded together to finance a political and philosophical book by a monomaniacal Marxist genius. Now opinions have changed, and support for the book comes at the price of moral indignation; the resulting disagreements lead to passion, hatred, a duel, murder, and a suicide pact.　　　　　*602 pages　　ISBN: 0-14-010470-4*　　**$8.95**

☐ GRAVITY'S RAINBOW
Thomas Pynchon

Thomas Pynchon's classic antihero is Tyrone Slothrop, an American lieutenant in London whose body anticipates German rocket launchings. Surely one of the most important works of fiction produced in the twentieth century, *Gravity's Rainbow* is a complex and awesome novel in the great tradition of James Joyce's *Ulysses*.　　　　　*768 pages　　ISBN: 0-14-010661-8*　　**$10.95**

☐ FIFTH BUSINESS
Robertson Davies

The first novel in the celebrated "Deptford Trilogy," which also includes *The Manticore* and *World of Wonders*, *Fifth Business* stands alone as the story of a rational man who discovers that the marvelous is only another aspect of the real.　　　　　*266 pages　　ISBN: 0-14-004387-X*　　**$4.95**

☐ WHITE NOISE
Don DeLillo

Jack Gladney, a professor of Hitler Studies in Middle America, and his fourth wife, Babette, navigate the usual rocky passages of family life in the television age. Then, their lives are threatened by an "airborne toxic event"—a more urgent and menacing version of the "white noise" of transmissions that typically engulfs them.　　　　　*326 pages　　ISBN: 0-14-007702-2*　　**$7.95**

You can find all these books at your local bookstore, or use this handy coupon for ordering:

Penguin Books By Mail
Dept. BA　Box 999
Bergenfield, NJ 07621-0999

Please send me the above title(s). I am enclosing _____ (please add sales tax if appropriate and $1.50 to cover postage and handling). Send check or money order—no CODs. Please allow four weeks for shipping. We cannot ship to post office boxes or addresses outside the USA. *Prices subject to change without notice.*

Ms./Mrs./Mr. _____

Address _____

City/State _____ Zip _____

Sales tax:　CA: 6.5%　NY: 8.25%　NJ: 6%　PA: 6%　TN: 5.5%

FOR THE BEST LITERATURE, LOOK FOR THE

☐ **A SPORT OF NATURE**
  Nadine Gordimer

Hillela, Nadine Gordimer's "sport of nature," is seductive and intuitively gifted at life. Casting herself adrift from her family at seventeen, she lives among political exiles on an East African beach, marries a black revolutionary, and ultimately plays a heroic role in the overthrow of apartheid.

  354 pages   ISBN: 0-14-008470-3   **$7.95**

☐ **THE COUNTERLIFE**
  Philip Roth

By far Philip Roth's most radical work of fiction, *The Counterlife* is a book of conflicting perspectives and points of view about people living out dreams of renewal and escape. Illuminating these lives is the skeptical, enveloping intelligence of the novelist Nathan Zuckerman, who calculates the price and examines the results of his characters' struggles for a change of personal fortune.

  372 pages   ISBN: 0-14-009769-4   **$4.95**

☐ **THE MONKEY'S WRENCH**
  Primo Levi

Through the mesmerizing tales told by two characters—one, a construction worker/philosopher who has built towers and bridges in India and Alaska; the other, a writer/chemist, rigger of words and molecules—Primo Levi celebrates the joys of work and the art of storytelling.

  174 pages   ISBN: 0-14-010357-0   **$6.95**

☐ **IRONWEED**
  William Kennedy

"Riding up the winding road of Saint Agnes Cemetery in the back of the rattling old truck, Francis Phelan became aware that the dead, even more than the living, settled down in neighborhoods." So begins William Kennedy's Pulitzer-Prize winning novel about an ex-ballplayer, part-time gravedigger, and full-time drunk, whose return to the haunts of his youth arouses the ghosts of his past and present.

  228 pages   ISBN: 0-14-007020-6   **$6.95**

☐ **THE COMEDIANS**
  Graham Greene

Set in Haiti under Duvalier's dictatorship, *The Comedians* is a story about the committed and the uncommitted. Actors with no control over their destiny, they play their parts in the foreground; experience love affairs rather than love; have enthusiasms but not faith; and if they die, they die like Mr. Jones, by accident.

  288 pages   ISBN: 0-14-002766-1   **$4.95**

FOR THE BEST LITERATURE, LOOK FOR THE

FOR THE BEST LITERATURE, LOOK FOR THE

☐ **THE LAST SONG OF MANUEL SENDERO**
Ariel Dorfman

In an unnamed country, in a time that might be now, the son of Manuel Sendero refuses to be born, beginning a revolution where generations of the future wait for a world without victims or oppressors.

464 pages   *ISBN: 0-14-008896-2*   **$7.95**

☐ **THE BOOK OF LAUGHTER AND FORGETTING**
Milan Kundera

In this collection of stories and sketches, Kundera addresses themes including sex and love, poetry and music, sadness and the power of laughter. "*The Book of Laughter and Forgetting* calls itself a novel," writes John Leonard of *The New York Times*, "although it is part fairly tale, part literary criticism, part political tract, part musicology, part autobiography. It can call itself whatever it wants to, because the whole is genius."

240 pages   *ISBN: 0-14-009693-0*   **$6.95**

☐ **TIRRA LIRRA BY THE RIVER**
Jessica Anderson

Winner of the Miles Franklin Award, Australia's most prestigious literary prize, *Tirra Lirra by the River* is the story of a woman's seventy-year search for the place where she truly belongs. Nora Porteous's series of escapes takes her from a small Australia town to the suburbs of Sydney to London, where she seems finally to become the woman she always wanted to be.

142 pages   *ISBN: 0-14-006945-3*   **$4.95**

☐ **LOVE UNKNOWN**
A. N. Wilson

In their sweetly wild youth, Monica, Belinda, and Richeldis shared a bachelor-girl flat and became friends for life. Now, twenty years later, A. N. Wilson charts the intersecting lives of the three women through the perilous waters of love, marriage, and adultery in this wry and moving modern comedy of manners.

202 pages   *ISBN: 0-14-010190-X*   **$6.95**

☐ **THE WELL**
Elizabeth Jolley

Against the stark beauty of the Australian farmlands, Elizabeth Jolley portrays an eccentric, affectionate relationship between the two women—Hester, a lonely spinster, and Katherine, a young orphan. Their pleasant, satisfyingly simple life is nearly perfect until a dark stranger invades their world in a most horrifying way.

176 pages   *ISBN: 0-14-008901-2*   **$6.95**